DIE OR NOT DIE

Is Death a MYTH, or a PORTAL TO ALTERNATIVE REALITY

By

MICAH SHANNON

Acknowledgment

My family for supporting and encouraging me despite all my frailties and sins. God bless them and my readers for devoting their valuable time to my efforts.

~

By breaking the power of sin, can he break the power of death? This is Jack's dilemma.

Jack Spec is a Washington DC Homicide detective chasing death from corpse to cadavers until the inevitability of Thanatos strikes him. God, Lucifer, and an alien being champion a quest to illuminate a pathway past death to the alternate universe of heavens God created.

Devotees of the paranormal power of death realize the thrill is in deciphering clues dropped to lead the reader to a shocking ending.

SYNOPSIS

Four months ago, Detective Jack Spec's life began to crumble as he lay wounded in a deserted warehouse, begging his dying partner not to die. Jack lost more than a partner and friend; he lost his soul. The Grim Reaper stalked Jack his whole life, and it worsened with his promotion to Homicide Detective. Jack felt out of sync with life, either just ahead or behind the Reaper. Each life corner portends a lifeless form, setting him to run toward or from death. Mortality morphs into a manifestation with metaphysical powers over all life forms. When he confronts the grave, he must face his internal self for understanding.

After attending a Christmas fair, Detective Jack Spec and his family were assaulted and lay in the city morgue over the coldest three-day Christmas weekend ever. Jack's dead body ascends on a transformational journey to a limbo state where God and the Devil greet him to explain his status. A glitch happened during his death transformation process, and he became trapped between life and the afterlife. This unknown phenomenon had never developed, and they would be doing everything to prevent it from happening again. God and the Devil were unsure of Jack's required placement, so they temporarily placed Jack back on earth until it was resolved. Jack returns to the morgue to melt and recuperate before the resumption of his duties, where he constantly meets interference from political, police, and religious corruption. His peers either seek spiritual guidance imparted from God's talks or are ridiculed for delusional, unnatural behavior. The skeptics' beliefs increased after another case led him to discover an alien that crashed on earth as he was coming to pursue solutions to earth's problems, especially climate control, which was the same phenomenon that had destroyed his alien world. He returned to duty after a thirty-month hiatus to meet a female psychologist and enter a complicated relationship. Can Love transcend death, and where do loyalties fall?

The author filled this novel with paranormal and spiritual activity to highlight alternate realities of life and death. To delightreaders in the discussions between the protagonist, Jack, and other Spiritual Leaders' perspectives and suspense. We will join Jack in questioning his religious beliefs, his mentality, and his own existence on a journey exploring the darkness of human fragilities.

The purpose of writing this book is to stimulate a reader's mind to foster their imagination and develop a positive mentality towards life's challenges. Color, gender, and equity are determined by the reader, as are the motives and morals of all characters. Decisions for the book lover are to uncover the clues to navigate life. The pattern of romance, science, and brotherhood, plus an ingrained spirituality, will capture the audience and will encourage enthusiasm to follow Jack Spec into the Light. The blend of the metaphysical and spiritual relationship of the characters will captivate the reader through the promise of life after death as a reality.

Bio

I have always been a prolific writer, having been educated by Catholic nuns and priests for 12 years plus at Carmelite Seminary, where composition in Latin, Greek, and English was demanded. Truthfully, I never finished "HOMER" for translation from Greek to Latin. After spending my term on transcription of ancient tablets and scrolls, I decided institutionalized religious thought was not for me. So, I was left to be drafted and sent to hell, which was also not for me. However, I went with a deeper appreciation for independent thinking and God's creative abilities. My religious background and tenure on the Human Rights Committee for 35 years defending the "God-given rights" of all individuals alongside medical professionals offer a deeper knowledge of the required material to author this book.

Table of Contents

PROLOGUE

Sleep is a period of indiscriminate physiological condition, where the consciousness of the world is replaced by a transient cessation of being analogous to lying in bed versus in a tomb. The dreams of this youth continually started with swimming downstream among worms, eels, and snakelike beings to escape eternal loss and survive. Survival is but only the entrance into a protracted conflict of right or wrong. Initially, the youth was awash in love and affection by his caretaker mother, raised to love and follow a Christian philosophy of loving God because he loves you. His dreams were filled with love and innocence until his only parent was given the burden of cancer by God.

Dreams reflect perceptions of life experiences. The youth's theological misconceptions as to suffering, death, and his dreams get darker with repetitive swimming through thick mucus-like streams filled with eel and worms to seek a way out. The aging of the youth expanded the conflict in his dreams and created questions with no answers. His life seemed a burden for the sins of others, as his dreams matured, as he did. He became a police officer and endured the continuous cycle of pain, suffering, and death associated with that career. Dreams of a youth, now an adult, named Jack Spec can instill trauma. Jack fought for his life as he reached to grasp the demons surrounding him, running as fast as he could, unable to determine if they chased him or if he chased them. He caught glimpses of saintly figures along the pathway and wondered if they were cheering or jeering for him. Suddenly, all was serene, and a voice spoke," You missed her and lost her forever because you failed her." Jack woke the same as all his dreams, crying, "GOD, why did you give her to just take her?"

Chapter 01: Darkness Descends

Jack hardly noticed the blackish ground cover piled along the curbs as he left the precinct. His ears still vibrated and recoiled from the tongue-lashing received from the office of his captain. Captain Kirby was his boss and had endured an expletive-filled chewing out from the chief supervisor about a lack of progress in Jack's cases. Hell, Congress had not done anything over these last two years, and now he is being berated like a child. Screw them all! He needed a drink.

He winced as he sat down on the bar stool, oblivious to the surrounding merriment. Around his third drink, through the fog, he heard a female voice screech "Merry Christmas" as she wrapped her arms around him and kissed his lips. Jack shoved her to the floor, saying, "Get away from me, you ugly bitch." He left her crying there in the spilled beer and walked out, his mood sourer than ever before. He hastened to the liquor store and bought a couple of packs of cigarettes and a cheap bottle of whiskey. His drive home was a guilt trip for his actions and the thought of having to take the family Christmas shopping and to the tree lighting ceremony downtown. Damn it, he said as he lit another cigarette. Why don't people get off my back stupid boss and a stupid wife nagging constantly and bitching at me. Screw them all. They were all right; he was burned out from the stress and the whiskey and life's everyday nightmares.

As he drove down his street and took notice of everything, instinctively seeking anything suspicious and out of the ordinary—a broken porch light on his neighbor's house or just like that big black car parked in the freshly shoveled-out parking space. The car was way too big to fit and stuck out into the roadway as if it did not belong there. With that motor running? Hah! He still had the instinct of a detective; screw them all and their stupid whiskey ideas. He walked up the slippery walkway through the three inches of new snow that had fallen since morning. He was going to have to shovel this, he thought, or else the family could not get out.

He stomped his boots to shake off the ice and snow accumulation on them. "Happy Christmas," he says as he entered his house. Rachel ran to him, yelling, "Daddy, it's Merry, not Happy," and she hugged him tight. Vivian came in carrying Jessica with a scowl on her face. "Why are you so late? Did you stop for drinks? Are you drunk? Glad to see you too," said Jack sarcastically. "No, I'm not drunk. Jessica was frantically reaching out for him, looking for a hug and to be held. "I think it is too cold to take the kids downtown tonight." This was met with a chorus of cries of, "No it is not daddy, please," and a further scowl from Viv as she gritted out, "You've got to be kidding. You promised since the opening of the village 3 weeks ago. It is always some excuse. We are going, no matter what the hell happens."

While I get the girls dressed, you shovel that damn walk. Jack put his coat back on and went out the damn door, cursing under his breath. Why does she have to be so bossy all the time? Do this and do that, never a decent word. He brings home pay to support all of them; what more does she need? Jack sometimes muses about the whys of marriage and can't understand. What stupidly motivated him to get married? It was not because Viv had gotten pregnant, so what was the reason? Was he really that stupid to treat it as the path of least resistance? If so, then all of this was his own fault, and it was too late to get out now. Bachelorhood was something he had lopsided been given a chance to experience, and he thought of all the young babes he met as an officer and the opportunities he missed. Damn, he was a fucking stupid idiot. Hell! Why does Vivian make it so difficult? If she was unhappy, why not leave and let him start over? That is not happening; she wants to make him miserable because he ruined her life and his, too.

The door opened, and out they came. Each girl was singing their favorite Christmas song out of tune, and Vivian had something on her mind for Jack. After they buckled the girls into the back seat, Vivian spoke softly to Jack. "Please, Jack, make tonight special for the girls; they sense the tension between us, and a truce would go a long way to easing that feeling and make for an enjoyable weekend for their sake, please." "OK, OK," was his response, "for the girls."

Inside the car, merriment began with the girls and Vivian telling stories, singing, and debating what to eat at the Christmas Village. While Scrooge drove, the traffic became heavy and required deeper concentration to avoid the cars and increased pedestrians. Occasionally, Jack was forced to quickly turn to avoid some fool or a pack of them stepping off the curb into the traffic lanes. Jack was quick to sound the horn and voice his anger. "Please, Jack, take it easy," Vivian would whisper. This reaction only increased Jack's agitation.

The drive back downtown was more drudgery and agitation from his wife and too much joy from the kids. How the hell is he supposed to pay for all this – another mortgage payment every month? How did he get himself into this fix? Think! Christ, he needs a drink, echoes in his mind repeatedly. I could sneak away and grab one at Jimmy's, the head local hot spot. It did not help that he also had this huge set of guilt about stopping for drinks and getting home late, way past the time he promised his daughters. And then he had to shovel that damn snow; the universe was out to make his life more miserable than it really was. Secret thoughts crept into his mind about what it would be like; it would be better if he were out of the picture and the kids would not suffer a lifetime of damage from the sour marriage, he had wrought himself, he knew. The drive took 20 minutes, so he slipped into his never-ending cell of misery and depression. The whiskey he had taken earlier took the edge off but also caused a lack of focus. He discounted a big car that passed him twice as he made his way through the maze of Christmas traffic and people rushing the closer to the center green they got. His reverie was broken by his wife's sudden lookout and the kids yelling, "Daddy, be careful!" as the car cut in front of him into the only open space to be seen. "Damn, we're going to have to drive around the block again. This is ridiculous; why did we come down here?" Rachel sat back and said, "Oh, Daddy, you are taking all the fun out of this. I looked so forward to being with you and having a fun time tonight of all nights; tomorrow is Christmas Eve. Don't you feel any happiness? I just want you to be happy and love us." His heart broke and felt crushed beneath the treads of the tires on the asphalt as he made his way down the backstreets of downtown.

The mall had been constructed on abandoned LED industrial ground, and an enormous parking lot existed, but the town fathers, in their infinite wisdom, had built a large staging area, vendor tents, and a winter snow village to replicate the North Pole. All of which occupied half of the space available for people. Where the hell did, they think people were going to park when they came? Take buses? I don't think so, shortsighted idiots, and with that, he had his first chuckle of the month, "Bah Humbug." Rachel started clapping and said, "See, daddy's happy; he's happy!" Daddy was only happy because his thoughts immediately had gone to Uncle Scrooge. "Bah humbug."

After another turn around the block, Jack spotted a spot, out of the way, next to a dumpster behind a vacant garage two streets over from the mall. He did not like the distance to walk, but there seemed to be lots of shoppers heading their way. The hairs on his neck stiffened from the apprehension coursing through his veins brought on by the situation the family was in. "Let's go, daddy. Yeah, I want to meet Santa!" Vivian said as she smiled happily at all of them. God, how happy and beautiful she and the girls were. I must take a picture to capture their look and remember it for the rest of our lives. They began their journey to the North Pole to meet Santa, and as Jack picked up Jessica in his arms, he looked up to the clear moonlit sky and pointed to the North Star gleaming. Jack said, "For the rest of your life, you can always follow that star home to daddy." Jessica hugged him tightly and said, "I love you." Vivian smiled and, for once, felt at peace. Things can be alright. The walk seemed much shorter to Jack as they laughed, sang Christmas carols, and watched Rachel and Jessica dance around them with other shoppers. Jess wanted to walk and dance all night. This suited Jack, even though she floated in his arms; defending his family was most important. His arms, hands, and body are the family's first line of defense and require freedom for a defensive posture. The family stepped from the darkened street into the blaze of sights and sounds of the Christmas Village. At first, Jessica recoiled, frightened, and squeezed her parent's hands tightly. "Don't be afraid," said her mom, "Daddy's got you!" and smiled at Jack. The world was glorious again.

Vivian slipped her arm around Jack's waist, saying, "Love you, and thanks." He kissed her. It's been a long time since that had happened, thought Jack, and he realized the thought of whiskey had not occurred for hours. Wow! It was late, and all should be in bed. It took at least another 40 minutes to round up and convince the need for bed. It was then Jack noticed the thinness of the crowd. The temperature had fallen, and coldness had set into everyone. Off we go, said Jack with a jauntier pace. Not far down the street, Jessica started to falter. "Daddy, I'm too tired to walk," she said. So up she came, and in a matter of steps, she was asleep peacefully on Jack's chest. The low muttering of the remaining shoppers slowly dissipated as Jack's thought process enveloped him. They had not been this happy in a long time, and this feeling must be the way genuine families are. While he investigated each beautiful face, a sudden sense of dread swept through his body. Why was it so muted? Jack swiveled his head, seeking sound or people.

Nobody was in sight. The street was deserted. The only sound was the ominous squeaking of the broken light pole chains as they dangled precariously over the street.

What the hell! Not now! Jack's sensory system exploded in fear for his family. The first to notice was Jessica, as she felt the pounding in Jack's chest. Vivian was next, sensing his alertness and pulling Rachel closer to afford a mother's protection. What's wrong, she whispered. Keep walking as quickly as we can; we need to get to the car. Jessica whimpered softly as their pace increased. A quick estimate told Jack, 5 minutes or six at most. Lord help us, his skull screamed. His head swiveled as he sought help. 4 minutes, please, no more. The cold was forgotten, only the need to get to the car, as the sweat dripped down his face. Are you crying, daddy? Asked Jess. No, baby, that's sweat, daddy's fine. Quick, swept the area. Nothing. Oh, God. Only 3 minutes left. Just around the next corner, he almost stumbled as he saw two men walking toward them, the left was an old man with a cane, and a slightly younger man shuffled along his side as if assisting him. Why are they both wearing oversized raincoats; it had stopped snowing hours ago? Vivian said, "Thank God, someone's here." Keep walking, Jack replied. Less than two minutes. Christ Jack, old man with a cane, come on. Stay close and stay aware. He spoke. Almost made it less than 1 minute.

Suddenly, the clock stopped as Jack heard the old man say, "Hello, Jack, good to meet the family."

Jack whispered to Vivian, "I need everyone to get behind me." He adjusted his position to protect his family from what was bound to happen. Jack gently placed Jess on the ground as tears streamed down her face. Just one damn minute, and only two of them. Out of nowhere, a man's voice declared, "They cannot." As the pipe crushed his skull, he dropped to his knees, unable to hold onto Jess as she appeared to float away. A collective scream erupted from his family. A shout came from the man behind. "Keep his head up~!" Keep his head up!" The boss doesn't want him to die yet. He wants this bastard to see his family being taken away from him, to suffer." Jack's dazed state focused on the snow beginning to fall. Jack threw all he had left in a primal show of strength and was rewarded with a pipe across the chest, breaking the ribs and against the legs breaking them and another crushing blow to the head. He lay beaten, and a witness to the beauty of the snow tainted red with his blood. The pain-filled fog swirled in his head, only penetrated by the screaming and the old bastard yelling, "Hold that kid! Hold that bitch! Cover her mouth. In Jack's mind was the sound of a clock ticking but not going anywhere. One lousy minute was all they needed. As time hung free, the sound ebbed and flowed between the bastard's laughter and the crying and screaming of the tortured family. An eternity later, Jack was jolted back to reality by the different screams and Rachel's voice, "Daddy, help! Please help, Daddy!" "Shut that kid up!" said the old man. "That bitch bit my hand and drew blood," was the response.

Jack heard his daughter's bones break as that butcher smashed his fists into her body, and her skull cracked as she was thrown into the dumpster.

Well, she's quiet now. She's dead! As they all chuckled.

Keep him awake, goddamn it. The old man approached carrying a pipe and said,

Jack, my lad, "your lovely wife does not look or feel so good- at least not now after my knife cut off her nose and cut out her tongue and eyes.

Did you hear the loud death rattle she gave?

Suddenly stiffing and slicking away. Jack's last thought was "a lousy stinking minute." Through the silence, Jack heard the crunch of footsteps in the snow and a familiar voice he did not now recognize. Jack, good to see you, said the voice.

With no movement from Jack's numb body, the voice yelled, He still better be able to hear me! Yeah! Yeah! He can't see you but hear you; he can.

Ok, Jack and I need to discuss some private issues. So, get to work and throw out the trash.

Their footsteps receded towards the dumpster and the bodies. Jack began to whimper at the thought of the family's bodies in the trash.

Jack, let us see if we can see eye to eye over some things. Oops, sorry, you have one eye left. I have been keeping my eyes on your family for a long time, and they were badly mistreated by you. You failed in promises to your wife and your daughters. Frankly, they all wanted a puppy, and you stood tall and shouted them down. TSK, TSK, TSK. Nobody should deny their daughters a puppy.

Wait, excuse me. As the voice turns and calls to workers, "You stupid clogs, throw all the garbage into the dumpster, even the bodies," Idiots!

Jack distinctly listened to the thud against metal from each body so he could say goodbye. He began to cry for them. Sorry, he thought. He'll soon be dead with them and try harder.

The voice crouched down to look in Jack's better eye and spoke. Not so tough now, but you were always weak and a lightweight. You really did not deserve a family.

You always let them down, not just tonight or last year but their whole life. Vivian placed her life and her children's lives into your hands. She trusted you. I only wish that you could look at her face and the result of her trusting you, you pathetic asshole. Why Jack? Why did you hurt them? What did they ever do wrong but love you? None of them deserve their end or fate of being dumped in a landfill. Their whole life to be unfulfilled. No happy moments, no grandchildren, and no weddings or memories.

Jack? Jack? Don't die. I have much more berating for you, you shithead!

Know this, Jack: I LIVE, I EXIST, and none of your seeds ever will! As you go, remember IT was me, all me the name is grrrr…………………

Chapter 02: Into the Dark Night

The sky had cleared overnight, causing a steep drop in temperature. Even though it was mid-day on Saturday, Dec. 24th (Christmas Eve), there was no joy inside the cold garbage truck. The driver, Mike, wore two sets of gloves to grip the steering wheel, and Oscar, his pickup man, swore he could see each word said to be written in their frozen breath. Damn, it was cold.

The streets of DC seemed abandoned, except for a few ambulances and morgue trucks seeking frozen bodies of those without shelters last night. Merry Christmas! Each stop grew more tenuous as the shift advanced, but what the hell, working today's half-day shift meant holiday pay for Christmas and the day after. This sounded great as an offer, but as they stepped outside their warm houses this morning, they cursed their luck.

On a day like this, garbage bags and cans would freeze to the ground, causing hernias or messy situations for pickup men. However, it was their fortune to be using a newer dumpster compaction truck (DCT). While they stayed warm inside the cab, the machine automatically picked up the dumpster, tilted it, and dumped everything into the rear, compacting the trash.

They cruised past the mall, with Oscar singing to a tape of Christmas carols, and both men joined in the spirit around.

"Jesus," Mike said as they looked out the windows at the huge piles of garbage strewn throughout the mall parking lots, "glad we're on the DCT shift. It'll be like working in a freezer out there today."

They turned the corner on the way to their next stop, again up an alleyway connector. Oscar said, "Be careful of those low-hanging light pole fixtures." "okay," replied Mike. When they pulled into the slot next to the dumpster, they were forced to squeeze past some fool's car. "Hell of a place to park. People must work. Damn rude bastard," complained Mike. They activated the machinery, which began to lift and tilt. The whining of the lift caused Oscar to look out the windshield, and he saw a ragdoll slide out onto the front end of the truck.

"Hold it! Hold it!" he screamed, "Not right!" Oh my God, Mike whirled to see Oscar starting to cry as he struggled to fight off his seatbelt and vacate the cab. A stunned Mike investigated the trash and immediately swore and wished he had not. Because of the holiday's light shift schedule, the police did not show until an hour later, and an ambulance took even longer.

Captain Kirby had just finished his holiday shift and looked forward to a restive, festive two days off. He listened to Christmas carols in his car as he rushed to the mall for shopping. He needed one more present for his wife. He spotted a space across the parking lot and stepped on the gas to beat some old people to his preferred spot. "Yeah!" He made it and jumped out, charging to an open door, he was stopped by a salesperson.

She said, "Sorry, sir, we are closed to the public." "Wait," he said, "I need a present, and I am a police officer!" "Officer, do you work here? Cause if you don't, I can't let you in. The store is only open to give a chance to employees to shop." With that, she politely said, "Merry Christmas," and closed the door. "BAH HUMBUG!" the captain said to no one in particular. "So much for the spirit of holidays." Upon reaching his car, he heard the speaker squawking his call sign. "Hell, what now?" While reaching for his mic, he hesitated and thought, "I need a present. CVS is still open? Kirby here."

"Sir, you are required at 122 Alley Connection Way around the corner from the mall." "What the hell! I'm off duty till Tuesday. Get somebody else." "Captain, this is all hands. Officer down! Repeat, officer down." The captain's blood turned colder than last night. He said, "How bad?" "Very," was the reply. "She caught swearing of SHIT! SHIT! SHIT! And tires screeching before the speaker went off."

The tires screamed, and the motor ran fast, but not as fast as the captain's mind. Warp speed is the term, as subconsciously he spun the wheel and swerved through traffic, honking his horn even with the siren screaming, "I'm coming, get out of the way!" Awhirl with questions, he jumped the next curb and asked himself, "Who was it? With a reduced schedule… Who? Did they die? Was there a wife? Did they have a family? God, no kids, please no. I can't go through that again."

Get out of the way as he blasted his horn to clear a path to the crime scene. No more thoughts of presents, no more holiday spirit! Goddamn, it is so cold. The captain's heart sank as he pulled up behind the old clunker parked next to the dumpster. Hell, kids, wife, and friend. It can't get worse. He slowly opened the car door and fumbled to release the damn seatbelt while a young officer waited. The captain looked up, and for an instant, thought he saw his son. Is this guy that young? okay, take me through it.

"Sir, Detective Olsen has an update and wants to speak with you on arrival," he replied.

"okay, but what did you see?"

"Nothing, sir. The first officers on the scene closed it down and denied me access, for my own good, they said." He thought, stepping around the truck. "What the hell happened? Olson."

"Sir, I am not sure yet. We are waiting on forensics to arrive. Who is it? What's your best guess?"

Olsen sat on a garbage bucket and slowly started. "It was Jack Spec and his family. The whole family," the captain incredulously asked.

"Sir, this is so difficult. May I please get through it without interruptions?"

"Sorry, Detective, I've done this myself. Only plain talk."

Detective Olson took a deep breath and sighed, "okay. It is an assassination, a trap. Carefully planned and conducted. There seem to be signs of at least four aggressors, and they waited patiently for the family. Yes, they knew and were prepared to torture and kill the wife and the children."

"Wait. Hold it," said the captain. "What are you implying?"

"Not implying, sir. The wife had her eyes gouged out as she lived, and her tongue was carved out, and nose cut off. The girls were brutally beaten with their skulls crushed." The captain reached for a can and turned it into a seat alongside Detective Olson, who started to cry.

"This is terrible," he spoke. "You did a wonderful job and deserved to cry and get it all out. You saved that rookie's career and others by shutting down and preventing them from seeing what you have. But, for now, we must be professional and go nail these fucking psychos. Then we are going to get wasted and puke out our guts, drink a shitload of antacid before we start the complete cycle over again. Thanks, buddy."

The captain stood up and shouted, "Get those fucking forensics people here now, at gunpoint if you have to. Hell, I want to shoot one myself."

The church bells had rung as a signal for midnight Mass to start. Few on-duty officers looked up; most had been at work for hours and hours, canvassing the total downtown area. They investigated every garbage pail and lifted all trash, looking for evidence left behind by the psyches, as they were now termed. The captain and his crew still at the scene paused between downing their 20th large coffee to join the police chaplain in praying for this family and silently for their own. The outreach of the community brought out of its citizens the brightness of the north star and flooded the first responders with provisions to share this season. Officially, a transference of holiday spirit onto a love of mankind has occurred, and generosity abounds.

Finally, forensics allowed the police to release the bodies. Though frozen in death with grotesque postures and covered with vestments loaned by the local clergy, a cadre of police and firefighters carried them to waiting ambulances. Tears flowed, and hand salutes were offered by everyone as the silent parade proceeded through the streets of DC, down the path to the morgue.

The police chief and the mayor were present at the morgue, along with another cadre of officers and firefighters.

Each shed tears and helped carry the wife, daughters, and one of their own into this chilly place. Many kneeled and said a silent prayer to their god for swift acceptance of these brethren into eternal life. Others stood silently throughout the morgue, as if the warmth of their own bodies could take the chill from the little girls' frozen bodies.

It was a night of humanity after last night's savagery. A night of love. Tomorrow comes the revelation, followed by hate and revenge.

Just before dawn, after everyone had gone and the bodies were covered for the future postmortem examination, it was determined that, because of the significance of this autopsy, it would be postponed until after the holiday to allow expert analysis onsite by many agencies.

The lights were shut off, darkness descended, and doors locked and guarded. The silence was only penetrated by the sound of ice dripping on the tile floor.

DRIP DRIP DRIP DRIP

Chapter 03: Into The Unknown

The mind is an incredible hunk of matter, truly the technology of the future, the distant past, or because of circular evolution. Enclosed in a primitive body and controlled by half a brain, it melds existence and extensional forces to generate thoughts, memories, and emotions. To protect the primitive encasement, the mind regulates the input and output of the functionality processes. Memories can be secreted in back recesses within its matter, only to regenerate in an overall defense posture to the body.

Jack's body lay dormant on a cold metal table, frozen in time; it continues to work in a subsistence state of suspended animation. Alone in this cold, dark room, with no outside stimuli, alternate processes within the internal organs respond in an inward fashion. Jack's mind regenerates forgotten capsules of memories and responses. Every so often, the mind releases sufficient capsules to encourage maintaining continuity of life on a basic level.

Jack's memory replicates past terrible occurrences to garner specific responses. Many occurred early in life when schoolmates mock him. Jack couldn't your family afford a full name. What kind of name is Spec? Did your dad have to pay by the letter? This went on all day. The later years saw the boys turn nasty. Hey Spec, you Jewish Specter, or German Herr Specular. Ostracized by communal consent, he never quite fit in, nor did he gain social skills. He always seemed out of balance with his environment. The mind used this themed approach as a survival technique. It hurt back then and still does.

Late Christmas day, the mind sensed a flurry of outside stimuli. This did not affect the body but lasted and was repeated later. Jack's exterior casement was still partially frozen, so no interaction occurred with the mind.

Sometime Monday, the mind sensed more stimuli input and received response signals back from the brain. A change in the atmospheric environment was detected, and sound was noted. Minor this was, but a start. The mind increased interior stimulation to cause brain activity.

The morgue assistants had been notified to come in early to clean body parts of frost or debris. Their job was to clean rectum residue and store, package, and label to be properly marked and ready for the coroner's use. Place syringes, tubes, probes, and other sterile items appropriately within reach. Towel and washcloths folded properly and placed nearby. The usual grousing took place, and after some time, the noise abated, but the lights remained on. Next came interns and nurses with doctors to do prior exams and supervise. The noise level increased, and the mind registered the responses. Some sound responses filtered through the brain, slightly discernable. A small segment response was detected about the girls' bodies being moved to another unit for examination. A large block of responses dealt with the wife's body, and great sadness spoke to everyone's compassion. Meanwhile, elevated levels of brain activity showed improvement to Jack's condition. Just maybe.

Soon new stimuli appeared, carried by new people, who spoke all at once. This garbled discussion overloaded an already weakened somatic network, causing delayed response, clogged interconnections. The afferent neurons in the body collect stimuli to send back to Jack's brain over his peripheral system, which is why he can receive small bundles of axons. While other neurons are still inoperable because of involuntary shutdown. Other systems will come online as the body regains various levels of functionality. If Jack had been a smaller man, his recovery chances might have increased.

Doctor, the autopsy team has completed their preliminary work on the female patient, and their rehearsal is ongoing. The doctor showed his upset. What the hell has taken so long? I have already got two more ops on tomorrow's schedule. Oh, ok. Tell them to get it over as soon as possible. Yes, doctor. Wait, is the other exam room open? Yes, doctor. ok. Get the male team over there to prepare, and we can rehearse as they do their job. We can get home before midnight.

Jack's mind was actively seeking pathways for query responses over the somatic nervous system from the spinal column nerves, which include motor nerves that stimulate skeletal muscular contraction, allowing for voluntary body movements. The mind and brain were simultaneously reactivating the body's Autonomic System, which regulates involuntary functionality, such as blood flow, heartbeat, and breathing. If either of these restarts, Jack has a chance.

The female team is finished, and staff has prepared her body for transfer to the funeral parlor. But for the male team, the long day continues.

"Listen up, everyone. I am the Assistant Medical Examiner for DC Metro, and my name is Doctor Meyers. I will oversee the Medico-Legal Autopsy. I would like to introduce Assistant Coroner Doctor Frantz, who will oversee the Forensic Coroner's Autopsy. Doctor Frantz will perform the actual dissection of the body. Soon, the niceties of legalize will be complete, and the dirty work will start.

The body will be meticulously scrubbed, and an external examination by the pathologist to include sampling, all without intrusion of the body. Doctor Frantz will draw the center dissect of the chest cavity. So, it goes over poor Jack's defrosting body, while internally the neurons and bundles of axons are racing through a revitalized network of nerves and junctions.

Jack's mind, and brain had been on overload for the last several hours for Jack's weakened body to survive and for a way to create a sign of life. While internally Jack's vital signs are showing, his body encasement requires extra time. The mind cannot see the clock, but internally can sense. The time is expiring.

If only this exam room came equipped with a magnetoencephalography (MEG) to capture all the electrical activity generated by the firing of billions of neural. The combination of high temporal resolution with the high spatial resolution displayed world was definitive proof of life. TOO Late!

"Please, will everyone step back and allow Doctor Frantz to begin the incision?" said Doctor Meyer in his loudest authoritarian voice. All present leaned forward as the doctor picked his preferred scalpel and straightened his shoulders and flexing his arms and leaned over Jack's still senseless body. The sharp blade barely touching the skin, like a pencil, left a mark of about twenty centimeters. All stared as nothing happened. Doctor said, I understand. The skin is frozen together. He looked around and chuckled through his mask.

Suddenly, everyone went into shock as the wound began to spray blood, quite high, as if to shout, "OW." Time started, 2 seconds, 3 seconds, and the room came back to life. The clamor of instantly talking at once caressed the walls and echoed off the ceiling. Finally, someone noticed!

The morgue was ablaze until way past next morning, as a quarter of the legal system and a half of the medical profession in Metro DC squeezed in to have their say. Jack! Where is Jack? The Metro Police Department swarmed in and stood guard until daylight. Then a huge hearse with Jack and guards took him to a secret area. It was not like Jack opened his eyes or raised a finger, like in the movies. Hell No. Outside of those early few drops of blood or blood-colored water, all is a secret. So, in answer to the question. It is unknown.

Jack's body was floating, and he was. He had minor cognitive ability, no more like a sense, a memory. Reality does not exist for Jack. He is nothing, not even a speck of dust. Poor Jack, but that is for the best. The brain can have substantial strength while being extremely fragile. It can face a horde of enemy troops without cringing but running over a little girl's puppy can bring the strongest to their knees.

Jack needs lots of counseling and care for his mind. However, his current needs are rebuilding his physicality, rehabilitation, and restructuring. His mind needs time and lots of rest. Jack's body is under repair, much like a smashed sports car. Reconstructive surgery is on the schedule and rehabilitation, but neither can be attempted until months have passed and his sedation is decreased for an assessment of his cognitive status.

Jack could again sense the sensation of floating, lasting an eternity. No noise, only darkness all around. Suddenly, a sense became a thought. Wow, weird! I must be dead, and this sensation of paralysis is all there is. Where am I going? This is too dark for heaven; besides, I don’t deserve it. Jack's senses reacted at a change. What was different? Goddamn, I wish they would turn on the lights or something. Jack felt like he was experiencing withdrawal symptoms, but from what? Was all this normal? What the hell was going on.

This was a hell of a way to run a railroad! Normal, there is no normal. When you die, the least they can do is provide a book or guide. Hold it! He thinks, No fire, heat, or pain, not hell. Nobody here empty; someone must deserve heaven.

Just then, an instant stabbing of pain washed through his senses, unlike earthly pain. Jack was back in his vegetative-like state.

Within any sense of time passing, Jack had no way to sense its passing. All he knew was the advancement in his mode of and to sensing increased perceptual abilities. Glimmers of sparkles and a feeling of early dawn grayness lent cognition to slightly appear. While Jack's world was still limited to his brain, a kernel of hope was being created. This world was limitless and seemed to expand every wake-up, which had become Jack's go-to measurement strategy. He felt like the Count of Monte Cristo, without understanding that meaning. It came to him from somewhere.

With each advancement came increased sensatory perceptions and virtuality plus hope. The grayness gave way to the beauty of the universe; somewhere out there might be heaven. This could be preparatory exercises for there. Like paying one's dues. Jack's current state was more a nirvana than vegetative. His mind expansion resulted from the seclusion environment. Without the clutter of extraneous external sensory perceptions, he is forced to think, and as with any muscle exercise, it increases capability. Not heaven, is this hell? Sensing around, a relative thing in an unreal situation, Jack.

Jack often sat on his slab, exploring the wondrous beauty surrounding him, which eventually creates thoughts of unknown memories of past encounters and resulting stabbing pains to oblivion. This time was different; a soft voice with deep tones spoke, "Beautiful, isn't it. The voice was all around, while he was on the slab in mid-air at the center of the universe. The voice said, look at that brightest of stars, which was the very first star, made to light the creative zone. You call it the North Star. But as creation continued to develop, more light was needed as well to create guidance to far stars and return. Thus, the North Star was tasked to send bursts or sparks to gather dust or debris to grow and generate light into all reaches into the Cosmos. The secondary issue was solved by developing gravitational fields around those stars to collect particles and fragments to form planetoid bases for potential habitation. As one question deserves an answer; so, does that resultant answer deserve a question? God's reasoning in creating "free will" in humanoid life forms was to instill the question-and-answer requirement as integral to the brain-to-mind relationship. Are you an angel? No answer, just the silence of the wonders surrounding me.

Awakened to a brilliant horizon, sounds pervading a sweet-smelling atmosphere, Jack was startled to hear a deep tenor voice speaking. God, he is finally awake. Turning around, nobody was there, and as he stood and looked down, the universe continued beneath his feet. Jack and his slab hung suspended in the middle of the universe.

Weird, very weird, said Jack out loud. Surprised to hear his own voice, Jack started speaking. Hello! Hello, is anybody around, here, anywhere. Since Jack did not understand or know where or how he was; his confusion came out. Again, that tenor voice called from afar. We are here, I am Luc. A strong baritone voice spoke, you know me--- You have not forgotten me GOD, incredulously. Baritone: YES, OLD FRIEND. Tenor said, so deep in thoughts, we did not want to disturb you. Who are you, asked Jack? Luc. Jack's voice jumped What the hell kind of name is Luc? Loudly, came a response, "You have a problem with short names, SPEC?" God steps in, Easy, Easy! Lucifer. Can I see you, asked Jack? Where are you? Luc's voice tersely replied. When you are ready, just go down the hall. Night seemed to fall; all was dark with tiny far away stars twinkling. Cannot see any damn hall, he muttered as he just started walking and walking. In the far distance, was a small glow which got bigger and brighter the more he walked. Funny, the walk did not tire him a bit. "After a million steps, welcome, come on in. It isn't often we get visitors up here. Most returnees go to PETER for reorientation." Curious Jack glanced around the universe and saw a pit of fire hanging in the air, which gave a partial glow to the three bodies present. "Would you like to sit and have a discussion" Jack looked at the baritone voice and answered 'Yes God, I think I might have some questions?" God seemed to chuckle to Jack." Please, have a seat." Jack saw nothing to sit on and took his clue from Luc and God. Both sat in a midair posture, as if in a comfortable chaise. Lucifer was first to start off. "Jack, you look like hell. You should learn to take better care of yourself. I know, your mother taught you better than you lived?" Hell, said Jack, "Then I am dead "God's baritone voice startled Jack, "NO! YOU ARE NOT DEAD!" Jack quickly focused on the face of God and slowly asks, "Am I alive?" "NOT EXACTLY," came the reply. A shocked Jack queried, "why do you appear so much like I imagined?" "Your imagination is based upon the imagination of countless their eyes and most saw love." Came his reply. "Love, love! Can a loving god allow sickness, wars, and brutality," said Jack, even as memories crushed his mind into oblivion?

He awoke alone on his slab, feeling the warmth of the fire. Still tingling from the surge of pain that was awash in his body, other thoughts unfolded in the mind. Jack's mother had taught him that God was benevolent, loving, and the creator of all life. His guidance was the path to salvation. Jack had questioned this because every time Jack had sought help from God, it had not come. Most especially when his mother's stricken cancerous disease and death occurred. A young boy left with a broken father struggling to keep a dysfunctional environment afloat. He suffered, and it was beyond his comprehension back then and even now those same feelings intertwine with current events to generate a dangerous and terrible sense, which is shrouded in fear.

Jack must have dozed off because as he reopened his eyes, Lucifer was speaking. "He deserves to know. Ok, Jack, I agree with Luc. "This situation has never come up before and so, we have to be creative in our approach." Jack interrupts, "Isn't that your specialty? What is my situation?" Luc quietly explains, "A severe problem arose during your processing. Mixed signals crisscrossed. You were dead, then alive, then dead, alive, dead, and then a shutdown occurred. In all the confusion and chaos, you disappeared. Is it clearer now? "Hell no, Jack said, jumping to his feet and walking in a circle. God said," I rarely get a chance to say, but I am sorry." "What, you both are telling me is that I am lost in space. Well ok, beam me the unknown territory to explore. You are trapped between heaven and hell. We're working hard to develop a path to either place. Jack's stunned expression would be comical if not tragic. "What will be done with me, is there a waiting room?" Luc stifled a smile as God said, "No, sorry. That is a dilemma, and our discussion warrants our combined efforts. Lucifer believes it is unfair to judge your life's experiences to warrant placement in hell, and yet it also falls far short of heaven." Again, Jack interrupts, "Who is he to Judge?" Lucifer steps in, "Interruption is bad manners, especially of GOD," Jack shows agitation and says, "Fucking Unreal" God provides an answer. "Yes, it is! God states. "Everything is artificially created to adjust for justification on frailties of life forms. Common belief to sin is the fault of the Devil, while to not sin is because of GOD. Both are based on life formation faults to fault transference. Humans should take responsibility for their actions." "Lucifer's mandate does not allow any attempt to coerce or tempt any sin in any form. Believe it, there was no apple nor evil snake in my garden. He has always been portrayed to be the antipathy to God, the evil scapegoat.

Reality in an unreal realm. Luc is smarter than he looks.' The discussion process continues with Jack pleading his case. I want to return home, go back to what I had. Luc politely says, "You can't. Nothing is left there for you." As Jack stammers and puts a hand to his head, God returns the discussion to focus on more options Jack may have. Each time Jack awakens for their discussions, a warm fire exurb a comfortable sense of safety and peace. This time, he only saw Lucifer's friendly smile across from him. Hello. as both silently gazed into the flames Jack asked if the fire ever goes out. Lucifer laughed and said, "I never need to worry fire going out. Hells fires were started by the sins of humans and will continue to blaze. Greater sins equate to greater flames, hotter heat, and greater pain to the souls in Hell. Have you given more thought to what you feel is best?" "Yes," said Jack, "I don't understand the reason it is taking so long." Can you just explain that.? "The Devil sits up in his seat and leans toward Jack. Listen, a problem happened, as you know; we are all trying to solve the issue and prevent it from happening to others. However, everything can take longer than you expect. Time does not exist here, as you know it. You are bound by celestial movements of the sun, the moon, and rotational elements. So, your frame of reference is nonexistent in your present state. We seek a level of fairness for you and assurance that this will never be replicated. You deserve our best so be patient. It only feels like forever. Much later, God and Luc stand by the fire viewing the vastness spread before them and speaking in tongues unknown to a sleeping Jack behind them. Lucifer is telling God his last thoughts of Jack's return. "I believe in Jack and of little worry about his retribution efforts. Revenge is dissected from the mind, and hatred is sequestered. My suggestion is to allow a pathway for our discussions to continue intermittently to monitor his progress We can table any final decision until Jack's actions warrant it. "God agrees.

Chapter 04:
A New Awakening

Jack, while in a comma-like state, is dreaming. It's like a TV show in fast motion. People in hospital garb flash across the screen of his mind, first in black, and white, and moving on to color. The only slow bits were discussions between the three.

The dialog was skimpy at first and partially garbled. Jack listened intently to make out what God was saying to him. Suddenly, the baritone voice came through, and too many have lost sight of the work of Christ. He preached an evolutionary independence, which meant not to seek everything from God. Don't seek everything from a government. Stand on your own feet and think, work, and pray for guidance. Don’t conflate help with guidance, as many try to do. The film sped up as Jack witnessed technicians placing bandages, splints, braces, and needles in the arm and in the back. This guy must have more holes than a pincushion.

At the next slowdown, Luc's tenor voice was heard speaking to complaining teenagers whining for the freedoms of adults. Those whiners are always the first ones to demand help. People's voiceovers of Mom. Can you watch the kids tonight?

Dad, can you and Mom take the kids for the weekend, or how about over our two-week vacation? All justified by Mom and Dad's love of having the kids. If this is so, why did they work so hard to send you away to camp, to college, to marry, and to retire so far away? Jack thought Luc could be cynical!

This scenario was repeated a few more times between the trainers and the three. The movie stopped, and Luc and God appeared.

God said, It is time, Jack. Luc said we agree you are ready to reenter a newer life with familiar faces and situations. Follow the teaching of your mother and of God to live successfully. God spoke up. Our presence is always available to provide guidance and comfort by the fire.

A jarring sensation of falling and voices crying out, Catch him, Gently, Easy. Bring me a wheelchair.

Jack opened his eyes to a strange face that was off-centered. Can you hear me or see me? Shouted the face. Goddamn, I am not deaf, Jack croaked. At that, the room erupted in clapping. Crying and backslapping as big smiles burst on all the faces.

After a while, as things calmed down, he was taken back to a room they said had been his for over ten months. After he was secreted in a private sanitorium to decide if he was worth saving and map a course for recovery, he had been moved several times for surgeries and to this modern rehabilitation. These clinicians had worked daily throughout his partial paralysis and comatose stupor to achieve mobility and functionality. Each day brought a parade of faces to congratulate, speculate, or just congregate. But today was different. The face he knew was staring back at him with big tears flowing down his cheeks, Captain Joshua Kirby. Hell, I truly am alive, Jack shouted. Later, after a kinship renewal, Josh, as he was now called, brought in a new face, a beautiful woman named Samantha Billings.

Josh, now a superintendent, explained Sam's job and her visit. Sam is the official DC Metro Police Psychologist sent to analyze Jack's sanity. I already told her you were a crazy bastard back then, so adjust her findings accordingly. The embarrassed laughter followed as Sam made herself comfortable. Her first words were, shall we get the elephant out of the room? "That is me," said Josh and got up.

No, I'd rather you stay, said Sam and Jack together. The silence permeated the room, from the sheets to the sound of simply breathing.

After a while, Jack spoke, can you give me the best news first? Sam began to choke up; Josh began to cry again and hissed. There was no news.

Everyone was still except for an occasional sniff or tissue use until Jack spoke. I lived each second of the attack, the screams, and cries for daddy, the cracking of my family's bones and every minute since. I waited to die, unhappy at my ultimate failure to savor death's breath and unable to unite with them. I will always live with it. But I must live to overcome practice my lessons taught in honor of their sufferings. Sam, you may think I am crazy for that lack of emotional response, but it was torn from my soul, and nothing is left.

Jack, this is standard procedure, and Sam is aware of everything in your file. Ok, Captain, if you say so, but everything! Yes, if printable; Josh said, Go ahead, Doc.

Dr. Sam Billings is attending for the recording record. Jack, what was your last memory? Jack thought like a detective, not a victim. Described the attack as he experienced it. From the first hit, the screams, Rachel's cries for help, and her biting the butcher's hand so deep the blood flowed, and the aberration of the Boss. No tears now. These professionals were focused. Jack had been a wealth of information. Finally, a direction and a path for pursuit. Josh grabbed the phone and drove forensics into a flurry. The technician grabbed stored boxes of evidence and swept them up in the early hours of the investigation. Carefully packed boxes contained garbage, vials contained trace elements from the frozen ground, and even particles of frozen ground, all kept in a temperature-controlled atmosphere. Special forensic technicians dug out the bags of the victim's clothes and checked each centimeter for DNA and blood residue. Now that they could perform analyses on saliva samples for a verification process, they could proceed.

Jack laid back and thought he had survived, and that alone, with his mind and memories, could be enough to punish everyone involved in this tragedy.

He chaffed at the slowness of progress in his case and the fact of his confinement in the hospital. Knowing the reasoning was of little comfort during these next months. Sam often came to sit, record, and talk, especially after he mentioned the discussions with God and the devil. The look on her face told volumes. She thought he was nuts after all. Sam tried to deny it, but there it was. After that, she took copious notes and even brought a friend who had bumped into her in the hospital lobby. I may be crazy, but not that crazy. They listened and questioned even more intently. Coincidentally, he was also a physiatrist and a minister. His great interest was in the how and why, plus all the details. He almost fell off the chair when I told him that both God and the Devil welcomed me back to sit by a warm fire to have a discussion anytime I wanted. After they left, I questioned the impression taken with them. Either I am really nuts, or they are.

Whatever, I was released the next day. Everyone from the hospital came by to wish me well. Some brought balloons and cards. A nurse wheeled me out to my ride, and as I rolled through the door, a strange tinkling pulsed through my whole body. I looked around to check if something had happened.

No! The only other presence was another patient, nodding off in a duplicate wheelchair. Who is that? I asked the nurse. Don't know, was her reply. I looked again and said he did it. Yup, he killed her.

Right after that, Josh came to pick me up with all smiles. The smiles quickly turned to frowns as I told him of my encounter. In deference to me, he went back believe he and the doctor had conversed on my stability. His face denied his smiles, and the worry lines were out in force. Ah, Jack, Sam asked if I could quickly visit to say hello if you are up for it. I replied, sure, I'd be glad to see her.

Off we went for a simple discussion, the good doctor, the friend, and the nut.

Jack, our relationship is beyond that of a doctor/patient but has developed into a deeper level of friendship. This is the reason I have asked some colleagues to intervene on your behalf to secure a level of objectivity for you.

Ok, whatever you say. This is not just my say but a consensus of expert advice. I asked her directly. No bullshit am I to be a test case to be dissected before religious zealots and other fools out to draft a book and present it as an example of madness and psychotic episodic remorse. Sam looked shocked and hurt. Jack, I did not mean to sound that way. I want what is best for you. I am so sorry. And choked up. Josh spoke up, Sorry, Jack, none of us mean to hurt. Our interest is to help you return to a livable environment. Before this all happened, we were concerned for your well-being and you went through. We worry, we care. The whole precinct gave blood, volunteered hours of service at your bedside, and took days off to continue looking for the suspect. That was not because of the charm and tact you displayed to any of them. You are a brother and always will be.

Jack suddenly felt remorse and shame. Josh was right. He was self-centered. Jack knew he owed so much to everyone, especially his brothers. They were his only family left. So, over the next several weeks, Jack endured countless sessions with the lucky chosen few. However, every day, luckier chosen few were added, and they even brought in an expert psychiatrist and neurologist to measure the interaction between my brain, mind, and being. I was hooked up to imagery EEG, EMG, and every kind of electronic gimmickry and poked and prodded in the recesses of my skull. I was a specimen and a spectacle to explore, whatever I was.

Unbeknownst to me, in the background raged a battle between two factions. One side believed my psychosis had developed from the combination of strong psychotic drugs, a drug-induced medical state, a thawing-out process, and pain suppressants. They had devolved into splitting among themselves to interpret the trauma of and coalescence of the continued use of electromagnetic measuring on the brain.

The other group combined science and religious opinions in the development of their theories. Both sides were of a Frankenstein mentality," IT IS ALIVE." Jack expressed his frustration to Sam and Josh. If I am not crazy, then they will make me crazy. Sam was sympathetic, while Josh saw the comical side.

What I want and need is to return to a sense of normalcy. They both ask, "HOW?" After an hour of deep discussion, Sam, speaking softly, says, A little guidance from above may help. Should I ask the minister? Jack sat quietly for a few minutes thinking and said, can't hurt.

Later, Jack laid in his new room at the 'NUT HOUSE," as he called it, for no apparent reason and thought of the reverend's words. I can speak to Jack, but it is best if he talks to whom he trusts the most. Jack drifted into the darkness, embraced by the room's warmth and the effects of the pain medication. Drifting along, Jack was filled with a comforting sense of home, evoking nostalgic sensations. As he opened his eyes, he was greeted by a breathtaking panorama. While seeking GOD, he was taken aback by the sight of Luc's smiling face.

Welcome Back. Are you lost? Jack stood and walked to his favorite spot beside the fire. Maybe, was the reply. They chuckled warmly. Talk to me said the Devil.

I thought I would meet God, began Jack. Well, you were told to talk to the one you trusted most, Surprise. You must still have concerns, not about God, but about yourself. These feelings you are having could be connected to human weaknesses and your beliefs. The rights and wrongs of your life's meanings within the context of your world. It is not about trusting God but who you trust more to resolve this dilemma.

We need to reach the center of the open wounds in our souls to realize why these feelings exist. When do you feel was the first-time God failed you?

Jack was a little boy again as he asked, "My mother's cancer and death. Why did he let that happen?" God does not let events happen. He does not plan for pain and suffering. He monitors all things as they unfold. Humans have free will to control their own lives. What happens comes about by their own actions. Our place is to monitor and regulate balance, not control. I have no control over the sins of humans, nor does God. That can frustrate, but there it is!

Jack asked, why is there so little evidence of life development in our dead-like portion of the universe? Did God abandon us out of frustration or anger? Why has he left us to self-destruct or worse? Is another section of the cosmos a more fertile setting to create?

No, said Luc, God will not abandon his children. We try to keep a sense of balance in the uncertain reality that exists.

Humans have a proverb, "When the door slams shut, listen carefully to hear the many doors opening." It is time for you to listen.

Listen, listen for what? I feel like a freak! Replied Jack. Listening is one of the easiest things to do and the hardest. Said Luc, according to Romans 10, 17, "Your faith comes from hearing through the word of Christ," and hearing faith is not an expression of our activity but our receiving the activity of others. Jack, puzzled, says, I don't understand. Luc continues, too many humans are terrible listeners. Too often, they are slow to hear, quick to refute, listen with one- half an ear, and are impatient to respond. Because they assume to know where the speaker is going and predetermine their response. Good listening requires a level of concentration with both ears. Many styles of hearing can be noted. Those who only want to hear the information that they care about do biased listening, which leads to distortion of facts and miscomprehension of what they heard. Critical listening is the one I am suggesting for you, Jack, to develop for problem-solving and a higher level of concentration to follow a logical sequence of events and concepts. These are to be wrapped in a vibrational frequency balance. Sorry, Luc, but now I am lost. What the hell is that? said Jack.

Jack, have you forgotten already? We spoke of this at one of our first meetings. Remember, you asked if we were really talking or reading minds? Oh, yeah. Vaguely! Responded Jack.

The Devil says, "Let me give you a refresher lesson. A human body comprises 70% water." It is an excellent conductive medium for sound and vibration, and since every living cell within that body, every organ and tissue, including the mental state and thought process, depends on a vibrational frequency or energy. The ears receive about 80% of all stimulation that enters the brain and provides the ability to start and monitor consciousness and the thought process. So, with this process of good listening and a proper vibrational balance between the voice's undertones and overtones in verbiage, informational data can be cross- referenced to stress the essence of communication. Did that clarify it? Oh yes, except for the way to interpret the data, replied Jack. Start with good listening, concentrate on vowels versus consonants' sounding plus the accent's tones. I get it, said Jack.

Jack, calm yourself. Your training and intellect will guide you. Jack awoke to the sun spilling into his room. All those experts were right, but he felt deeply the presence was real and therapeutic. He resolved to remain silent over this latest discussion with everyone. The day progressed as usual until his afternoon function with Josh and Sam. The time is right, Jack said. I believe a little familiar work will restate my sanity and focus me on what is important to me personally. How? Jack asked Josh. If I went back to just reviewing old files, I might slip into a comfort level and a sense of achievement in returning something back to my brothers. We'll see, they said.

Chapter 05:
Into The Fray!

Two weeks later, Jack returned to his precinct amid mass clapping and speeches and a level of comradeship and kinship reserved for survivors and a brotherhood borne of the trenches. Detective Olsen, now a Captain, took Jack downstairs. Ok, Jack, This is our morgue! He stopped and sheepishly sighed. I am sorry, Jack, old habits. Jack smiled and congratulated him on a promotion to replace Kirby. Yeah, feels good. Here are the old files and a desk we moved down here. Make yourself comfortable. The coffee is in the same place as the stale pastry. Watch out for rookie Jim. He likes sweets. As he departed, Jack looked around, taking everything in, even the awful smells. He smiled as he opened the first drawer and picked out a handful of files.

After three weeks, he had whittled down many of the files to about twelve of interest. Sitting alone in his solitude had been a blessing. Little noise and piles of work had been beneficial to a resharpening of his skill sets.

He has highly advanced synastry perceptions, and his hearing is equivalent to that of a blind person. His sense of touch and smell are exceptional. The reconstructive surgery on his nasal cavities, ear canals, and face manages this miraculous recovery. His corrective eye surgeries and lens have given him a 20/10 vision rating to complement everything. Unfortunately, they deferred from including tremendous speed in his package. No 6-million-dollar man!

Hell, it felt good to be alive, but that is where it ends. The feelings had regressed too far to repair, and he was afraid. The phone on his desk rang, and he jumped to pick it up. Spec here. This is Olson. We have got an old body dredged out of the river, and I'd like you to come with me. Jack replied, Ok, Captain, and sprinted up the stairs. The drive was uneventful as they both listened to dispatch over the radio. Only 10 minutes to cross midtown DC was unusual for this time. The sun had not set, and traffic was slowing down. A rookie uniform waved them in, and the captain stopped just short of the pier end. A dredger had deposited a pile of bottom crap on the pier's edge, and a foul stench filled the air. Torn plastic bags with a body were visible, along with forensics techs and the ME standing, waiting for their arrival. I said hello, captain, and looked into Frank's eyes as he said; I am so sorry, Jack! Good to see you back. With that over, everyone lowered the veil of professionalism and went about processing the crime scene. The body was unrecognizable because of an elongated period of submission. Everything was bagged, labeled, and photographed, and by then, the sun had set. Jack suddenly said, damn, I need a drink, and all seemed to stiffen at once. The coffee wagon is here, and I'll buy. A laughter of relief filled the air. Thanks, came a chorus of voices. Two days later, ME's report hit Olson's desk. His immediate reaction, after reading through the report, was to call the superintendent's office for an immediate appointment. Come on, come up. Josh Kirby meets him at the door. He asked, What's up?

Captain Olson said, handing over the report, check this out. Josh quickly glanced through the report and mentioned that he fell into the water 3 years ago and was wearing a raincoat. Ok, what of it? Think it was one of his cases. Olson said. Read on and check out any distinguishing characteristics. The hands were badly bruised, as if in a fight, and Josh froze. Fuck, whatever you need. Get it, spend it. We must know.

Yeah, I wonder! I want an abrasion test. That special type used a femoral cell on a host. The bit marks and residue of salvia or blood or cell molecules in his hand.

If we get a match, we get a start. Let us not get ahead of ourselves. We'll need a response from the Justice Department central directory for the final ID.

Meanwhile, let us sanction this investigation for our eyes only.

Jack continued reviewing cold cases, especially three, that involved several missing children in a suburb in the metro area. It caught his eye because it involved a little girl of six. Rachel would have been six. All three belonged to the same small church and went to the same religious school. The incident involving a little girl of six caught Jack's attention and aroused his instinct. He seeks the investigating detective and finds out more.

Searching the record file, Jack discovered Detective William Bushes had retired just two years ago and still lived at his old address. As Jack drove, he wondered how it might feel to retire with his wife, Vivian, and see his daughters grow, get married, and have grandkids. To have grandsons carry his name was too much, and tears welled in Jack's eyes. Jack smothered the sudden thoughts and did not let them penetrate his consciousness. Fear of an unknown and unstable future closed out this entire train of thought. He stopped in front of a small, comfortable cape cod-style house, much like his own. But not quite. His was a dead house, not a warm home as this was.

The door opened, and a partially recognizable man, slightly older than Jack, stuck out his hand in friendship and said, Hi Jack, long time. They went inside to sit and reminisce about past times and an old case both teamed up to solve. Eventually, the talk settled on the reason for Jack's visit. Detective Bushes had an obvious recognition of the facts and placed them before Jack as any officer would. Afterward, a question-and-answer period began, with Jack's mind absorbing conflicting evidence and processing small, interconnected details to evolve themes and several thesis. Then, they introduced Bill's wife after she came home from work. She asked Jack if he would stay for supper. No, thank you. I need to get back to you. They all shook hands, and as they walked to the door, she looked at Jack. We went to the memorial services held for your family, and it was beautiful. I remember coming home with Bill. That was when I asked him to retire. I insisted. I did not want to end up alone. I am sorry. Jack hugged her and said, no one aspires to be alone. It's unnatural.

The trip back to town dwelled on the information in his mind about the case and only the case. Bill's help and the rehashing had fostered several theories for his pursuit. The lack of recovered bodies meant they had little evidence available. This meant a great difficulty in prosecuting a perpetrator. So, retracing any potential steps was his priority. Start with what you know and branch out from there. Each fact established is another step to completion.

Jack drew up a strategic plan of activities to follow, and over the next two weeks, he followed and surmised each child's path from home to the last verified destination, the church. Next door to the school and the rectory.

This led to a canvas of persons involved in and around that specific area during the period of the crime's occurrence.

The little girl was first at just past ten years, with a boy one year later and another boy after another year had passed, then it stopped as quickly as it had begun. The investigation did not lead to any explanation, and it was abandoned until Jack picked it up.

Jack's senses shouted begin here and work back. With no place else to go, he thought, What the hell!

Jack spent the next several weeks reviewing old files, conversing with other detectives, looking for leads or receiving them from Jack, and following up on canvassing the area around the church. The police believed that all three disappearances started there. However, Jack at this point was of the opinion it was truly the end.

Finally, an older parishioner pointed Jack to the retired rectory director of nursing as the one with the most knowledge. So, another step uncovered, and off Jack went. Jack discovered that older women no longer sat at home knitting. Jack tried contacting her every day for the next two weeks to no avail. Obviously, she did not believe in answering machines. Finally, he went to her address, and to no surprise, she was not home. The next-door neighbor explained she was a volunteer at the library on Tuesdays, at the soup kitchen on Wednesdays, on Thursdays yoga, and Friday was at the local hospice. Jack felt tired and asked, do you think she'll be home next Monday? Oh no, she replied, that's the day her grandkids take her to doctors, lunch, and a movie. Best to leave your number with me. I'll see if she calls you. Jack chuckled as he drove away. Jesus, retirement is challenging work.

Early the next am, the phone rang, and it was Flo, the retired Matron. Sorry I missed you, but I can make time next Wednesday at 3:45 pm.

Promptly, on the next Wednesday, Jack rang Flo's doorbell. When Jack rang Flo's doorbell on Wednesday, a lovely older lady of grace greeted him with a cheerful voice, saying, "Welcome, come in, Mr. Jack Spec!" I am glad to meet you. Please sit down. Jack marveled at the ease with which she placed him. What can I help you with?

Jack explained his quest, slowly at first and then as if to a confidant. They bantered back and forth over details and what-ifs. Jack learned about past priests, which made the time well spent. Father Banc and his many moods and hobbies. The hobby of a garden, in the far corner of the rectory's backyard. His private doll collection he kept, and different clothes to dress and redress them. For holidays, of course.

Jack inquired about what happened to Father Banc. Flo spoke softer than usual. I was confused when he went on a sabbatical to Rome. He did not seem the type to just get up and leave his garden and his collections, and it was a long time before his return, over a year. A year and half. Other priests filled in for him and continued throughout his hospitalization. How long after these disappearances did Father Banc go on his trip? About a year., Flo replied. Was he hospitalized for long? Quite some time, she said. I never had time to say goodbye. I did not see him on his return from Rome, my 2-week vacation, nor after his illness. What was the matter with him? Jack asked. Never really found out. But it was serious enough to force him to retire from the priesthood. She spoke. Jack had lots to think about on his drive back to the city.

The next morning, saw Jack at the diocesan offices to review their records. After three hours in the basement, he had learned little. Only some notes from a Reverend about someone kept repeating, "The Devil made me do it over and over". Sloppy record-keeping, mistakes, redactions, and missing documents were of no help. Jack pondered, Do I have to make a mental note of all of it to set before God or the Devil? On his way out, the bishop's secretary stopped Jack. "Can you spare a few moments to see the bishop", was the question? The bishop's secretary led Jack into an opulent office with walls lined with pictures of ceremonies performed by the bishop. The bishop will see you in a few minutes. Said the secretary as he closed the door. Jack wandered the room, viewing each picture disinterestedly, and waited and waited patiently until god's work took time. Startled, Jack stopped before a picture of young men surrounding the bishop as they were about to be ordained. Gazing intently, Jack picked out one with the name of Jonathan Bancorello.

The door opened, and Jack was in the bishop's presence. Please forgive me for keeping you waiting. Sit down, please. The bishop, not one to waste his valuable time, asked directly, what brought you here today?

Jack spoke of his search for documentation regarding old cold cases and the need to complete any that can be. The bishop stated, my people have told me of your discussion with God and the Devil. It's rare I get to talk to such an illustrious person. Jack felt tired. They say you can go back any time you want. What will you talk about next time you visit? Jack blandly said, well, Certainly about sloppy record keeping.

The bishop looked directly into Jack's eyes and said, I presided at the memorial services for your family. It was beautiful.

He stood and said goodbye. Jack left, wondering, What the Hell!

When Jack got back to the precinct, he found a note on his desk. See Captain!

As Jack walked into the captain's office, Olson said, follow me. They both, without a word, walked to the superintendent's office. Hello Jack, sit down. Olson took a seat opposite Jack. I just got off the phone with the bishop's secretary. What the hell did you stir up? I don't know. He then updated them on his investigation into the three children's disappearance and the subsequent finding of it centered, of now, in the church's area, most especially within the confines of the rear garden. They spent the next hour discussing Jack's suspicions and evaluating their merits. They reached a conclusion to send out a search team equipped with ground imaging equipment to survey the entire area around the church. Getting a court order was the captain's last words.

After Jack left, Olson said, Any new development back on the scan? Yeah, lots of data to discern and process, but no word back from Justice yet on a match to our body. Olson spoke up to announce that they had just identified the body as one David Blaine, a local strong-arm man for hire. Let us continue quietly to prevent leaks and issues, said Superintendent Kirby, and then asked? What was the original name Jack gave as a potential for that priest? Olson said, Jonathan Bancorello. Damn, that has a familiar ring.

The next day, Jack receives news all day long. First came the news of an arrest of a suspect in a cold case Jack had developed into a prosecutable file. Then, the authorities granted the court order to search the church grounds and scheduled a meeting with the search team for next Monday. Around mid-afternoon, another of his detectives called him to pronounce the filing of an arrest warrant in another cold case. Well, Happy Days are here again. Jack piled his nightly reading material into his car, to go home. His thoughts had just turned to a dinner of sardines on a peanut butter sandwich when his cell phone rang. Hi Sam, he said, what can I do for you? Her voice came back. Take me to dinner? Sure, I'll pick you up.

Jack smiled and thought, this day keeps getting better and better.

Monday morning saw a heavy mist, with slight sprinkles, as if the skies were crying, as the search began. The heavy dampness caused only a little interference with the images, and a sweep of the front saw several old statues in pieces buried at various depths. The right side gave way to a view of a couple of dogs' burial spots. The bones created a flurry of excitement for a time. Upon arrival at the entrance to the garden, everyone's instincts were on high alert. Mapping out and documenting each sweep per square inch was done carefully by them. First one and then another, and another faint form appeared. Tears of joy at their findings quickly turned to tears of sorrow as each small bundle rose to the surface. The enormity of the situation crushed down upon each present, causing every step to be labored as they carried each tiny bundle to the morgue wagon. Today was a day of pain and sadness.

Late that Monday, Jack drove up to the nursing home and walked up the ramp to a wide porch. There, he spotted an old man in a wheelchair. Jack kneeled before the old man and spoke. Father Banco? The old man looked up to Jack, and his eyes momentarily cleared. With tears flowing down his craggy cheeks as if they were the draining of the mist from his eyes, he spoke. I did it; I did it. Then he slipped from his sudden lucidity into the abyss of his own hell. Jack stood and, after a second, said, Sergeant, read him his rights. A lot of good they'll do him.

Jack drove slowly back to the precinct, wondering what could have influenced the priest to decry. The devil made me do it, and now, as the man repented to say I did it, I did it. What caused this new realization? Did a discussion occur about it with someone? Also, why had the church leadership and the bishop accepted the explanation of "the devil made me do it" as a justification for protecting him?

Just before arriving at the precinct, Jack thought back to the other night with Sam. The dinner was superb, as was her company, but something was missing. Vivian. He missed her and thought of his complaints about the marriage and the girls. What a fool he was to lament what he had. When he really had everything, he ever wanted, and now he had lost it all. He vowed to work hard to remember the words the devil had said to guide his way forward.

Sam is great, but not Vivian. What had Sam discussed? He had asked about her life since she had total knowledge of his. She explained that her mother had died early, giving birth to a baby brother, who also died. Her father failed to fully recover from it and sought solace in his work. He had been a police officer assigned to an organized crime unit. Sam seemed passionately interested in Jack's current work and his coping with all going on in his life. There seemed to be so much more out there for him.

Chapter 06: Too Much Of A Good Thing

The bosses kept Jack in the cellar, where he was out of the way and still produced noteworthy results. It was a win for everyone. Jack was happy with this arrangement since they mostly left him on his own. He could pursue his choice of cases. God knows, there were plenty of cold files available. A month later, and four more referrals resulting in arrests, Jack became a celebrity and a go-to man. More and more detectives, when stumped on a case, quickly visited to pick Jack's brain. His going fee was a large coffee and two doughnuts. His chairs were never empty. Another big case came his way from two districts outside the Metro area, so he required approval from Super Kirby. Jack called Josh's office to see if he was available. How about we grab a coffee in your office around 10:30 am? Not today, though? Jack was now free to research other case logs until around six tonight, when he was going to dinner with Sam.

He sat back and thought about the endgame with Sam? Can this go anywhere? Is it fair to Sam if he can't move on after Vivian? A strange thought theme for Jack to pursue. Is he growing or just maturing? Must be a maturation process. He has felt devoid of any emotional involvement since the family's death and his return. It really is too late for him. His musing faded away, and he picked up a file marked special care, eyes only. He was unaware of anything that existed. What the hell. He opened it up and started reading about the unsolved murder of a news reporter and a cop. The police found the bodies of a female reporter named Jamie Katch and a detective in a motel at the north end of the metro area. They suspected an affair, but they could not identify any potential jealous lovers. Since Detective Billing was a widower, there were no obvious leads to review. Jack forced himself to reread this several times. Was this detective, Sam's father? The department failed to pursue it, and the case could go cold. Jack sat back, stunned by this coincidence. Or was it a coincidence? He mulled the situation over in his mind several times and resolved to seek information on Sam's feelings about Jack investigating the case. He left to go home, shower, and get dressed to pick up Sam.

Later that evening, after Sam and Jack had settled into their seats and ordered cocktails, Jack spoke of what had transpired that afternoon. Did your father go by the name Detective Billing? I found a mention of him in a file I opened today. After her brief pause came. Yes, he is my father, and I never spoke of him because I did not want to burden you more with my personal issues. You need to resolve your own grief, not mine. Jack thinks for a while and says, "I wonder how it ended up on the top of the pile of cold cases on my desk?" It's not my style, Jack, to sneak around and manipulate someone behind their back. Ok. Besides, here are our drinks to focus on. A more normal, joyful banter continued, but in the back of Jack's mind waged a battle of questions. He knew the file appearing was not a coincidence, and someone placed it, but whom? What was the reason? That person might have information they wanted him to investigate. Could he still not betray Sam? All of this was filed for later. Now, he focused on making Sam relaxed and happy. Afterwards, Jack dropped her off. His brain mused about his reluctance to delve into Sam's deeper feelings around her dad's death and its manner. Why was that case lost? So many details to answer. Suddenly, Jack had an instinctive worry for Sam's well-being. Whoever had sought his family out as a target of such extreme had intense hatred and anger toward Jack. If they discerned an interest in Jack's part for Sam? She could become a target. Fear choked up in Jack's throat. Thoughts continued to churn as if in a fermentation process. Finally, settling on one absolute. Sam's personal feelings were subservient to her safety. He also concluded that the person who placed that file for him wanted his involvement to proceed. For what reason? That will reveal itself in due time.

Jack settled into his chair as his friend and boss came in carrying two coffees and a bag of doughnuts. Morning, Jack.

Late at night, he asked. Don't smile at me, Josh, we are just getting to be good friends.

Ok, I am glad for both of you. Don't take the chocolate ones. They are my favorites. Give me an update on these two other cases. I don't want you spreading yourself too thin. I keep my ear to the pipeline, and I hear all the chatter about your super detective skills. Let others do their jobs. It's ok to point them in one direction or prod them into a U-turn in another, but don't let them take advantage of you. Josh, I am touched by your concern, but this is still me. One guy seems to me to be too close to see a tree. A tall tree has some apprehension about charging after it.

The other one is making rookie errors, even after 5 years as a detective. I think I might help them with a little diplomacy. Really, Jack, you! Yeah, me. Did you change your discussion with God? Partially, more so, by private talks with Luc, the Devil. Josh, spilling coffee on his tie, replies, Jack of all people, the Devil, come on! Jack laughs out loud. Josh, you are old-fashioned. It's the 20th century. The Devil has matured. He got rid of the tail. Cloven hoofs and horns. Now he has a mustache and goatee, all finely trimmed, and speaks a little like Cesar Romero. Jesus Christ and I rely on you to train detectives, said Josh, placing his hands high in the air. Both laughed. Try not to tell them that, please. I'll adjust your timecard. Be careful.

Detective Superintendent Kirby left, shaking his head, and muttering to himself. Jack chuckled and returned to work.

Hi Frank, I was going to call you this afternoon. Josh granted his approval and intended to contact your boss via email. So, let us talk. Upon continuous persuasion from Jack for an hour, Frank realized he should investigate other suspects he had previously dismissed too quickly. That the father-in-law had discovered his son-in- law's body was not automatically reason enough to prevent him from an investigation. The fact he fired him the day before the murder was curious. Why was the firing, and what was the basis and subsequent reasoning for firing, as it is pertinent? Were there issues with the man's daughter? Was family discourse or violence a problem?

All potential motives. Another potential problem was the release of a brother known to have it in for the victim. Frank saw some logic and thanked Jack. I'll keep you appraised of events; he told Jack as he hung up.

Late afternoon saw Jack vacillating between reviewing other old cases or spending time on Sam's father. Since, once again, the file was at the top of the stack, he read the dissertation of the case. The synopsis was on the first three pages, and he briefly glanced at each page. Next came background. The female was doing a journalistic essay into the murder and arrest of a young page on Capitol Hill. The supposition was that he inadvertently noticed or became privy to information about connections between organized crime figures and people of influence on the hill.

The focus of the piece was that certain people profited by passing future contract approvals or holdups in approvals to others for profiteering schemes. No one discovered her drafts. They surmised that Detective Billing had helped her in the investigation and had become romantically involved with her. Because he was doing this on his own time and it did not interfere with his professional work, there were never any notes or records found. Jack sat back to focus on several oddities and irregularities, many left unsaid. Why is so little information on suspects to actual murders, of the suspected wrongdoing and on the investigation process itself. No notes on the interviews held are mentioned. Background on the page and a dossier on his investigation? Too much missing.

Jack began a whirlwind tour of the library, the archives on Capitol Hill, and ended with the newspaper's files. This produced several thick files of copies to keep him up all night. Later the next morning, having overslept, Jack walked up the steps to seek and clarify information in the paper's files once again. Some were on microfiche, so he could not copy them yesterday. After 3 hours of cranking the handle and squinting to view the blurred pages had given him a headache and a hungry stomach. The local café gave him respite and momentary relaxation. While he sat at a corner table, Mr. Bushes, an old, retired detective friend, walked in. Hello, they said in unison, why are you downtown, asked Jack. My annual appointment to have my eyes checked. A previous appointment discovered small indications of future glaucoma, and now, about every six months, I check. Promising idea, said Jack, I hear that nowadays there is a lot that they can achieve if caught early. How is your wife? Happy, in another 2 years, she'll retire. I can't wait. I am going crazy, sitting home alone with nothing to do. Jack laughed and spoke of dreams never to be fulfilled. The conversation turned to the reasons Jack was here. After listening intently, Bill said, I vaguely remember that case. The entire department was up in arms when the brass let it die slowly. Many friends of his continued to investigate on their own time. Hell has no fury, like the brass, when they say drop it! Huh, do you remember who that was, asked Jack. Do you mean the brass or the cops? The hell with the brass.

Groused Jack, OK, OK! I had to ask. I'll check around, and if I find anything, I will talk to you. I will set up a meet and greet at my house one day. Enough! More than enough, thanks! replied Jack. He felt a sense of accomplishment as he drifted off to sleep around midnight.

He awoke early, surprised at how well he had slept. When he dropped off to sleep, he had a premise of a meeting to discuss some things, but they were too busy Congress was in session.

Nobody can stir up trouble and global problems like those idiots. Jack got shaved and showered as he absently listened to the TV and the morning news. Nothing seemed to have fallen apart overnight, so they were just busy elsewhere. Jack met several detectives in the precinct at the top of the stairs leading down to his office, as everyone referred to the basement now. Well, it was quite a reception committee for me this morning. Said Jack. Your famous Jack can't live it down. They all laughed.

Jack inquired, who is first? Frank chimed up. I am seeking a car chopping operation in the Atlas District and Noma section. The district has a reputation for making cars disappear, and the residents have noticed vehicles from all over the Metro area vanish. They just vanish, said Detective Jaz Further. And sat down. Jack thought I need an appointment secretary. Jack spent about 20 minutes with each man reviewing and discussing their file. He told each of them what his quick thoughts were and gave directions with follow-ups in a set number of days. Each man was glad of his suggestions and agreed to a future time. Jack was glad to help but also glad to see them grow. It was one thing to become the department's guy, but another to become their scapegoat. Josh was right.

Jack's phone rang, and Jack said, Spec here. A young rookie's voice spoke up. I am sorry to disturb you, Detective Spec, but I need your help. What is the problem? asked Jack. I was assigned my first case as a detective, and it turned into a homicide. I am at the scene and lost. Where's your training partner, asked Jack? He left for home sick earlier and then the call came in, and everyone else was busy. Ok, give me the address, and I'll come right over. Touch nothing, Ok. Good.

Fifteen minutes had Jack climbing a set of rickety wood stairs. Standing, as if on guard, stood a baby-faced plain clothes man. Your name? John Renton, 4 years. He replied. You look old for four. Sorry, sir. ok, just making a joke was Jack's reply.

Where's the victim? Renton led the way to the front of the apartment. Jack kneeled next to the young girl of about ten. What do you see and hear? Asked Jack. Renton looked around and said nothing. Jack felt old as he said. The couch legs had caused the rug to bunch, having been moved. The window behind the couch was half open, and the lamp next to the couch was partially behind it. The girl might have startled someone when they came in through the open window to commit robbery. A struggle had occurred, as indicated by the torn and displaced neckline around her neck. Look around for what is missing. Check for telltale dustless spaces to signify a moved item. The detective smiled and said, Yes Sir, as he began searching. Jack put on his gloves and picked up the phone to call for a forensics unit to respond.

After about 15 minutes of looking around, Renton came back and reported that dust smears on a bureau indicated a possible stolen TV, a metal jewelry box left open on the floor may yield fingerprints and a handprint on a mirror over the bed looked promising. During the next 10 minutes, Jack had John Renton check the phonebook for a pawn shop in the area. When forensics came up, Detective Renton told them what to look for and process as they would check out leads, just as Jack had told him.

One shop was less than 3 blocks away, so they walked. Jack explained the reasoning used up to now and told John about being a listener to gain insight into whether the interrogated person could be lying. They entered the shop, and John immediately located a portable TV, which was still covered with dust and hand smudges. Jack let the rookie be the lead investigator. And John spoke about whether any jewelry came in yesterday. The owner, surprised, said no, that was not yesterday. Ok, today? Yeah, just some old costume pieces. May I see them? John asked. Yeah, sure, I have nothing to hide. John then asked for the pawn sheet and information about the person's address and telephone number. They called for a patrol car to pick up the loot and tag it into the precinct. The forensics unit was hardly done as they got back. Waiting for the morgue wagon, Jack congratulates Renton on his fortune and reminds him that his intellect and luck ruled on the day. After everyone finishes, report back in and check to verify those prints to apply for a warrant. Before he left, the rookie told Jack his story of how Detective Olson had kept him away from the crime scene as a precaution until Captain Kirby had arrived. No, he was not allowed to view any bodies or the scene.

Thanks, said Jack. A tired Jack made his way home to get some rest. Creating a peanut butter sandwich and getting some iced tea was enough to exhaust Jack. His eyes drooped before he was half finished and slowly drifting away. Hi, Jack said Luc, not lost, are you? Jack says, No, I am fine, but I have been meaning to ask you about Jesus. I have not met him yet. Luc replied, Remember our last discussion and the reasons for our meetings, the glitch. The main issue is to allow the three of us to reach a solution together.

I did not forget! Luc continues, he does not need to be involved in, say, "Damage Control". This is a priority matter that necessitates the consent, analysis, and discussion of our personnel. God represents the upside. I focus on the opposite opinions and the severity of infractions and damage assessment. Pardon my expression, Jack, you are the joker, the active participant. You are providing the movement and activities to allow us to reach a correct decision.

I worry about that. Said Jack, how much time do I have left to rebalance and offset my experiences? Is there enough time for a family and a career?

Luc says, everyone has that worry, Jack. All I can say is, "So far, the jury is still out."

The word spread quickly, up and down the chain of command, about the rookie's success and he projected it all to Jack's brilliance. Superintendent Josh Kirby was waiting to congratulate him upon his return. Oh, my god said Jack.

Did God tell you who did it, or was it really you?' chuckled Josh. It's not funny, grumbled Jack. I want to keep a low profile; he said.

Too late, let us get some lunch.

Over lunch, they talked the usual shop talk, with Josh expounding on the success Jack was getting with the other detectives. I only give some advice or point them in a direction. Said Jack. Josh came back with, according to all of them, it is so much more. They think you have gained a second sight and sense. Some wonder if a spirit is guiding you or telling you directly. That's all nonsense, said Jack, the only thing I have gained is a better need to listen and concentrate on minute details. Whatever, the department is all impressed. Don't get an enormous head. I like the new you, Josh said. Sam was at my office and spoke to me about you. Really, said Jack. Yes, she was a little concerned because you have not called her in a while. I don't know what to say. I am worried about seeing too much of her and the possibility of whoever came after my family and me would take issue and seek to hurt her. Frankly,

I am afraid for her. So how do I tell her that? My superpowers, you surmise, haven't given me a suitable response yet. I can't tell you what to do. I am lost replied Josh. That other detective called me today to report an arrest on that carjacking and chop shop ring you helped him on. Another decent job, Jack.

Next, we'll have to hang a flag over the front door, Jack's Place!

Ok, I want to ask you about Sam's father and what happened?

Jack, that is a sealed case. Not to be reopened. Jack looked directly into Josh's eyes and firmly said, WHAT HAPPENED? Josh asked if Sam had brought it up? Jack interrupted, No, Not her style. Ok, forget the rumors, began Josh.

They were not having an affair. Tom took a turn for the worse after his wife died in the birth of their son, Sam's baby brother. He also passed away about 3 weeks after the mother. He got so bad that he was suspended. To pay the bills, during the suspension, he freelanced at the paper. After his 6-month suspension was up, he just continued the side with a few of the reporters. She was one.

They became consumed with the crimes and the people responsible. Unfortunately, they were influential and well-connected on both sides of the street. It was a setup planned to provide the appearance of a love triangle gone bad, all bull shit. Who was in on it, asked Jack. Never found out, yet Josh said softly, Well protected, and high placed at that. I remember some thought that police involvement covered it all up to continue the operation.

Jack sensed Josh was less than forthcoming and pushed harder. Josh, answer me, please. How did it affect Sam? She was devastated and out of control for over a year. I arrested her for drunk driving and hardly recognized her. My wife and I took her in and got her treatment. This sparked her interest in her work. It is all behind her now. No, just below the surface, thought Jack. They continued to talk, and Jack sought to just review all Josh had on that case. Maybe let us wait a little while till some things calm down or become clearer.

Next morning, Jack read and perused a book about the workings of Capitol Hill.

Chapter 07:
How Things Calm Down!

Mr. Bushes had called early that AM to see if Jack could stop by around 1 pm. Jack returned the call and left a message that he would be there. Jack spent the next hour returning messages and then turned to the files for that afternoon's meet. Jack's mind sought the minor details when rereading files. He tried a form of logical sequence based on the minor details and followed those to a conclusion. Jack brought several scenarios to the surface and discarded them. The arrest of the young Page and the murder thereof was still in question. Also, the name of the page, plus the arresting officer, how and when was he murdered? Exactly the who, the how and the location of that murder were pertinent to the facts of that case. Before pursuing the second case. All this took Jack to lunch and getting ready for the meet.

Promptly at 1 pm, Jack rang the doorbell. Jack was surprised by the turnout when Bill called out, "Open the door, come on in!" Bill made the introductions all around. On the left side of the couch is Ray Hertz. Next is Samuel Klutz, and the right cushion is Randolph Butz; this is Jack Spec, everybody. All said hello. The large coffee pot and cups were on a credenza, along with cookies against the wall. They exchanged little pleasantries to loosen up everyone's tongues.

As that faded, Bill got into the actual reasons for this meeting. Jack here asked me about the Billings matter, and I collected all of you for a proper briefing for him. Great idea, said Randy, seconded by the others. So, let me start as I was first on the scene with my partner. Upon entering the room, Sven noticed that the front door was slightly open and immediately yells, "There's someone running outside the back window!" I immediately gave the chase around the motel to go to the back, but halfway, I heard and then saw a runner. I chased after him, but the bastard was too fast for me. When I returned, backup had arrived, and they were searching for the scene. Sven was sitting on the bed, shaking. Blood was everywhere. On both victims and on Sven, he had tried to resuscitate each. The rest is in our reports. A copy is on the table, next to the cookies. Wait, said Jack, I looked through the files and was told they had vanished. Yeah, all our files plus had vanished. Luckily, we each had our own copies for protection. They all laughed. Who was your partner, Sven? Yeah, Sven Olson, now Captain Olson.

Ok, Jack wrote that plus everything else in his note pad for review later.

Samuel was the lead investigator on the Capitol Hill murder and made the arrest of the Page. I was the responsible one. I gathered the evidence and booked him. A nice enough lad, ambitious and worked hard with late hours. That led to his discovery of corruption and subsequent recovery of private documents outlining, the who and what of the operation. I felt something out of place, not proper, but not enough to pursue. Only enough to get the hair up! Have you included all of this in your copied files? asked Jack.

Hesitantly, Sam replied, most of it. I did not want to open the evidence bag until necessary. Ok, I understand, Jack said. If you find it is required, I'll get it. Jack nodded assent. Raymond, what do you have? I oversaw the case on the woman's part. Jack, there was not a romantic involvement between the two of them. Just a bunch of noise from the brass. We all thought that it was all iffy. Concocted to divert and place a smoke screen to hide what really went down. Be careful, Jack. Influential people are going to be upset to see any of this surface. You should be careful, Jack. If any of this comes to the surface, it could ruin several careers, including yours, and some people may end up in jail for a long time or worse. This will all be underwater. I want everything kept muted, even your wife's. Raised eyebrows all around signaled an elevated level of anxiousness. Bill spoke up, well. I hope everyone enjoyed the poker games, and let us do this again. Jack, call when ready to win back all you lost. Goodbyes were said, and consolation was presented to Jack. Every one of them had attended the memorial services for his family.

Jack cradled his packets and left, wiser and with more questions than as he had gone in with.

Bill was a very smart guy, not just for hosting but for getting the best men to speak and providing a successful cover story.

Jack called Sam on his way home but had to leave a message. Where was she?

On a date? Who? Jack, none of your business. She is free, as, are you? Is that what you want? He continues to drive, thinking through some confusion. Jack entered his building with a little trepidation about the valuable data under his arm. He continued glancing back and forth for anything untoward until he had entered and locked his front door. It was paranoid, but he felt better for it.

He sat down and opened the first packet and the file, reading the ending of two people's lives. The unfolding story was as Randy had said, except for some of those pesky minor details. If Randy was the lead, why had Olson stepped to the front? Did he want to enter first to check out the room? Did he think fast and divert Randy away long enough to do what? Was someone else in the room and needed time to escape? Was any pertinent evidence trashed or hidden? Question, looking for suitable answers. Nothing or something. Jack had another note to make, Olson was first on the scene of my attack.

Next up was the file by Samuel, another smart guy. The Page's arrest resulted from his rifling several desks of (REDACTED) and (REDACTED) in Congressman's (REDACTED) office. Jack thought, boy, this redacted guy must get around. He had stayed to work late, as he usually did, and was caught going snooping, which the boy did not have permission nor authority to perform such actions. The police took the perpetrator into custody and obtained a search warrant for his apartment. (REDACTED) seemed extremely anxious and terse in his responses. The search team found some minor documents and items during the search. The authorities subsequently granted bail to the individual, and he left the precinct by taxi around 4 pm. That night, they discovered his body behind the monument under some bushes. A conducted search showed little avail. No further details were discovered, and the file was turned over to the other detectives for investigation. Minor details left to nag at Jack.

What else did Sam know and what privy documentation had he held on to? Any evidence, still in the bag, and if so, what? Why did Samuel hold back from placing everything on the record? As smart as he was, what activity had aroused Samuel's instincts. Raymond's file contained newspaper clippings, reporter's notes, and a draft of the article. There was more background data about the daughter and her past adventures and about the father's degrading actions and reconstructing his life and a place for his daughter and him. Most showed the heartache and pain of life's pressures on Sam and her dad. Much of the same about the reporter Jamie Ketch.

Past midnight caught Jack dozing, and he sleepily went off to bed.

Jack woke in his favorite spot beside a blazing fire.

A younger variation of the other two sat across from Jack. Luc has told me about you and your curiosity about me. Jack responded, Jesus Christ! Was that a surprise exclamation, or did you recognize me? Both, said Jack, smiling. The hair pulled back in a ponytail threw me a little. Luc's influence, he seeks a more modernistic look and returned a smiling Jesus. He believed I should clarify your perception of my purpose and my experiences. Starting at the beginning of earth, man was created and a woman. Everything they required was available, so all their needs were met. One night, the man sat alone on a hilltop, looking over the beautiful valley below, slowly raising his gaze to the brilliantly lit heavens above. Suddenly, a sensation came upon him, his first attempt at thought. The vastness above caused him to ponder. What or who had made all this and placed those twinkles so precisely so high? That greatness deserves honor and gratitude for everything. There was only the man and his God. Continuously, God and man interreacted and co-existed to evolve together until an abundance of other men recorded and put down the teaching being handed down generation by generation. This was harder than first thought. Since no actual record existed, it called for interpretation. Don't blame them, reality creates many problems.

Just think, if I gave you a pad and asked if a man and woman became stranded on a deserted island, tell me, what happens? Correct, only those two can tell exactly. They did the best they could. Most might have been based on their lifestyles and known qualities, and much would be embellishment or fiction. All good-intentioned prophets and scholars, with little or no factual knowledge of the facts, worked hard to chronical and build a basis for religious interpretations. This is where bias comes into play. Each sect arrived at different conclusions and interpretations fitting their own narrative, not intentionally, but causing consternation and confusion among the masses. An evolutionary process began as each sought to gain congregants. Does that clarify the background? Jack spoke up. I was never a real religious person; it was too confusing. I saw God at a more personal level for me. Good for you. said Jesus.

Jack questioned whether this implies that all the miracles and written reports are not dependable.

Jack, miracles happened, especially during the early years. After the crowds grew, interest grew also, by all types. There were opposing factions seeking to spread their own ideologies, and they discovered the most pressing need for each was a charismatic leader. I continued to grow, as did my influence with the masses, so their operatives targeted for intrusion and I was targeted by their operatives. They supported my stance, linking their agenda to my ideology. Spread descent for the Romans and Harrod's reign as King of the Jews. Eventually, I enjoyed the notoriety and was honored by the attention, but soon it became too much. An example was the wedding supper and changing water to wine. Operatives had hidden several jugs in the basement and placed sprigs, branches, and herbs to increase fermentation and enhance alcohol content before the reception. When the wine was gone, they produced several containers of this new replacement and claimed it came from the jugs of water. Highly effective. My disciples, especially Judas, were more perceptive and told me, among other instances, of the activity behind my back. After that warning, I became disenfranchised by the entire process. I needed time to think. The pressure got worse each day, and I ordered my disciples to guard the paths and let no one follow me up the mountain. In my solace, I sought to think and write a sermon to explain my feelings and thoughts. When I came down, the crowd was at a fever pitch, wrought to not listen or comprehend my sermon. As the days went on, the operatives continued to offer their own interpretation of my word. Changing vague references to them to be representatives of the Devil, and the Devil tempted me to be King in place of Harrod. Well, this incensed all concerned: Harrod and his faction, the Romans, and all members of the disillusioned mob. The end was near, and at the Last Supper, I told all my disciples my decision. The garden was where we often prayed, but that night was incredibly sad for all. The disciples became fearful of what was to become of them, as shown by Peter's sudden denial of knowing me. The rest is well known via accurate historical records by the Romans. They knew what had happened, and the soldiers presence on the hill. Placed a placard on my cross to embarrass Harrod that said, King of the Jews.

I felt lost, and as I struggled to breathe, called out, Father, why hath thou forsaken me? His richness came back to me. I welcome you back to my arms, my son.

We all can become or feel lost, Jack. That feeling manifests in a question. Seek your own answers. Think, it is your free will.

There it is, Jack, my story. Presently, I am in charge of promoting free will and a corrective process as a path to the future. Catchy title. Luc produced it.

We'll meet again, I am sure. And Jesus faded away.

Jack became awake. No warning, no lights in the eyes, and very few sounds. What the hell were Jack's first words of this day? He peered into the darkness of the room and out the windows. The power must be off in the area. Jack picked up his phone and read an alert message. ALL HANDS! POWER OFF! The time was 3:52 am. He promptly got out of bed and walked into the closet door. Goddamn! He said, then quickly, a SORRY, GOD. As he stretched out his arms to find the bathroom. He came out to look for clothes and grabbed yesterday's pants. They still had the belt attached. Socks, shoes, and a shirt completed the day's needs, and off he went to the precinct. He had only driven about a mile when a barricade blocked his path. Rolling down the window to speak to the officer guarding the intersection, he recognized an old colleague. Taylor Pierce, I thought you retired years ago. What the hell are you doing watching over a barricade? Hi, Jack, how are you? The power suddenly cut off all over town and sent all into a panic. I mean, why are you back here? Asked Jack. Long story, Tay replied. I am on my way to the station to see if they need help. Not two old farts like us, Jack, he replied. Jack investigated Taylor's face and said, yeah, I hear you. Any place with power to get us some coffee and... The convenience store one block over, said Tay. Be right back, how… Tay smiled and said black two sugars, Ok.

Ten minutes later, Jack was back with the lifesaving coffee and a smile. As Jack set the coffee on the hood of his car, he said, ok, tell me the complete story. Taylor took a sip and winced. Damn, that is hot. About 4 years or more, I took early retirement because my Jen got cancer, and I needed to provide home service. It is permissible under the contract. We went south to cut our expenses and rented out the house. Well, around 18 months ago, she passed. It was for the best, too much pain and drugs to even speak anymore. She wasted away to nothing. Finally, I cleared up everything down there and, with a return waiver, could return to active duty. Jack softly said, Sorry to hear all of this. Jack, as bad as I feel and all I went through, pales next to your losses. I wish I had been there for you. Ok, don't cry, or we'll turn our coffee cold. They both smiled at the return of a friendship.

Has someone placed you yet, or is this all they have available? Asked Jack. Nobody wants an old has-been like me, it's a younger department with latest ideas. I am like the typewriter, yesterday's tech, outmoded. Jack looked at his old friend and asked, any gas left? Enough to chase with you, and Tay asked, what do you have on your mind? Jack smiled again, broader than before and said, just thinking, just thinking!

Shortly later, with coffee time over and lights reappearing, Jack shook hands and continued his way.

Settling in, he picked up a pad of messages for return and the phone to start calls. Halfway down the pad was a message from Sam. Call me if you can? Jack leaned back in his chair to reflect on his thoughts and concerns.

An hour plus of self-recriminations left Jack unconvinced as to the best way to protect Sam. However, he had concluded that hurt by him could be inevitable. While he may protect her from others, this time, he would try harder.

Jack picked up his phone. After four rings, Sam lifted the receiver and said, hello, this is Sam. Jack here, was his response. So formal, she said, how are you? He laughed and repented. I did not mean to be. It's just a habit. No one calls unless it's business. Business good, since I have not had a call in a while. Jack blushed as he said, stop teasing. So, the conversation lasted another quick 10 minutes with them arranging a dinner date for later. Jack spent the rest of his day smiling.

He picked her up promptly at 8:30 pm and was blown away by how beautiful she looked. While walking to the car, she asked, what is the matter, Jack? You are staring.

No, he said, these eyeballs are fake. Mine popped out when I saw how gorgeous you look, and they are still on your sidewalk. Sam looked at him and spoke. Sweet talk will get you everywhere. I am glad you like it. This took me over an hour to get perfect. They both laughed and knew the night was off to a great start. After seating and ordering cocktails, Jack got right to the point. Sam, I really like being with you and would like to see where we can proceed. But I have some concerns? Sam hesitated with her glass partially to her mouth and said, go for it, you know I like to talk plain, no BS.

Yes, and it is most appealing. Jack began, since you are aware of my past, you also know of the attack. People planned and conducted an attempt on my life and the people I loved. I don't want to place you in any line of fire. I am still worried about my total return, and any resultant rematch. I would like to go forward; my feelings go deeper than I believed possible. But I can't place you in danger. Sam raised her arm, and Jack continued, Wait, I am not finished. I know I failed my wife and kids. As a trained cop, I should have done better. With tears in his eyes, he said I am not sure I can totally protect you. The server's question broke the silence,

"Are you ready to order?" Sam looked up and said, one more minute and get us another round. The night was calm and slightly muted by Jack's expression of doubt and concern. Small talk remained about the quality of the food and, the richness of the dessert, and the potential for both to diet together. Finally, Sam spoke about the possibility of seeking closure of the attack and subsequent losses by actively devolving into the actual how and why of the whole situation. Jack slowly lifted his eyes to meet Sam's and said, is that what you did for your father? A tear appeared on Sam's cheek, and she replied, we should combine our efforts to help each other.

Chapter 08: Follow The Money

Next morning, as Jack was exiting his vehicle, he spied Superintendent Kirby about to go into the building. Jack called out, SIR! Can I have a word? Sure, Jack, anytime, but can it wait till later? No problem came Jack's reply. I'll call when I am ready. Jack saluted and continued his way to his office.

Sometime later that morning, Jack received a call from retired Detective Samuel about setting a meeting. Jack was glad to agree and asked the where and when? Samuel suggested the café, where Jack and Bill Bushes had met at 3:30 pm. Fine and hung up. Something must be up.

Promptly at 3:30, Jack entered the café and spotted Samuel. Jack excused himself to take the call that just came in. Jack here, Kirby here, can you come up? Sorry, not in the building, but I'll take you to dinner tonight if you are available. Great, I'll miss out on the hotdogs and beans my wife left. Jack laughed and named the place and time. Ok, and Kirby hung up. Hello, said Jack as he approached Samuel. They ordered coffee and a buttered roll for a snack. This reminds me of the old days. God, how I miss them, said Samuel. I investigated our issues and uncovered some crap, so I got that evidence bag. Here, take it! Reaching under the table to give Jack. In a muffled voice, he leaned in slightly and recounted all he had discovered. He also handed over the evidence bag containing the evidence that had been mislaid.

Jack was shocked and dismayed by the names and dates passed over to him. He thanked Samuel for all his help. Jack, Samuel went on, this shit is dynamite, be careful! Don't take chances, and if you need help or backup, Call. We all agreed. If you need us, we are there. Luck Buddy. Jack sat there, deep in thought at the wonders of a brotherhood, joined in strength and solidarity. It almost required tears. Jack read all he could throughout the rest of the afternoon.

Finally, he arrived at the restaurant to greet Josh Kirby, his friend.

Josh sat in a far corner, away from the front windows, to ensure privacy. Josh spoke as Jack approached and ordered the drinks to get us started. And as Jack sat, he asked, what is the matter? You don’t look so happy, Jack.

Jack certainly did not feel happy he had read. Jack started with a statement of their friendship and his concerns going forward. Jack spoke of the coverup and Josh's part in it. Why, when you found out the dirty deals in the case I was working on and the obstruction involved with the case, did you chastise me and berate me for his lack of progress? What did you know, and were you in on the attack?

Josh waved the server over and told him to bring two more of the same. He then began a low soliloquy of explanation.

Jack, I did not know of the behind-the-scenes activity until after the attack was all done. Those above lowered the hammer, and my family was threatened, and they became the potential victims. Jack, you were already dead, along with your family. My wife, my kids; I needed to be there for their protection, no matter the cost. There was and is no way out! Do you know those involved? Asked Jack. Some, and I suspect others. I am getting as much as I can. After you returned, I needed to do something. You are too good a detective not to find out all those who did this and think they got away. I'll do whatever you want, Jack, but I can't put my family in your place. I would rather kill myself now. I know, Josh. I am in my place and worry about any consequences, but I know they can't rest until I am in the ground.

You are in or out. I need your help, quietly, but I need it. No one will know from me about any help you give. The only thing I ask is you protect Sam and your family. The hell with the rest of us. Josh looked around and said I am hungry.

One favor Jack sought was for Taylor Pierce to be reinstated as a detective and made his partner. He knew he could trust him. Josh agreed. He was a good man. Jack replied, He still is!

After several drinks with Josh on top of a very filling steak dinner, Jack welcomed his bed early.

Jack spent most of the next day at the library and then at the archives, reviewing all the players and their backgrounds. His next stop, late in the day, was to search the dead letter office in search of mail not picked up or left addressed to the dead letter file. Eureka. Something remained, along with a self-addressed certified letter. Jack was happy with himself. Bet you no newbie would think of that. His file was fattening up. He signed the required form of concern that the PO inspector had given him and was told to expect a letter of explanation and the missing mail within 3 days.

After supper, his phone rang from Sam, wanting to know if he would go to the cemetery with her to visit and pray over her father's grave. Of course, Jack replied, what time?

The rest of the night was spent reading and creating a dossier to relate evidence to each case and cross-reference to.

Jack laid his head on the pillow and eased into thought. He was recharging his physical presence and allowing his mind to think freely.

The reasoning behind processing a case was like building a ladder out of wooden matchsticks. Too many assumptions and suppositions can cause crumbles and go up in flames when the weight of evidence is brought to bear. Evidence is the binding factor behind real justice. What any detective must do is recover the evidence and follow its path. Much like the adage,

Follow the Money. Jack's next thoughts were more basic. If the world was diverse and different, why are we all striving to evolve into one? Celebrate our diversity, each difference, culture, color, and person. Culture, color, and person make up material differences that affect the fabric of all life and are required to blend into the one. The perfection comes from our diversity blending. Like an artist molding a cake batter, we blend our diversity into a beautiful and perfect creation.

Jack's free thought next wandered into a realm of pain and sorrow. He thought of his daughter's frozen in a metal garbage dumpster. Sam was right, he needed to discover the place they now lay. He knew the way to reach the closure of their passing.

He spent the next morning calling around to set an appointment with the department necessary to reach closure. Josh called to tell him, Taylor Pierce was being upgraded and would be his partner by the end of the week. Jack said, thanks Josh, to which he received a reply to be careful and warning him to watch his back. I'll read him into everything he needs to know. Goodbye, said Josh.

He then glanced around his basement office and thought, the start is over, now comes the hunt!

His first hunt was to get a coffee, but the coffee can was empty. So, he climbed upstairs to replace his supply. Loud voices drifted down the steps as if a Class A chewing out was going on in the squad room. Jack listened to see if he really wanted to get involved. Olson was bitching about practical jokes, not funny, and he wanted to find the culprit. Jack walked in and said, morning all, just need some coffee and sugar. Everyone froze. The captain stood with his hand in the air, holding a large walnut between his fingers. Hay, said Jack, you found my nut. Yeah, someone had hung it over your door, some joke. Sorry. I hung it, said Jack. I wanted to remind myself that whatever anyone else thought, there was only one nut downstairs, and this was it. Thanks,

Capt., I'll put it back up, said Jack, turning to go and as he left, he gave a smile and a wink to the boys. Olson's voice followed down the stairs. I'll be a son of a bitch!

The desk soon became covered with cold files as Jack sorted out any that could have pertained to Taylor Pierce or his partners. He wanted to review them with Tay for any fresh ideas and, between them, gain insights for further investigation. About two hours in, his phone rang. Sam here, and her voice was on the other end of the line. You beat me, said Jack, and they both laughed. Sam went on. I wanted to set some time for us to visit my dad's grave. Saturday afternoon it's supposed to be a beautiful day, at least, that's what I hear. Fine with me. I can pick you up at about 12:30. Sounds good, was Jack's response. Great. Everything else. Ok, yeah, and Jack told her of the episode in the squad room. She asks, who did it? I don't know nor care. A joke is a joke. It's comical. Olson is always busting on them. Makes him feel more important, I guess. Ok! Got to run, bye. Jack smiled, busy girl, I like that, and he went back to dissecting the files sorted for those that showed promise. It was late when he finished. So, placing the chosen three files, he tucked them under his arm and went for food.

The sun rose on time, and so did Jack. He spent extra time this morning to dress professionally to impress Tay and a few potential interviewees they may see. While driving into work, he reflected on a case that had caught his eye. It involved several witnesses from Capitol Hill and some robberies and cyber-related shenanigans. Another involved a Page which lived in the same complex as the lad found dead behind the Washington Monument. Jack despised coincidences.

Tay and Jack spent Thursday and Friday investigating other cold case files. The first on top was a reported missing person case by his wife. One morning after breakfast, he walked out the door without a word and was never seen again. This happened, and the wife just thought he had been in an accident and caught amnesia. She assumed that someday he would recover, like in the movies, but he never came home again. Let us talk to the lady and find out what really happened?

On the drive over, Jack spoke of the change that had occurred in the department and the precinct. readjustments to staff and the several marriages. Tay was shocked to discover that little introvert Evelyn Rose had gotten a breast reduction and Big Mike, all 300 lbs. of him, had asked her to marry him. Holy cow, said Tay, she was only about 95 lbs. and skinny as a rail. Jack laughed and said that after her surgery, she had lost 10 lbs. and needed to put on weight. No shit, 5 lbs. each was Tay's reply. They both laughed at the thought of them together. Jack states, for the record, Evelyn is the boss, and Mike loves that. The happiest couple in the department by far. After Kirby's promotion, the department promoted Olson to Captain. Tay nodded his head in agreement and spoke highly about Josh's promotion. Olson was always an ass-kisser. He had his nose so far up Swanson's ass that if Olson had sneezed, Swanson's hat would blow off. Accurate statement both said Jack and Swanson is now going to retire as Assistant Chief of the Department. Not soon enough responded Tay. The car stopped at the address listed on the complaint, and they rang the bell. Mrs. Colby was an older lady of tall stature, slender, and spoke in a high squeaky tone. Police, did you find Mort's body? Tay said, No, we just want to talk about what happened to him. I don't know, came a return shriller voice. He just went out the door. I had to pay all the bills by myself, that bastard. This happened around 5 years ago. Jack said, No! No! came a shout. He left over 8 years ago. Jack and Tay looked at each other with bewilderment and a perplexed state. How about it? said Tay, Why did you wait 3 years to report him missing? That stupid government required a missing person report to get on welfare and to stop them sending Absentee Ballots for him at every damn election. They still do, idiots. Ok, we will get the picture and get back to you. The shrill voice followed them out the door and down the steps. If you talk to those election people, tell them to stop sending all that crap here.

Back at the station, Tay called the Election Bureau and made an appointment for 11:45 tomorrow, Friday. Jack had already gone back to file searching. He handed two files to Tay and kept two for himself. Two hours later, both had finished and traded each review. Jack was first to note one case was for a missing wife lost three years prior, but the computer upgrade has been redone and her body was discovered on a roadside in Vermont. A victim of a hit and run, caught, and convicted, now serving six in Vermont's prison system. The armed robbery case was transferred by the Justice Department to be prosecuted as part of a RICO case.

We are making progress, said Tay, both mine show up on the computer, closed via conviction. Is it dinner time yet? Was Tay's end of review?

Saturday morning is beautiful, just as Sam had promised. Jack set off on his errand list. The deli was first to get a picnic basket, next came the florist, to place on the grave and give to Sam, finally the wine specialty store. Not like in the old days, when a common liquor place would do. No, he wanted special wine for them to commemorate today. So promptly at 12:30 pm he rang the bell and waited. The door opened, and there stood the loveliest woman Jack had ever seen. WOW was the only thing he could say. Sam said, that's it, all my work for just that. Jack smiled and said, it was worth the effort to render me speechless. Damn you! You can be so romantic when you want to.

Off they went on a lovely day for an excursion. They laughed, flirted, and made friendly banter until arrival at the cemetery gate. They parked and entered a small care keepers' cottage constructed from field stone found around the property. It was a quaint and quite beautiful setting. The cottage contained a large, numbered map that designated the burial sites of each party. A corresponding list was to the right, alphabetically providing parties' names and a number to locate each site. After a quick glance, Jack spotted the Billings name and location. When they reached the car, Jack told Sam of the flowers he had brought to place at her father's grave, and she cried. Jack drove silently around the driveway, past manicured grass, and tall headstones of carved marble. To eventually halt at marker number 2313, this is it, said Jack. Opening the trunk and getting flowers for placement. They walked up a level of grass to stand before a granite headstone with the inscription of Matthew Billings from his loving daughter, Samantha Billing, with some dates underneath it.

Sam cried. Jack mumbled, Sam, I'll give you a few minutes alone. Be right back.

Jack returned to the car to get the basket and flowers for Sam. Upon his return to Sam's side, he said I brought your own flowers and a picnic basket. I thought this was a lovely spot to sit with your father to discuss things and laugh. I am sure he would like that to spend some with you and hear your voice. Sam turned to Jack and burst into tears. Jack was floored. Ok, we'll find someplace else. No, she said. What a wonderful gesture by you. I have dreaded this day and avoided it till now because I feared my reaction. This is the most spectacular gift you could have presented to me. Thank you so much. Sam turned and spoke to her father softly; Jack could not hear a word. Jack busied himself with opening the basket, getting out, and unfolding the blanket. He placed everything at the bottom of the grave so Sam could look to her father. Jack opened the wine and poured each a glass.

Standing beside Sam, he took her in his arms and kissed her with a big hug. Sam caught her breath and said, that is the first time you ever kissed me like that, with a smile. Jack turned and spoke, right pops your daughter brought a gentleman for her first visit. Sam burst out laughing and said,

I love you. Jack, startled, responded I do too! Sam sat down, well are not you the glib one. You love you too.

After about 30 minutes of sweet conversation, Jack spoke, your father is happy in heaven. Really, did you see him up there? "I lost my passport, and they denied me entrance," says Jack in response. I already said I was dead, then alive, then dead, and again alive. This caused some sort of time rift, which trapped me in an open void or something. They tried to explain, but I was confused. Sam spoke, I don't get it. Join the club, said Jack. Who tried to explain what to you? Oh. Brother. In an apparitional environment, both GOD, and the Devil appeared and spoke to me to explain. They spoke to you. Not exactly spoken words, but more of a vibrational frequency of musical tones. Open or low. Sam yelled, Jack, you waited till after I committed to loving you to tell me this. Right in front of my father? He'll think we are both nuts. Sam, he is up there and will know what I am talking about. Ok, Jack, say this again, more slowly, with each syllable distinctly pronounced.

Jack began again. God, Luc, short for Lucifer and Jesus, are required to speak to all tongues, not just on earth but throughout the cosmos. This requires a monolithic language of the language first uncovered in ancient times by using a Pythagorean method in a redaction scale to get a number code and was introduced and developed by a Benedictine monk called the 'Solfeggio Scale', around 991AD. This correspondence to a six-note music scale gave a vibrational tone to notes and consequently gave fruit to syllables for word transmit historical records. Best preserved example is the hymn of St. John. Leading doctors translated Paul's message to St John the Baptist into vibrational electromagnetic sound frequencies. Really, Jack, said Sam. Yes, leading scientists, like Dr. Carl Sagan and Albert Einstein have supported and written extensively about this. Einstein has been quoted as saying, "He was mistaken; there is no real matter, anticipated matter vibrates at specific rates, and everything has its own melody. The Musical nature of nuclear matter from atoms to galaxies is now finally being recognized by science."

Radio telescopes pick up the vibrational melodic tone of all heavenly spheres to generate a balanced resonance for the universe. Research is being carried out with the Solfeggio music code to develop the key to the cosmos, Heaven communicates through vibrational frequencies, I hear what I perceive is God's or the Devil's voice on a multi-conversational network, for lack of a better term. Sorry, the best I can do. Research this on your own so you can better explain it to me. Next time I visit them, I'll ask for a reference book to give you. Hilarious, said Sam. How about another glass of wine with some food this time? Jack uncorked the bottle and, poured two glasses and reopened the basket to pull out some hors d'oeuvres.

Sam sipped some wine, deep in thought for some minutes, as Jack sliced some melon. Finally, she asked, do you think my father can talk to me from beyond the grave? I can't say, but everything I have read and researched allows for that possibility. Researchers have documented many instances where people claim to have received contact from their deceased loved ones. Scientific knowledge is still too early for definitive answers, but many experts espouse conceptually that a universal cosmos language could exist. The melodic vibrational tone nation exists, and a partial translation attempt has been completed. Is an actual ability to converse with the divinity or trees far away? That, my dear, is above my pay grade. Far smarter people than I should be trying. Sam persisted. It is surprising that despite a few thousand years, no noteworthy progress has been made. There is the belief that much had been done until the Imperial Library of Constantinople was purposely burned in 473AD, and over 120,000 volumes were lost. The Crusaders captured the city in 1253AD during the Crusades and burned the library, resulting in the loss of all its archives. Papyrus manuscripts and the teachings of the ancients were destroyed. However, some historians recorded it as being at the behest of the pope and religious leaders. The Vatican does not allow access to the ultimate lower levels, and some people believe that the most valuable documents are still hidden there. Some say that even Hitler sought access to those sealed chambers, and that's why Pope Pius XII made terrible compromises to forestall that eventuality.

Sam looked at Jack with a soulful expression and asked, why is there so much deceit and hate in the world? Why does God allow it? Don't blame God! Humans often abuse their greatest gift of free will. We choose our actions, and that can create moral conflicts. Like many in the world, the Pope faced a moral quandary on how to address the maniacal tendencies of the day. Allow mass destruction and servitude of the known world or stall as best as he could. What would you do? Like I said, above our pay grade. Don't judge, let Luc do it. It is his job!

More wine. Sam smiled and asked, are you trying to get me drunk? Me never replied Jack innocently with a leer. Seriously, thank you for this day, and I hope to reciprocate with you at your family's resting place. They kissed and set about packing.

The day turned out awesome, and the evening appeared even better. Warm temperatures, low breeze wafting through the windows, and soft music on the radio set a romantic mood for just enjoying. Jack, are you really telling me that music like this can contain hidden messages? I am not saying all music can or speaks to everyone, but many people have said that a song or type of music speaks to them. They experience certain feelings from some songs. I don't think these kinds, like on the radio with words, are the ones about which I am talking. It is a tone issue. I intertwined the vibration produced by upper or lower tones on different frequencies to resonate in the brain as different symbols, memories, and representations evolving into vocalization or a type of speech differentiated at a specific segment of the brain. The mind reads this into our psyche, by-passing the ears. Did I explain too much and bore you? said Jack. No, I enjoy hearing your voice, and your thoughts impress and provide interest for me to think about.

Monday morning brought both back to reality and work. Jack and Tay set off first thing to visit the apartment of Howard Martin, the lost Page.

Upon entering the building, the superintendent met them with an immense ring of keys on his hip. Can you show us these two apartments, flashing their badges? Sure, glad to help. Anything wrong with those tenants I should know about. Tay spoke first it's about two previous tenants that lived here. One, Howard Martin, a Page from Capitol Hill, lived here around 4 years ago. Do you mean the kid found murdered at the monument, interrupted the super? Yeah, that one and another, Jason Cole, they did not find him, just disappeared. Yeah, the cops searched and found nothing. Can we just look? Ok, but a fire destroyed the apartments about 3 years ago. Alarm bells, whistles, and tingles coursed through both detectives. How did that happen, asked both at once? They were doing renovations to that side, and someone left two gas heaters on overnight, and everything was gone. After a quick walk-through, they left wondering. Was this an accident or a coverup? They discussed both alternatives on the way over to the Hill.

At the entrance to the secure parking lot stood a gatehouse with a capitol police officer to check credentials, they showed their badges and announced the time of the appointment with Senator Reilly's Chief of Staff, only to be told that it had been cancelled. No notes of explanation, just cancelled. Something stinks, said Tay.

Back to the station and a message for Jack. Call Swares at the scan office. The call to Officer Swares was not, as Jack expected. The authorities did not allow him to visit his family's graves because of his purpose. He sought to have an imaging scan done on the graves to provide a last viewing of their bodies and allow closure. Talking to Swares led to lots of trouble from the diocesan office, which controlled all property owned by the diocese. It would disrupt all other occupants of adjacent plots. What the hell is incorrect with these people? Jack yelled at Swares over the phone. They are afraid of noise complaints from those neighbors, came the response. Jack yelled again, They are all dead, for Christ's sake!The day ended not on a positive note.

As Jack lay down for the night, his thoughts were of his dead family, and rage welled up in his body against anyone involved in the attack. It was the first feeling of anger, long repressed by traumatized emotions. Closure was not as far as it seemed right now.

Jack walked in to find a postal envelope on his desk. He picked it up and thought, not three days, but four to get across town: definitely, from the post office. Jack gingerly turned over the large envelope for irregularities and reached for the knife. Tilting it into the waste basket for debris to drop into as protection. Jack shook the envelope as an added precaution before slitting it's side open.

Jack sat back and read, Dear Sir, this is a response to your letter of concern placed with our department about any lost mail addressed to Mr. Howard Martin, now deceased.

We have located one piece of certified registered mail. We apologize for this error. Our investigation discovered a discrepancy in the address. A neighbor's number was noted for the apartment. Mr. Martin was never home to get the receipt, and when the delivery person discovered said transposition, multiple failed attempts also proved fruitless. The delivery person marked the letter undeliverable and sent it to the dead letter file department since Mr. Martin was never home to receive it, and multiple attempts failed. Sorry for any inconvenience.

Ok, good job. Explains a lot, I hope it produces a lot. Dear Mom, I am so sorry I have not written more often, just stupidity on my part. Everything just gets away from you in DC. It's all-consuming, starting with time and morality. DC, correction, the Capitol corrupts all. Its magnetic forces steal your time, your thoughts, your passions, everything. Like a giant monster eating your very soul. If I could, I would run, but I can't. Especially not back to you. It has become too late for me and way too dangerous to evolve into you. I LOVE YOU, and I am sorry for all I have caused you in the past, and that is yet to come. I fear for my very life. I am convinced an old man was following me tonight to do me harm. I am locked away in my apartment, but inwardly know, I am helpless.

I will seal this letter in an envelope addressed to you and place it in another one addressed to my neighbor for safekeeping until I take it back or cannot.

If I survive till tomorrow, I will call you on a payphone to protect you, GOODBYE HOWIE, your loving son.

Many other papers were enclosed, mostly an account of statements, ledgers, and letters.

Jack sat back and thought, this took two lives. Boy, was he right and knew it numbered his days. Jack sat alone in the basement in silent prayer and thinking? Ten minutes later, Tay came in and asked what was wrong.

Jack growled. Let us go for coffee. He went out and picked up the envelope.

Chapter 09: Secret Music

As they drove out of the driveway, Tay spoke. Jack put a finger to his lips and handed over the envelope with mouthing lips, stating, READ, don't talk.

Jack was not sure if Howard's paranoia was real or just catchy, but he did not want to take chances. Taylor finished the letter, the files, and just sat thinking, taking his cue from Jack. One-half hour saw them pull into Sam's father's cemetery and to his grave. Jack got out, after turning the radio on loud to the religious station. They looked at Matthew's stone, and Jack said Mat, we have made some progress in Howard Martin's murder and in your situation. Just wanted you to know, we have not forgotten you or Jamie Ketch. Both men walked to the shade of the tree.

And leaned on it for support. Taylor then spoke, what's with the cloak and dagger stuff. Jack explained his caution and his experiences so far. There is some sort of connection between his murder and Howard's, pointing a thumb back toward the grave. If so, it may include high-placed officials, in or out of government.

Welcome Home! They both chuckled. After an hour of strategizing, they had two plans. One was offensive, to destroy all involved, and the second was defensive, to remain cautious and protect everyone connected to this operation. The plan involved not discussing this case in or around the car or office, even on their phones. Walking back to the car, Tay asked, what is that on the radio? Jack smiled, God talking, chanting and hymnals, directly from the bishop.

Seriously, Jack, I have heard talk about you and God conversing and being dead and alive simultaneously. What gives?

They left me for dead after the attack; it was the coldest night in a century. I was freeze-dried, like the coffee. Two days later, I thawed out in the morgue. The coroner cut me open, and a blood well sprayed straight up and over everyone. They stitched me and cleaned everything up. Took me to a clinic, and 18 months later, I suddenly awoke and finished rehab, psyched out and cleared for special duty. In a NUT shell.

Come on, what about God? Jack began soberly explaining. I believe that when a person dies, an interlude occurs for just that instant of passing. During that period, nothing remains of the past and nothing is yet to the future. It is a moment of non-existence, profound loss, and nothing. It is supposed to last a split second. Mine lasted forever! Drifting in a non-existing void. I floated on a slab with no extraneous stimuli, nothing in reference. At some point, my senses became alert to a surrounding of lights and later to a visual representation of the beauty of God's cosmos. Gradually other senses came back on various levels. Finally, sound registered, and the angel's wonderful melodic voices chanted vibrational tones, developing into word structure. Later, God and Lucifer spoke. Wow! What are some things they spoke about? There was a lot, they stored many in a restorative state to listen when needed.

Give me something, please, begged Taylor?

Jack replied, ok. Here goes. Luc, Lucifer, was philosophizing about our world and that it's controlled by fear. Everyone looks to a leadership for answers and the leaders don't even understand the right questions. All too often, these leaders pontificate and do their little boy antics. The Devil smiled at me and said, when a little boy comes to a can in the road, he must kick in a game to see who can kick it the farthest and declared the winner. All jump up and down in joy. They then go to the can and start over. None realizes that they can keep getting bigger and bigger until someday it can crush all under its weight. When that day comes, who will decide whose children will get to drink the last remaining water, gasp the last non- contaminated air and who will be left to live. Someone must pick up those cans.

Understand, asked Jack. Yeah, that was the reply. We need to think more and kick less.

Ok, time for lunch and after we eat, we go to the voting booth.

When they met for their appointment, there were two employees waiting. Hello detectives, I am Joseph Foils, and this is Supervisor Lands of Voting Controls. We understand your interest and can assure you we also were concerned. However, sometime back, we performed an validated and confirmed Mr. Colby's absence from that address. Great, is he dead? Asked Taylor. Not exactly, came the answer from the supervisor. Really? Both exclaimed! We went and spoke with him for verification, which he had and provided. He begged us not to disclose any information since our research did not find any criminal activity. We agreed and had not recontacted Mrs. Colby.

They walked out and down the broad steps, shaking their heads. Tay said, it's a great city. People hide in plain sight, and others scurry around in the dark, like rats. Yeah, and we get to deal with both. Replied Jack.

On the way back to the precinct, more chanting was playing over the radio. Come on, Jack, how about some blues, maybe? But Jack replied, I am trying to develop the ability to feel the vibrational tone relayed in the music. Any luck said, Tay. Yeah, watch my hand and each over-tone, the hand will swing up and down on the undertone. The drive was quiet and proved confusing to Taylor, but Jack seemed happy, so Tay was satisfied.

After an hour of case review, they had closed out three more cold files. Two individuals confessed on two cases plus additional crimes unknown to plead out the conviction of greater offenses to gain leniency in sentencing. They transferred the other case to another district for the same reason to gain leniency in sentencing in an original case.

The phone rang, and Josh wanted to meet with Jack. They agreed Jack was to be in front of his house at 6 pm. Jack went home to clean up and wait.

Josh came right on time, and Jack slid into his seat with a smile. Good to see you, Josh. Yeah, same here. I need your help on a grave issue. Ok, said Jack, you got it. What can I do? As they drove, Josh explained his urgent problem. My twenty-fifth wedding anniversary is at the end of next month. I only have six weeks to plan and get a place for the party, caterers, band, and send out invitations. Much less waiting on RSVPs for confirmation. Ok. said Jack, I am out! Are you nuts? Why did you wait so long? Josh whimpered back. I thought all I had to do was make reservations for dinner. Where are we going? First to get some drinks and then check out potential spots. Do you have thoughts on where to look? Josh pointed to the glove compartment, and Jack reached in and pulled out a bunch of papers with names and addresses that matched. Skip stopping for drinks. We'll fill up along the way.

After a few minutes, Jack said pullup. Here's Casa Royale. They parked and went in and sat at the bar. They ordered drinks and requested to meet the party planner. When the drinks came, the bartender said she would be out as soon as her appointment was over. They discussed business as they waited. First subject was about Mrs. Colby's missing husband. I remember that case, about 5 years ago, he just walked out., said Josh. Yes and No. replied Jack. Yes, he walked out, but it was 8 years ago. I am confused about Josh's comment. He left her 8 yrs. ago, but she did not report him gone. She thought he would come back or bout of amnesia. That did not happen, so when she applied for welfare, she needed verification of his absence. She filed to have proof of welfare. Successful, case closed. No Josh, said Jack, the election board had gone seeking him in the meantime, and they ultimately found him less than a mile away. He did not want to go back and begged them not to betray him. They closed the case after they decided no crimes had been committed, just like we had. Josh laughed and said, he hated his old lady? Did he get a new one? Yes, they are just living together happily.

Man, boys are dumb, but men get no smarter. Jack raises his glass, and I'll drink to that. With that, a smiling face appeared and introduced herself as, Jennie, the party planner. They all went into the back to the reception hall to go over the needs. Well, to get started, Josh began, we have a wedding anniversary next month. Jennie said, congratulations, how long have the two of you been married? Josh turned bright red and choked on his drink, spilling it over himself and onto the table. While Josh tried to recover, Jack said, just my friend and his wife. I do like him but fancy his wife better. Josh choked again and mumbled, you are not helping, damn you. Jennie laughed and got up and went out to the bar. She returned immediately with several bar towels and said, I ordered refills, and these towels will come in handy, the way this discussion is going. They all laughed together and got down to the details. After the next hour, they left with brochures, menus, and a price quote. Look around and get other quotes. Please be sure that the other quotes match all what we are including. Some will not mention the need to have attendants for parking, and we provide parking and attendants in our pricing and all other details as outlined in our inclusive quote. Please come back with questions?

As they left, Josh felt impressed and ready to sign. Jack said, tomorrow will be better, but she was very professional. Josh grins and says, that's why I brought you. Jack brought Josh up to date on the murder at the monument, as it was now referred to. Josh also got that tingling up his back at the fact that there might be some connection or link between the two Pages. He gave his critique and suggestions before dropping Jack back home.

Exhaustion overcame Jack, and he needed to sleep. Jack did not know if it was the drinks or the day's work, but he felt exhausted. As Jack was slipping into the haze of sleep, he thought of Sam and wished he had called her earlier.

Thursday

Early Thursday morning saw Jack performing his normal ritual of morning coffee, two cups, pastry, and reading files in his office chair. Nine am on the dot had him calling Sam, and he was glad to hear her respond, Sam here. Jack replied, Jack here. She laughed, as he knew she would. I am sorry I missed you last night, but wait, you were out partying with the boys. Don't lie. Jack sat back and said how could you ever think that of me? I am crushed. Sam giggled and responded with, my spies are everywhere and told me the entire story. Jack replied, well, you should tell me of my wild night. Sam began with him and Josh drinking at a bar and met a girl, a beauty at that, and then all three disappeared into a back room for over an hour. Jack was flabbergasted and did not know what to say. How am I doing? Sam said teasingly. Finally came the dawn, Jack said, you know, Jennie.

Jennie, who came? The reply, ok. Did she tell you why we were there? It is a secret party, and Josh wants to surprise her. I will not tell, but if you need any help, just call. Jack smiles and says, in the movie, Bacall says, just whistle! Two young boys like you two don’t know how yet. Stumped for a reply,

Jack changed the subject. He spoke of the denial by the diocese to go to the graves. She suggested he go to the bishop directly for permission. Great idea, but did she want to go with him to see the bishop? Not such a clever idea. When my father's funeral was over, I made a fuss about the church being offended by having to bury an adulterer next to the saintly patrons. I get it; I had a hiccup with him, too. When we can go, I will keep you updated. Sam replied ok, but remember a girl gets hungry too. I'll call, was his reply. Bye.

Tay came in and placed a sheaf of papers on his desk, motioning him to review. The first was an accounting sheet of payments coinciding with monies received by the parties named. Jack failed to recognize the names, flipping the page. Jack noticed a graph of multiple companies on a hierarchical display. Names of the named owners were under each company's listing and numbers. The name at the top of the page was ARROYO. Jack looked across at Tay, sipping the coffee. Nothing said, so Jack continued searching for links. Next two were letters from a foreign concern about some friction within ARROYO and what can be done. Last was a letter from ARROYO to Congressmen Catcher's office, with a notation on it, spoke to the boss man, and he said not to worry, He will end the problem. Taylor stood up and said, if you are just going to sit on your ass and read all day, I'll go to work. And started for the door. Jack said wait, I am done, and we must meet the informant. Tay took the wheel today to give Jack a chance to assimilate all he had read. Taylor pulled into the Jefferson Memorial parking lot. They stepped outside to catch some cool air and discuss this additional evidence.

What the hell have we stepped into? Asked Tay. I don't know, but it's a gigantic pile of something, and we are it. Taylor spoke up, Jack, saying that this might be too big, and everything seems to interconnect. Some go up, but how high, and others go down. Who can we trust? Jack looked at Tay and answered US, we got the short straw. The next hour was spent going in circles. Finally, Jack broke the spell and spoke. We are looking for the wrong answer. Tay looked perplexed while Jack continued. We are looking for a way out and not a resolution. They left to place a call to the bishop. As they left the memorial parking lot, Jack turned on the radio to his new favorite station, and as the sound of chanting filled the car, Tay cried, Come on, Jack. The smile appeared on Jack's face as he replied, if this will drive us nuts, think what it will do for eavesdroppers. They started in the precinct's direction when suddenly Jack put out his hand as if to say, muted, be still. Tay hardly breathed. After a few minutes of slow drive, Jack spun around and headed back towards the direction they had just come from.

Chapter 10: When Does Defender become the Offender?

It soon became clear the direction and then the destination of the car. Jack did not speak and, in an almost trance-like state, driven by instinct, steered through the gate past the beautiful lawn and marble statuary to stop at the grave of Matthew Billings. Jack stepped from the vehicle while turning the radio louder and walked up and sat on the headstone, all without a word.

Jack saw all this as if in an out-of-body status. The feeling was halfway between life and death, as if he were being pulled toward something or someone. The pull grew stronger as he reached out his hand to steady himself as he sat down.

The voice, in a slightly melodic tone, was soft and calming. Nice to meet you, Jack. Please be kind to her! I have been allowed to use this channel to communicate some interest to you. Beware of getting ahead of yourself in the investigation. It can mislead you, and danger awaits. Stay alert to all the facts and consider each separately and in combination as part of the giant puzzle. The truth will be your path to the answers you seek, all of them.

Remember that Systemic Logic will sometimes lead to a point of delimitation when is too much; too much? When does the defender become the offender?

Matt began by admonishing me, too.

Jack felt himself falling, and as he lay on the beautiful green grass, he heard Tay's powerful voice, which brought him back to reality. Jack, what in the hell is the matter with you?

Jack, with Tay's help, stumbled back to the car. His only words were, damn, I need some coffee. Tay replied, that makes two of us. You scared the hell out of me. Jack smiled at his friend and said, I am ok, really.

Once Jack got his second refill at the coffee shop, he began interpreting the events that took place. The music's rhythm, melody, and expression captured a feeling in a harmonious way. I apologize, but that's the best explanation I can provide. My mind was divided into two distinct realities by my state of being, leading me to follow the messenger to the grave. Matthew spoke to me to assist with our investigation. Jack! Jack, I am taking you to the hospital? No, don't be silly, I am ok, and this really happened. The chanting can provide a vessel for spiritual guidance, which is the best I can figure. Tay breaks in to say, how about I take over, at least, to visit Sam?

No! said Jack, standing abruptly.

What would we say? We just left your dad, and Jack had a long talk with him about you. Yeah, great, she already leans towards me being crazy.

Tay smiles at Jack and says, she may not be alone in that. Sit back down and relax. Jack sits and restarts his narration of events. Matthew began with an admonishment to be good and kind to Sam, and that he could use a channel to communicate. Not to get ahead of ourselves, because we can easily be misled and run into danger, we should check all the facts to verify the authenticity and always keep the big picture in mind. Follow the truth to get your answers. Last, was like a proverb; when is too much, too much. When does the defender become the offender? They sat across from each other, both lost in thought, for almost 5 minutes. My mind is swirling around, Jack. The number of answers is infinite. Jack said, not really. Think about some other conversations I have heard. One comes to mind. Good questions deserve good answers, and so good answers lead to good questions. Focus and use "free will" to simplify and clarify the good ones. Taylor looked and said, That's the first damn thing I can understand and see its value to our predicament. Why don't we start at the beginning and filter all we know through this advice for good answers? So, the day ended with both men bleary-eyed and bewildered by all the assumptions and suppositions they had made and placed on paper. The notepad had circles around the bishop, Olson, and Capitol Hill??? Follow the line of time between Howard Martin's death and the disappearance of Jason Cole. Somewhere during that period, an excellent answer was waiting to be found. They left the office thinking of a nice bed, but by the rumble from both abdominal regions had overcome all mental faculties. Tay asked Jack, I hear you, and we should listen to each other and get some food. Jack laughed and agreed. I know a great pub in Georgetown with a delicious roast beef sandwich and roasted potatoes as a side, countered Tay. Do you think our stomachs will make it, was Jack's only reply? 20 minutes later saw them sliding into a booth to delicious smells of beef and beers. They ordered immediately and got two cold beers within seconds.

My kind of place, said Jack, clearly relaxing. Some young lady with a steno pad on her lap called out in a loud voice, can you turn up the volume of the TV? She gave the impression of being a journalist. The voice on the TV was of a religious dignitary at a news conference. They listened until their meal arrived. Tay asked, what was all the fuss about. The server shrugged and spoke. Some bishops or cardinals are defending the church against criticism regarding their lack of concern for human rights for those immigrants risking their lives to trek through dangerous territory and floods to get here with no hope. He is expressing the church's dismay and frustration over the difficulties and obstacles to providing any help or support. Just

BS, same old, same old. Taylor asks, where is God now? Ask him next time you visit, will you? Jack looked up to Tay and said, don't blame God, or Jesus, or even the Devil. Leaders, whether religious, are most often the problem. God and Jesus make and made all things simple and easy for humans! Humans create difficulties for other humans with no external influence. Remember your early catechism teachings. Nothing could have been easier than in The Garden of Eden. God gave for nothing. All God asks is for them to use his gift of "Free Will" to think and make rational decisions. They abused his generosity and forced him to punish his creations for the rejection of their father. Sure, the myth is they bit an apple after being told not to. Well, every day, people make the choices and bite that damn apple. WOW, Jack, if you don't like the sandwich, just say so. Both sat back, laughed, and ordered coffee and a big dessert.

One hour later, Jack was sound asleep and ready to resume his hunt. While he slept, his mind wondered where he developed those thoughts and feelings that he espoused to his friend in such a vehement manner that it did not sound like God or the Devil. More like a loving son defending his beloved father.

Friday morning saw Tay and Jack starting all over again.

They began at the beginning by seeking any connections between the bishop and Captain Sven Olsen, looking for any commonality as clubs, choir, or charities involved in and many other simple meeting places.

Next came a survey of documents about cross-connections between the bishop and Capitol Hill staff. This was more complicated. Names of mutual acquaintances on the Hill and in religious exposures. Any memberships of community service or standing committees. We found many connections between the bishop and Howard Martin or Jason Cole. Olson to Martin or Olson to Cole. Olson to members of Congress and all required investigations.

Jack called Sam to invite her on a private personal tour of the monuments around the mall. Sam seemed hesitant. You know, I have lived in DC most of my life and have seen all of them many times. Jack retorted, you, like most natives and visitors, see them in passing or just sprinting to each to have a cursory look, take some pictures as proof of being there, and rush to get to the next stop. Never enjoying the experience or beauty, artistry, and efforts of those who worked so hard to represent our history and sacrifices of bravery that made our country the place it really is. Wow, Jack, do you moonlight as a tour guide? Asked Sam. Just for you, was the reply. A personal private tour sounds interesting. What time? Tomorrow around 2:30, said Jack. I have Josh coming over to fill out the invitations, sign and do RSVP"s all morning. So, I'll pick you up, and maybe we'll miss the early morning crowds. Ok, she said, should we take your car or mine? Jack hesitated and asked, quizzed, you don't have a car? She laughed and said, Jack, it's the thought that counts. Smartass, he said, we'll take mine. It's easier to find parking for a police car, even unmarked, in DC.

Josh arrived late, and everything was more difficult than they had believed. Josh, visibly upset grimaced out the words, we should have gotten Sam to help us. Jack responded, no, you said it will be easy, she'll mock anything we say or do. You know how women are. They have this belief that men are useless. Jack retorted, they are right, at least with this sort of thing. Josh laughed and said, ok, but give me a hammer and watch out. Yeah, watch you bust your thumb, and both grinned broadly.

Jack drove up to Sam's place just in time for her exit and walk towards his car. He thought, boy! She can walk. Sam slid into the car and leaned over to kiss his cheek, and said, you have got a sheepish grin on your face. What are you thinking? Jack cleared his throat and said, man, can that babe walk? He gunned the car and made a sharp turn as Sam gave a dirty little laugh. After finding an available spot to park, they walked across the vibrant green grass of the mall until reaching the World War II Memorial. Walking between and around this beautiful spot created a most calming and exuded reverence, inviting soft speech and respect.

They sat together on the steps of the giant fountain with their feet in the beautiful water, touching toes in a silent, very romantic manner, surrounded by the feeling of love generated within this monument to brave souls. Suddenly, the multiple spigots hidden under the water spouted geysers of cascading droplets into the air high above and showered down as tears of rain. A wondrous experience missed by so many. As they sat, Jack spoke of his last visit here. He began with twilight creeping over the monument's tops, and as he sat in the muted and solitude, listening to the rustle of the wind in the trees, he heard a faint voice, like from a frail woman calling a name. As I listened more intently, I again felt the resonance of a name and a response this time. More names and replies of here, present, and yea. Some things or some presence tugged at me. I rose and walked toward the voices, getting louder and stronger with each step, past the reflecting pool, Constitution Gardens, and Lincoln Memorial was The Vietnam Memorial Wall and there, and a cascading refrain of a name and a corresponding reply, answering their call to duty one last time. Sorry, said Jack as tears flowed down his cheeks. I rarely show my emotions like this. Sam placed her arms around his and whispered in his ear. Jack, this is good for you. It is a manifestation of all the grief, anger, and trauma pent up inside from the attack and ensuing violence. You continue to feel guilt and frustration towards yourself about everything. Let it out, and if anyone is watching or comments, I'll tell them to go F*** themselves.

After resting and drying off, they strolled toward the Lincoln Memorial, where they sat in a darkened corner. Speaking softly, Sam used her wares and professional acuity to help Jack deal with and dispose of some anger and angst. Later, outside, she offered to buy him a drink. Jack, brightening up, said great! Sam let the way to the coffee van and ordered two hot chocolates with whipped cream. As Jack accepted his drink, he said, Big Spender! They read all the inscriptions and speeches of Honest Abe before saluting and heading over to the Vietnam Memorial.

People, including families, busloads of students, and lingerers, crowded the Vietnam Memorial. They stood on the slight hill above the entrance path to get an unobstructed view of everyone walking through. Many were crying, some were etching the name of a loved one with a paper and pencil supplied by the park department, and some stood in silent prayer. The silence was only broken by an occasional voice crying out a loved one's name as if on a roll call.

One such mother leaned on the wall with her hand resting on her son's name and cried out his name. An alternate younger voice startled the crowd. In a loud voice, one teenager yelled HERE, and another called present in reply. Many turned and gave looks of disgust or despair. All the teenagers in the group laughed, some out of embarrassment. Jack frowned and approached the group, saying, are you mocking that mother's sorrow? The big mouth says, What's it to you! Sam moves closer to Jack, and Jack takes a step forward as the group bands together. I am Detective Sergeant Jack Spec of the DC Metro Police, and that officer, gesturing him to come forward, is a member of the Federal Park Police. He takes offense at all smartasses disturbing family members attending the parks. Right Officer? Yes, that was the reply, and as a veteran, I hate smartasses! Jack and Sam walked away to the sweet sound of an irate officer demanding IDs from everyone and asking. Where was their keeper? He would have to explain to him the crimes committed and why they might spend the night in jail. Both Jack and Sam were laughing and enjoying their feelings.

Hungry, my turn to buy, said Jack. Sam reminded, "Keep in mind, this is an expensive date."

They doubled back, and on the way to the Jefferson Memorial, passed the Martin Luther King Memorial, and Jack stopped at a vendor cart. Two long dogs with mustard, relish, onions, and ketchup. Jack asked Sam, need sauerkraut, she replied, only if you can afford it, dear. The vendor served while laughing and asked if they needed any soda? Sam replied, just one, as she took a plastic cup. Coke ok, sure said Mr. Big Spender, and they sat on a bench overlooking the beautiful Tidal Basin. They talked over many items, especially the feeling between them. Time seemed to vanish, and darkness descended. Jack felt apprehension rise in his body and kept glancing around. Sam sensed his anxiety and decided she was too tired to visit any more memorials, and they walked the short distance along a brightly lit path. Jack walked Sam to her door and kissed her deeply. After several minutes, he asked her to go with him to a special place tomorrow. Sam said, anywhere, anytime. Jack smiled and said dress up, and I will see you at 2 pm.

Sunday afternoon at 2 pm had Jack ringing her doorbell. The door opened, and a lovely vision met his gaze. Perfect, was all he said, taking her hand and leading her to the car.

Fifteen minutes later, he parked in front of the Cathedral and said, Special Service Mass for the Pope's recovery. ok, said Sam. And in they went. Jack noticed that only about half the seats were filled and led the way down front. None other than the bishop himself conducted the service. The service was brief and provided updates on the Pope's condition and level of recovery. The refugees seeking asylum and protection offered prayers to the Pope and made sacrifices. After mass, the Pope greeted those present and blessed all individually. Jack shook the bishop's hand firmly and introduced Sam as his psychologist. He then asked if the bishop could arrange his schedule to include a meeting with

Jack later this week. The bishop said it was an inconvenient time, but he would try. Jack replied Thank you, and we received our complimentary blessing.

Outside, Sam chided at Jack. Is that the only reason we are out today? I am used as an adornment to display to the bishop for an appointment.

No, not at all. I was coming before I asked last night, and it gave me more time to spend with you. Jack explains they are visiting her father's grave again to think about and discuss matters of significant importance to them both. Sam was muted, and Jack knew she was worried, as he was, and to ease tension, he turned on the radio, more chants. Sam looked at Jack several times and wondered about Jack's state of mind and the resultant impact upon her.

Finally, the longer-than-usual drive ended, and as they approached the grave, Jack left the radio on loud. Taking her hand, he led her to the gravestone and sat her on it. She squirmed in Jack's arms and responded with, I am not comfortable with this, Jack. Jack tries to speak and explain his actions. Sam says, no, Let's just go! A melodic voice recites, for Christ's sake, just sit and listen for once, Kitten. Sam slips and slumps to the ground and asks, what did you call me? Jack remarks. It was not me, but your father calling you Kitten. I don't know why? Jack, is this some sick game or joke? Not funny, said Sam angrily. What the hell is going on? Did you slip something in my drink? Am I as crazy as you are? Is it contagious? Continuing talking to no one, just rambling. Suddenly, the voice declares, Kitten, get off my grass!

Sam slumps over in a faint. The voice is of Matthew, her father, and he says to Jack, that's my girl, never could shut up. She'll come around shortly. Jack and Matt then continue uninterrupted to speak of many things, such as the conveyance of information, passing of messages, and strategizing between old comrades separated yet alike. Sam awoke and asked if this was real? Jack helped her up and tried to explain. He told her to listen for the vibrational musical tones on a low scale and to define meaning. Sam jumped back onto the grass, and her father's voice announced, Kitten, get off my grass, I fertilized it myself. Jack grabbed Sam as she bent at the knees. Matt, Jack said she's had a tough day, and her mind is recoiling from the indecision of whether she is crazy or not. Yes, he is, too, now. Am I crazy? Matt's laughter flows through, and he addresses his daughter. Your mom is with me, and we both love you and Jack. Listen to his instruction and his crazy chanting. This is real and available for transcription. He is real. Look forward to seeing you both again soon. The radio shut off, and only low static remained. Sam leaned against Jack and asked if they were going to get married in an asylum.

The night was still young, and the silence of solace wafted in the air.

Jack met Taylor at their favored café for breakfast and to discuss the weekend and the information compiled. However, no mention of Sam, his visit to the grave, or subsequent events was given. They discussed the leads generated Friday and what Tay had developed. Tay began with a synopsis of two informants' confessions to being arrested many years ago and trading information to" get out of jail free." The information involved David Blaine, the body found dumped in the river and recovered about 8 months ago. Blaine was a small-time collection agent (enforcer for the mob), and he branched off for consulting gigs. They did not know who? They heard he was part of the gang that attacked you. He fucked up and went for a swim. We have got to squeeze them, said Jack, sitting up straighter in his chair. No can do! They are protected. I talked to them via an old contact, who just dropped a shipment of fent to them. Can not burn her, too valuable an asset. They were so high; they took me for a brother. Anyway, they disclosed some info on the protector they own. Their words and some of his vices. Both are in management and Swedish, the blonde-haired bastards. Their words. Do you think what I am thinking, asked Jack? Tay replied, you were right to go cloak and dagger. Taylor leaned over to softly ask Jack, do you suppose Blaine killed your daughter by accident, and that was his fuckup.

Jack sat back in stunned disbelief and sought to re-question everything he thought had happened, really happened. We need to focus on everything associated with the two Swedes, said Jack. Ok, but something else produced those two creeps. When one puked all over the couch, the other threw him out. He then went on a rant about the stupidity of the asshole. He let it slip that Blaine knew of you and participated in killing that Page in a fit of anger at the boy's whimpering and trying to get loose. He stopped the car and beat the shit out of him, thinking he could make people believe a robber had done it and left the body behind the monument. Shit, hell, and damn, exclaimed Jack, now two connections to me and to three murders. He also intimated that the puker assisted in the disposal of another one. Jack spun around and said one word, Jason?

Tay shrugged his shoulders and took out his wallet to pay. Jack said whoa, on me, you earned it today. Tay replied, we must protect my friend. Jack paid and said he was much too valuable to risk.

Bypassing the office, they proceeded to central records and spent most of the day searching old cases, files, and any cross references. The difficulty was in providing a screen or filter to cover their tracks in case anyone got suspicious and came looking. Taylor produced a radical idea to contact Jack's poker buddies to pick their brains. When they took a break for lunch, they called Bill Brushes and set a meet for a game with the boys. They followed different lead trails. Tay followed Swanson's trail, and Olson became the quest for Jack. Jack was especially concerned by Olson's activities prior to and directly after the attack. How did he become "first on the scene" at the murder of Matthew and Jamie, plus my family's attack? Note to oneself, speak to Josh, and get the names of everyone onsite that night.

Remembering Matt's counsel to follow the truth to verifiable answers, and the logical reasoning in his brain kept repeating. When does the defender become the offender? Spurs Jack on the hunt to create a timeline of anything about Olson and combine it with Assistant Chief Swanson.

The two detectives met at the library and sat at a back reading table with a computer on it in front of Jack and another next to him for Tay.

They choose the location to decrease anyone deciphering their search parameters, of anything they searched for.

Jack searched for any events that Detective Olson attended or presided over during the period before or after the disappearance of one Jason Cole or the death of Howard Martin. The screen listed several items with no mention of Olson or Swanson. However, page two had an article about

Captain Swanson being Knighted in the Order of the Knights of Columbus, with a picture of the annual dinner. Front and center was the bishop himself, with Swanson sitting on his right and third from the left sat a smug Olson. Jack hit the print button and continued his search. Jack hit upon several more pictures of the bishop and either Olson or Swanson. Taylor had also been busy pushing his print button, and finally, the librarian announced closing and thanked them for utilizing their library. They switched files so both would know the contents and could review them for tomorrow's breakfast. On his way home, he called Sam to verify she was alright and asked her to dinner Thursday night. She laughed and told him she was busy at a function and was going to call him as an escort. Wonderful, email me the details. She said ok and dress up. That is one smart girl and a looker.

Turning the radio on, with chants. Suddenly, a voice startled Jack as he heard a priest say this is WRCH serving the metro area with the sounds of God. His Excellency, the Bishop of Washington, DC, brings tonight's broadcast to you.

Tuesday morning, Jack caught Josh as he was going into his office and asked, Got time? Josh, while taking his jacket off and sitting down, said, grab a understood the reasons Josh was cornered into being a passive participant, but now his knowledge of David Blaine's connection to the death of Howard Martin and the disappearance of Jason Cole, after hesitating, he went on to mention the connection between Rachel and David. Josh was upset and reiterated his grief and guilt for placing everyone in jeopardy and going along. Josh then asked Jack to meet him for lunch today or tomorrow, and said he'd have copies of everything he knew about and surmised about the events during that chaotic time. Jack agreed to meet for an early bird dinner at 4:30 and then departed. Jack believed that it was justified not to involve Olson, as it gave Josh the opportunity to prove himself and strengthen Jack's trust in him. Reviewing the little evidence accumulated to date for the two cases and searching for any other connections occupied the rest of their day. In checking time records for the date of Howard Martin's murder, Jack saw the duty roster. It showed Olson on the night shift, starting at 11 pm, and at 12:45 am he logged off to check suspicious activity and did not log on again until 3:30 am. Note to Tay to check the officer's logbook of all persons at the crime scene. Jack pulled out his notebook to discuss his thoughts with Tay from Brushes files, which now made more sense when combined with the newest information. He still must produce something to convince the bishop to allow access to scan the graves.

He received an invitation on the office phone to attend a poker game at Mr. Brushes' place at 11 am tomorrow and requested to bring his friend.

Chapter 11: Hold Them or Fold Them

Meet for poker at 11 am on Wednesday. Bill Brushes opened the door right away and welcomed them. You know where the chips and dip are and the coffee pot and cake on the table. Tay asks, are we really going to play poker? House rules came to a chorus of replies. Ok, we are in. Once the first deal was done, the cards lay on the table. To enhance their cover, these were experienced men and took no chances. The talk was low, and a radio played in the background. Tay asked, can you get, like, the Bee Gees or the like. Jack asked about hymnal music. Tay relented and said, ok to this. All the talk went directly to what everyone was fascinated in. Some spoke of cross- connections developed by each. One had talked to the officers at the crime scene at the monument, and Jack asked if anyone had witnessed Olson onsite. Olson had stopped but did not get out of his car. He called officers over to his car to question each present but refused to get out to investigate anything. The contention and general impression was that he seemed nervous and specific as to all found items. Two members remembered that he was concerned about any cards or personal items that might have been found. He even described several places to verify where we had searched or found. One officer got the impression that the detective had already been there. Jack made a note to carefully review all collected evidence from all locations for potential fingerprints or DNA to connect to Olson, Swanson, or anyone not supposed to be there.

Jack had Randy carefully retell his story of events from memory. This was while Tay read the actual event sequence report and made notations. Then Tay questioned some memories of events to recover lost memories and provide an increased level of accuracy and depth to the report. The other men then chimed in with their reflections of all conversions during the events and after around the station as gossip, facts, or conjectures. The conversion provides fruitful and much more discoveries. They combined singular timelines for each event and readjusted them by reassembling some facts. A productive afternoon for all. Each man left a twenty on the table not as lost money but out of respect for Bill's generosity. As Jack was leaving, he said, if anything comes up. All replied Call, we want more of your money. As the door opened, they went out.

Josh at 4 pm Wednesday.

Josh knocked on Jack's door and came in to see Jack asleep on the couch. Jack, wake up, wake up. Jack opened his bleary-looking eyes; I am awake. Sure, you are. Got any coffee leftover, Josh asked. In the pot was Jack's reply. It's cold, came back a yell. Put the damn shit in the microwave.

The coffee tasted like shit, as Jack had said, but it did the trick. Jack was wide awake now and took a shower before dressing for dinner with Josh. While driving to the Steak House, Jack turns on his favorite channel, and Josh says oh brother, I have been warned about your obsession. Jack turned to look at Josh and innocently asked, What? Josh said, this is the way to talk to God. No, it is one way he can communicate with us. I don't believe that crap. Ok, you are right via free will that God gave you to disagree. Josh asks, can you put it into a simple explanation for a dumb cop? First, Josh, don't BS me about you being simple.

All is so, just imagine sound is a vibration of air while vibrations in the energetic field are primal and affect everything because, as physics and metaphysics agree, absolutely everything, including mankind, is vibrating energy. So, imagine encapsulating the power by use of the 'Solfeggio Frequencies' energetically instead of as mere sounds. The possibilities are infinite.

Early on, the musical scale was called, Just Intonation and fell below the A417 Hz. More modern music is within a scale A440 Hz frequency, and a seventh note, "TI," was added, and the first changed from "UT" to a higher "doe." This allowed an additional" DO" for greater vocal range and is more dissonant as it is based upon "Twelve-Tone Equal Temperament."

Successful music lesson, but how does that allow God to talk to us? Jack says that lower frequencies can create quality and perception.

Human ears can register sounds from about 20 Hz in frequency up to 20,000 Hz, depending, of course, upon the hearer. People with hearing loss usually have trouble hearing sounds in the higher frequency range. Speech usually falls within the 100 and 8000 Hz range. People may have difficulty discerning speech once it exceeds about 3000-4000 Hz. The ancient 'Solfeggio Scale' is renowned for its use in the Gregorian Chants, but its history can be traced back to Biblical times. Many musicologists and scientists consider the 6-tone scale, and an additional three tones discovered since, to have a positive effect on the mind and body.

Back in the 11th century, a Benedictine monk named Guido D'Arezzo introduced the musical scale we now know as the 'Solfeggio Frequencies' – though modern research contests that the scale dates back much further. The monks used the original six 'Solfeggio Notes' in their Gregorian chants, which we now know to comprise the frequencies 396, 417, 528, 639, 741, and 852 (Hertz).

For thousands of years, from Egypt to Greece, a different frequency was used. The Schiller Institute and various physicists and scientists contend the 440 Hz frequency not only lacks mathematical or scientific significance but is also actually out of tune with the natural world and wider universe because of the mathematical consistency 432 Hz has with the vibrations of the natural universe.

Some argue the 440 Hz tuning keeps us closed off from a higher sense of meaning and disconnected from our surroundings. Mozart and Italian opera composer Giuseppe Fortunio Francesco Verdi used the natural 432 Hz vibration. Researchers have found that it tuned the singing bowls and other instruments of Tibetan monks to 432 Hz. People also believe that the harmonic frequency was used to tune the instruments of the ancient Greek God of music, Orpheus.

Explorers and religious missionaries recount stories of native tribes using the scale based upon the notes of the 'Solfeggio Scale'. You have seen untold movies and shows where the native tribes used chanting and drumbeats for ceremonies and to cure sick or infirmed members. They are all based on the same scale: from the farthest areas of Africa to Asia, to far northern sections and isolated islands in the Pacific comes the same sounds occurring in repetitious origin along with harmonious sounds to assist the body recuperation or to place before their deities' requests in seek of answers. Researchers have uncovered an accentuation of audio vocal patterns that can resonate at 10 to 15 Hz, and modulation can occur at 7.83 Hz frequency, which is the resonant frequency of earth's naturally occurring intensity magnetic radiation value.

Please answer me, Josh, how this phenomenon could have existed? Sam's correct, we are all going to end up as crazy as you. Jack says simply, All I know is that when I listen to these chants, they touch my soul unlike any other music, and my spirit soars. And that's good.

The reservation sat them in a muted corner to give them space to do their business.

Drinks were ordered; it was down to business.

Without hesitation, he begins with his suspicions about Captain Olson and Assistant Chief Swanson. He discusses his initial vague worries and how they kept coming back repeatedly. He began his cautionary procedures just before the attack. If he had any inkling of the impending scenario, he would have gone public and wished he had. After the damage was done, he was caught in it, whether he liked it or not. I was promoted, and Olson took over. You survived, and the shit hit the fan. The original case you were looking into led to a congressional chief of staff, a congressional representative, and only God knows who else. Why don't you just ask and save us a lot of trouble? More drinks came, and the meal started. While eating, Jack laid out all he had discovered. Leaving out the boys and most of Tay's help. Better to protect them than be sorry later. He told about Olson's activities at the murder of both Jamie and Detective Matthew and sending his senior partner around the back to chase a suspect. Which left Olson inside alone for at least 10 minutes. He also told Josh about the incident at the murder crime scene and the fellow officers' concerns, the impression of Olson being on site early, and his failing to exit his vehicle. One officer saw Olson changing after a quick shower at the station and bundling his clothes into a plastic bag. Another sore subject was the fact that Olson denied anyone other than himself to one observe his family's bodies and that Swanson had paused at that scene to verify that everything was taken care of, as noted by the officer on traffic control. Jack ended with the news regarding Howard Martin's letter, warning of his impending death, and an old man following him. Josh was heartbroken and warned Jack to play it all close to the vest. He understood if Jack wanted to limit feeding data to his superiors, including himself. They stood and shook hands for a while, and understand and know you are behind me. Yes, mouthed Josh, call me for backup when you need it.

Jack drove slowly and called Sam. Are you ready for tomorrow, he asked? Sam said yes, and I bought a new dress to impress, so be impressed. Goes home to digest his supper and all he learned from Josh. Still unsure of what to say to persuade the bishop. weaknesses and fears, the reason for the path to proceed. Speak to his ministry and personal beliefs. Do that, and you will get answers to your correct questions. Went to sleep and felt that feeling of floating and thought, not tonight,

I can't meet God with a hangover. Those were his last conscious words. Floating along, drifting into the sleep of utter relaxation. A friendly voice says, Hi Jack, thinks he's lucky, not God. Luc sits next to the flaming firepit and gestures toward Jack's favorite chair. Jack, did you enjoy your evening? Yes, was the reply, as much as I remember. Luc smiles at Jack and tells Jack to pay attention to these facts, that whatever you think or fear of the bishop, he is an ordained minister of GOD! You feel a direction. Strength and faith are on your side. Trust God's wisdom. We will all meet soon, and darkness settles to fade back to the sublime stillness of dawn.

As the day progresses, Jack gets hungry, and he realizes it's already late. He races home to change and gets ready to be impressed and, of course, be impressive himself. Jack soon picks Sam up who looks gorgeous and drives to the hospital. He remembers so well. Will there be anyone I know there? Besides me, the bishop, and a dozen nurses and doctors who can bear witness to have not any idea. Great, said Jack, which is a confidence booster.

Sam giggled and sat closer to Jack and provided background information about the dignitaries and staff that would be present. She warned him of the butt kissers and the snobs and to avoid any greasy items if he was going to drink.

Jack said thank you and felt suitably prepared to face the lion's den.

They arrived at the appointed time and correctly walked the reception line, shaking all hands, as each remarked on how beautiful Sam looked and Jack was a catch in passing. The large open lobby area was expansive, even when filled with tables, chairs, bars, and guests. The servants were just accessorial and required to perform their duties without being seen or in the way. No expense was spared, and the checkbooks were open for donations to use, as the silent auction had already been open and busy. Jack was finishing his second drink when Swanson and Olson arrived. They saw him and whispered between themselves. Jack slowly circled the room, closing in on the tight circle surrounding the bishop as if he were the center of a wagon train or the world. Tough to penetrate, so Jack bided his time. Two more drinks came and disposed before the bishop spoke out beyond his barricade. Jack Spec, I am glad to see you could make it. Yes, sir, a wonderful gathering, and edifice to your commitment to the health care of your flock! Thanks, Jack. When you have a free moment, I wish to discuss something with you. Jack smiles and says, call me over when you are free. I will guard my companion.

Half an hour later, dinner started, and everyone sat down to boring conversations and false platitudes. Jack's face seemed frozen in his smile, and Sam kicked him, more than once under the table. With half the dinner complete came the obligatory speeches by several individuals that slurred parts and sipped too often along the way. The bishop spoke briefly and rose to leave. Jack was prepared and had the door covered. The bishop, called out as he was leaving, glad you caught me! Be at my office tomorrow morning at 10:15 am exactly. I have a luncheon meeting with several congressmen, and they are always in a hurry. He was gone as if a wisp of smoke. Jack looked around for Sam, who was congratulating all and saying goodbyes. They walked down the center stair and out the big automatic doors into the parking area. I'll take your keys, said Sam. Whoa, came his reply. Sam stood defiantly and told Jack, just because I don't want a car does not mean I don't have a license. Sam drives Jack home and helps him upstairs to her apartment. Jack stands on wobbly legs and grins sheepishly and stupidly. Sam says, Jack, you can't risk driving, so you will stay the night. Jack asks if that is so you can take advantage of me. Sam turns to look at him and says, NO, only in your dreams. Take your clothes off, again with an idiotic smile. I need to hang them up so you can still wear them out in the morning. Jack lay on the couch and was covered by Sam, who kissed him good night.

He went to sleep and felt that feeling of floating and thought not again, but Jack was wrong. Instead of God or

Lucifer, his mother spoke to him in terms and tone as only a mother could use. She spoke of the immense love and pride that flourished within her. Her words caution not to accept finite fears, and never lose infinite hope. Our hope is the ability to see there is light, despite all the darkness. Her soft tones conveys volumes about her alternate reality after death in a multi-dimensional spatial space where time does not exist. I can call out names, Vivian and she'll appear and speak with me, or my mother, your grandmother. Many discussions about family members, but we all are proud of you. Especially Vivian, she likes your choice and believes in you.

Jack gets up and dresses as quietly as possible to avoid disturbing Sam, who is sleeping. He grabs a bagel and coffee, still partially hungover, and makes his way through the early DC traffic. He scrutinizes each word uttered by his mother, while cherishing all of them.

Jack looks forward to another chance to ask for some clarifications on the strategies to enforce his will and make the bishop reconsider his prior decision to disallow access to his family's graves.

Arriving at exactly 10 am at the diocesan offices, he entered the bishop's private sanctuary. He was alone and walked around, viewing the enormity of the bishop's presence, represented by the gallery of pictures of the bishop on his altar, surrounded by his flock, and in revered postures or scenarios by encircling throngs of people. Good questions reveal excellent answers.

Ten minutes later, in came the bishop with his coat already on and hat in hand.

Sorry, Jack running late as usual. Jack puts out his hand for the bishop to shake and begins to quickly explain his predicament. The attack, which killed his family, also left him unconscious, bleeding, and unable to see. He heard the screams of his children and their last gasps but nothing from his wife. The torturer cut out her tongue and cut her face, which left her unable to scream or gasp, only a gurgling noise. There was not any closure. They believed he was dead, and when he returned to life, there was nothing left. He now has recovered, to an extent, and has met someone to restore his values and life. You met Sam last night. However, it seems impossible to submerge or put past feelings behind him. That is not fair to a wife or to an honest marriage. He can't have a relationship if he buries his emotions in the past. He needs to have a visible representation of their bodies to become fully sane and squash the thoughts of suicide that haunt him. That would be a sin and condemn him to hell, never to see his family again.

The bishop speaks softly to Jack. I understand the hurt you have gone through and the pain you still suffer. Monsignor Chase is concerned that your plan will cause disruption and undue damage. They buried his mother near your family's graves. Don't worry, I will take the heat, and you will receive notice of the appointment. If you have any problems, I am here. Please only scan your wife's gravesite to placate the monsignor. His mother is on the far side. Thank you, bishop, this has lifted a heavy weight from my soul. God Bless, and out he went, hat and all. As the bishop was driven away in his official limousine, he thought, had he done right? He had cleansed his own soul of fault in Jack's suicidal thoughts, but as he left an opening for Jack to encroach into the world, the bishop in habituated. He must seek guidance from superiors.

True to his word, an email message came to Jack that very afternoon. It requested several times of availability and a listing of instructions.

Jack called Swares office to leave a message and forwarded the email. Tay came in and had some news, he wanted to convey, just not in the office. Beautiful day out, Jack. Let us walk over to the deli and grab something. Ok said Jack, rising to follow Tay outside. After they had left the building, Tay spoke to the news he had garnered from informants. The dead guy, Blaine, performed odd jobs for the diocese and even the bishop. Olson was also mentioned as having a connection. Jack almost tripped at this news and trudged onward. Is the circle widening or closing? asked Tay. Too soon to tell, came Jack's reply. They ordered and waited outside at a picnic bench with their drinks. Tay filled in lots of details and some gossip with background. It seems as if Blaine had done some deeds for Swanson through the bishop and somehow got caught by Olson. This led to a protective informant status for Blaine and Olson. Everyone became ensnared in a bigger net then they realized. Who pulls the strings and calls the shots? Tay did not know. How deep is way beyond them? Jack, unwrapping his grinder, sat deep in thought. After a few minutes, he told Tay that we have to find out at least anyone involved in the local dealings just to have a secure path to involve upper levels of investigative services. Tay nodded. Jack continued to lay out the bishop's position and the resultant email. They discussed options and repercussions of certain scenarios that might unfold. Least of which was the protection of the information and evidence they may uncover. The most critical issue dealt with was the way they guarded each other and Sam. It was too early to indicate which known parties were dirty and were not corrupted. They will focus on this issue during their operation until they complete the scans and receive further instructions.

After an exhausting day, both men were left numb and unable to think properly, so they each went home.

To bed to rest, his brain was too tired to think. Jack lay for hours, seeking access to answers to questions spilling forth from his overworked, troubled mind. Finally, a kind of awkward haze-like sleep descended over him. Not restful nor uneasy, just a half-sleep state continually interrupted by memories of conversations past.

Half asleep and half awake, Jack broke the spider-web spell he was in and awoke to groggily get up and dressed in the predawn light. He made coffee, had some toast, and resolved to focus on getting through the day, one step at a time. It was going to be one of those days.

Getting into the office, he was halfway down the stairs when he heard his phone ring. Hustling, he grabbed the receiver and said, Jack here. Swares, speaking into the machine, was startled to hear Jack's real voice. Jack, is that really you? Yes, I recognize Swares. I was going to call you this morning. I thought you might. I have your email and one from a monsignor laying down the law on what and how to scan my scan. We must abide by his wishes and still get all we want, came Jack's comment. I have some dates to scan. Do you want to let me know? Can I come over right now, asked Jack? Sure, I am free.

Jack quickly glanced through his messages and grabbed his cup of coffee on his way over. Swares was tinkering on a machine as Jack arrived. Hi, looking like shit today. No sleep, Jack. Jack mumbled and sat next to Swares. Explain to me exactly what and how much I'll see from the grave. Well, I'll do my best, replied Swares.

Ground penetrating radar performs best in locating bodies wrapped in something, as it provides a good reflective surface. Machines that measure electrical resistivity can detect fluids such as blood from a cadaver where the body is still decomposing - these machines measure how strongly a material opposes the flow of an electric current. In a recent study, we showed that conductivity in grave soil water rapidly increases up to two years after burial. We don't care because we are in a graveyard and precisely know the variables necessary for the ground-penetrating radar and electrical resistivity to allow optimum detection.

DC district requires internment in a simple pine box. They rent a coffin and place the box inside it. The actual burial is of the pine box alone, after the removal of extraneous disturbances, like all handles, cushions, and other sorts of impediments to proper imaging. We should have a successful definition with our high-resolution technology. Great, when can we proceed? Asked Jack. Next week is open. Good, set it up. Do we need to scan as much as you can get away with, understand? Understood, came a reply!

Jack stopped back at the office to see Tay. He gave him a rundown and asked Tay to contact the boys and ask if they had any news or wanted to play poker soon.

Next, Jack called Sam while driving, chanting on the radio. He spoke of all that had transpired with the bishop and the approval to scan. They chattered the language of closeness and set a time to have dinner. Jack continued down the street, his eyes focused squarely on the capitol building straight ahead. He pursued the lead. They have all tiptoed around, the Chief of Staff that had Page Howard Martin arrested and an easy target to find. He bypassed the private parking lot with the guard and, through a miracle, entered an empty slot in the first row. Jack always felt a sense of awe when climbing the Capitol Steps and a pride in what the Capitol stood for. He only wished his daughters could be here climbing with him. After the scorching sun, the air inside the halls felt cool. Echoes filtered out of the tundra and rooms open to the public. He asked a guard for directions to Congressman Catcher's suite of offices after placing his badge on his lapel. The man was quick to direct Jack in the proper direction.

Jack took an elevator up to the designated floor after being told not to use the reserved one. It was only for the elected officials. Jack wandered around until he found a door with Catcher's name on it. The door opened into the receptionist area; he asked to first meet with the congressmen and then with his chief of staff. Can you give his name to me? As Jack withdrew his pad to print the name. Jack wrote in big letters at the top of Sorry, the congressional representative is in a session, but his Chief of Staff, Reginald Dwyer, will be out shortly. Have a seat, please.

While waiting, Jack wandered around the office and looked at the many pictures along the walls. One picture of the congressional representative, and the bishop and chief of staff received a prominent placing, mid-center of the wall. Jack slowly turned at the sound of a man's voice, which said pompously, I am Reginald Dwyer, the Chief of Staff to Congressmen Catcher. Jack's first urge was not pleasant, as he responded politely. I am Detective Spec, and I am investigating several cold cases, one of which requires me to speak to you and the congressman. Is there someplace we can get started? If you just seek preliminary information, I have a few moments. No, it involves more than that, and I would rather speak to both of you at once. Impossible was the reply. Excuse me, do you refuse to be questioned in the middle of a murder investigation? The silence of all available audience members gave a sharp pause to Reginald, and he quickly responded, no, that's not what I meant. The congressional representative cannot leave this session and will be glad to schedule an appointment with you and me as soon as possible. Great, said Jack, with the appointment secretary right here. We can get it approved and scheduled. How about next Tuesday? Jack asked, leaning over the reception desk. Jack thanked the COS and the receptionist for their quick attention and vowed to see them all next Tuesday at 10 am.

Jack next went downstairs, walking this time, now the section that controlled human resources to discover where exactly Jason Cole had worked. He worked in a senator's committee room. They informed him to fill out a form to gain any further information and to include dates in which he was interested. The reason for this was that several dates were reserved for different caucus meetings and party training. Jack needed to complete a form to obtain more information, including the dates he wanted,

Jack left to find a ticket on the windshield of his unmarked police car. It had a DC marker plate, which was listed on the ticket.

He drove back to the office to see if Josh was around. He was not. This was an opportunity to call Samuel and check out his impression of Mr. Reginald Dwyer.

Samuel was of the opinion as Jack, Reginald was a pompous ass and a lackey for Congressional Representative Catcher to wipe his boots off on. Samuel's belief was that Catcher was a corrupted politician and up to his neck in graft. He's good at it and seems to have a respectful persona. His first wife died over a decade ago, and after 4 years, he remarried. Catcher is wealthy and has connections. A perfect fit for a rising star. Jack asked if he had any children. No, came the response. His first wife was pregnant, and both she and the newborn died in childbirth. His second wife can't have any kids. Wait a minute, Jack. Jack hears talking from afar, and soon Samuel returns. Samuel says, I am sorry, Jack, but Edie tells me she read the couple adopted a child a while ago. and thanks, Edie. Brief time later, Josh called to inform Jack of the news. Bishop Fry's is to be elevated to the archbishop's status early next year. Thanks, successful news, said Jack, looking heavenward.

Next morning saw Jack heading to his office when Josh called and said they needed to talk. Ok, I'll stop up a little later, replied Jack, and hung up. Later, working at his desk, he remembered and picked up his phone to check with Josh's schedule. Suddenly, Olson comes in on Jack and says, put down the phone, we got to talk. I want a list of all the cases you are working on placed on my desk by tonight. It is coming on budget time, and I need to know exactly what everyone is working at and properly spending their time productively. TONIGHT, and out he went. Ok said Jack, standing up and starting down the hall. Halfway, he meets Swares, who says, WE need to talk. Not here, says Jack, be outside in an hour, and I'll pick you up for lunch. Jack continues up to Josh's office and tells him to meet for lunch at Nick's in an hour. After an hour, Jack picked up Swares and took him to Nick's for lunch, where they met Josh. Each had a lot to say. Jack went first and talked about Swares' involvement up to now and spoke about Olson's bizarre speech earlier.

Josh then questioned Swares but stopped and asked, What the hell is his first name, anyway? I keep seeing your name tag with Swares on it, and everyone calls you that, so? Swares smiles and begins, my full name is Doctor Budusto Swares. I don't like Budusto because people shorten it to Buddy, believe it or not. I have some people I don't like and don't want them referring to me as their Buddy. Both of you can use that term anytime.

Jack asked Tay if he had any available time Saturday to take a walk and reconnoiter a potential crime scene, among other interests? Tay nodded, good, now I know., and went on. Swanson called me this morning and laid grief on me about you stalking the bishop. What gives? Jack spills his added information just as he hears it. Josh says, Christ. Jack says, exactly. Buddy Swares blesses himself and says, Jack, it is best for us. You have got an in with GOD. They all laugh and eat lunch as they discuss strategy. Swares explains the directive from Olson this morning. He came in to scold me and tell me not to take the scanner out unless allowed to. Shit, said Jack. Don't worry, my friend. I have a plan, said Buddy. He outlined his plan to seek approval from Jack and Josh. First step was to accompany him and his pilot friend to Rock Creek Park this weekend and walk the area the Government Geological Aerial Soil Survey Mapping had indicated as positive for underground masses three or four feet down. We will stake out any that look promising for further processing. If we come across something, I will place a report for Josh to approve going ahead with the investigation, as they will be cold cases. Jack grabs Buddy by the shoulder and says, you are a genius. Josh states that is good, but what if you find nothing? Leave that to me, says Dr. Swares.

Jack went back and outlined a bunch of missing persons and potential murder cases he was processing and filed them up to Olson. Taylor was in before Jack. He had been to see the poker players and picked up some old files relating to lost or missing persons, agreed to be picked up by Jack around 10:30 am, ready to hike.

Chapter 12: Digging for Treasure

Saturday morning at 10:30 am, they all stood in a circle at the old Rock Creek Bridge. The pilot, Brad Hanson, looked around and wistfully spoke of the rumors surrounding this place. He told of the days prior to the Civil War when this was the favored dueling location in DC. Most liked the solitude and its proximity to escape into Maryland in two different directions if authorities came calling. In the old days, before Walter Reed Hospital, a small hospital could provide care to either party with little fanfare. Yes, it was the perfect place to die or live, depending on your luck or aim. Buddy, is that the reason you believe you'll find at least one body out here? Swares laughed, no I have faith in my science and in Brad's gut feelings. Jack asked, which direction? Brad bent down and opened his backpack. He pulled out a map and a compass. After a minute, he pointed north and said, walk 2,486 paces till X marks the spot. They all looked at Brad and, in unison, loudly said, Sure! Brad laughed and said follow me, spread out in a horizontal line about five steps apart. He continued; you all know the drill. Look for any depressions where the ground has settled or openings and evidence of erosion. As they walked, each picked up a stick to poke the ground. They were professional men on a specific mission, finding the bodies and granting peace to someone. Two hours later, they had developed a methodical pattern due north. They then turned right and walked about twenty five steps and turned right again began walking due south. In this way they created a geometric square pattern of searched ground. Suddenly, Doc Swares yells out, here, here, I got something. They looked at Buddy and his stick stuck into the ground he was pointing at. They all rushed to him and stood quietly as he said a prayer in his native tongue. When he had finished, each began a pre-defined ritual of marking the spot with spray paint and creating an identification map of exact measurements of any identifying objects. 175 yards to Riley Spring Bridge. And distance between trees of note, to water, garbage cans, and anything visible. After completing the task, Swares moved five steps ahead, Jack followed with five more steps in the same direction, then Brad, and finally Taylor was at the end of the line. They walked in a large circle around the original spot. They identified several more potential spots for further investigation by the time they finished. Enough for the day came the call from Doc Swares. Jack suggested they adjourn to this local pub he knew to wash up and eat since they all were starved. After the hot wings, several large beers, and a giant half-pound burger covered in onions, peppers, lettuce/ tomato with onion rings on the side, each struggled from the booth and went home to a well-deserved rest.

Monday morning saw Olson at Jack's door early, demanding an update by Wednesday night. No problem was Jack's response. The rest of Monday saw Tay and Jack reviewing their folders to find a list of victims for potential identification. Compiling a list such as this meant searching for items worn when last seen if that item could survive underground, and for how long. Jack's top name was Jason Cole.

Jack took a shower after calling Sam and recounting the day to her. She was eager and happy at all the progress; she realized the importance of Jack's pursuit to find closure for all the families left with a void towards their loved ones. This is one of the many reasons she is in love with Jack. Jack and Sam talk with no concept of time. They would speak till dawn and beyond. However, Jack still had shaving cream drying on his face and a shower running, so he told her his love and explained the shower was running out of hot water. She called him a dope and said, Love goodnight. Fortunately, the lateness of the hour resulted in no one else using hot water, so he could linger and relax. This created a mellow feeling, along with the beers consumed, and placed him in a deep sleep.

He was experiencing a feeling of floating and thought. Why does this always happen when I have had too much to drink? They'll think I am an alcoholic.

The floating stopped, and Jack sat upright. Never failing to appreciate the beautiful galactic view before him, Jack looked to the firepit and saw all three sitting and talking together. Jack walked apprehensively towards them. The flames appeared higher than Jack remembered. They smiled and waved hands in greeting, Jack worried. Something was up. The Devil began, relax, don't worry. The jury is still out. We wanted to clarify something in your mind. People are thinking you may be crazy. This is their issue, not yours. However, we don't want you to have any doubts or misconceptions. We know you are a sane, well-balanced human. You are asking questions and seeking suitable answers. Logical pursuit of the truth is never crazy.

Jesus spoke, the neuroscientists and scientists within your reality are just catching up to the Astro Physicists regarding their levels of discoveries. Both are reaching out to open their minds to unknown theories and hypotheses of the greatest and vastness of God's creativity and plans for the cosmos. Many are still at a level equivalent to your considered 17th-century medical procedures. Many still have not yet formed a correct question or a proper answer.

God has the last word, of course. Jack, continue with great care along your path. Trust in your logic, free will, and the belief in God's presence beside you.

Your faith and love will guide your steps along your path. All our love.

Jack slept late and called Sam around noon. Well sleepy head, about time are we going to lunch or a late breakfast. Jack groaned. My head hurts. Jack felt the frown on Sam's face through the phone. So, he quickly said, brunch, like I planned. I'll pick you up in 20 minutes, ok. Make it half hour, I'll be waiting.

Whew, quick thinking Jack, as he hustled to find suitable clothes for a Sunday date.

Half an hour later, Jack was outside Sam's place watching her stroll towards the car. She can walk. They walked and discussed her week and all she had done. When she raised a fuss about dominating the conversation, Jack replied, I love everything about you. From your walk to your voice and your career. How am I to know if I want to marry you if I don't know your interests and your beautiful soul? Sam replies Damn you; do you have to always say things to melt me? I will try, was Jack's only reply. This time, he splurged, and they ate at an excellent restaurant overlooking the basin, not a truck.

The date ended too soon, and as they sat on a bench watching the sun sail along with the Potomac River toward the beauty of the red horizon, they both wondered at the gifts and bounty of the vastness of God's creativity.

Jack stood on the doorstep and hugged and kissed her goodnight. He asked, do you want me to come in, Yes was her reply.

Monday was a redo of Friday. Tay and Jack reviewed and drafted reports to files around 2 pm. They went upstairs to provide a briefing to Josh on all that happened on Saturday and requested a full complement of cadets to clear, search, and shovel any potential graves. Josh almost falls out of his chair when Doc Swares says at least nine suspected spots. Are you shitting me, was his response? Jack, are you digging up the cemetery, for Christ's sake. All of you are as crazy as he is, pointing to Jack. Go with the science, sir. It was Docs' comment. I am at a loss as to how to proceed with the size operation. Jack grins. If Olson questions this, just tell him to keep his trap shut and be careful what he asks for. They all had a good laugh.

Jack hands over a proposal written up by Doc Swares for forensic personnel and equipment for approval, time, and expense account and facility usage.

Ok, just explain the how and where you'll start and proceed. They lay out the scenario so Josh can protect himself. Josh looks around and says, you guys, better find something or. Buddy interrupts to say we will, and many people are going to piss in their pants. That's fine. Came back Josh, just so it's not us.

The authorities approved the preparations and scheduled them for Wednesday through Saturday.

Jack met Taylor first thing in the morning. At their coffee shoppe, Samuel was sitting having a cup to himself already. They walked to him and said, mind if we sit with you? Samuel stood and shook hands. Of course not. Glad to see you and winked. I went to the diocesan office yesterday to get some records for my local priest. While there, I just came across the appointment book for the bishop. Once every two years, a new one is issued, and the old one goes to the archives. I noticed it just sitting there, and I trolled a few dates to see who he met. A young friend of ours, Jason Cole, had an appointment a few days before he disappeared. What! Yes, went on Samuel, and the next day, Bishop Frys attended a meeting with the K of C. Sorry guys, this keeps growing. The Capitol, and the police and a religious leader is as deep as the shit can get. What's next, the White House. Excellent job. Check on getting another game set up for next week; that was Tay's only comment. What is the matter with Samuel asking this week? Busy, about to open the graves.

After Samuel left, the two talked briefly, and Jack drove to his meeting with a COS and a congressional representative.

The receptionist was waiting behind her desk, and before Jack spoke, she reported that both the COS and Congressional Representative Catcher had been called to the White House for a meeting, which was expected to last awhile.

Congressional Representative Catcher apologized and said he would contact you later to reschedule.

Jack bit his tongue and courteously responded with a Thank you! Wednesday

Next day dawned, much like every day in the past month, dry and warm. The District of Columbia, as well as most of the northeast, was in a long drought. Good and Bad. The bad was the browning of all grassy surfaces and a deep subsurface of dry sand and dirt. This was a perfect time to dig and search beneath the crust. Jack, Tay, and Swares rolled out a tricycle-like carriage containing an elaborate contraption nicknamed the "Mole". And loaded it into the specialized transport for the trip to Rock Creek Park. Jack's car followed the van up to the bridge. They marked the area with large yellow luminous tape and restricted access, and the police department oversaw it. They drove over the grass to get a better access point for the contraption and its cables.

After about an hour of testing and reviewing images, Swares declared, we are ready men as if to mount a cavalry charge. Turning on the machine amid the noise of a whirring sound, an electric mower motor and beeping and buzzing, the contraption moved out slowly, slowly toward the initial spot. It could be the last spot filled or the first. The doctor traversed the uneven ground as carefully as a surgeon, stopping often to push a button and generate a pictorial image of grainy content. Taylor numbered these based on their size and position within the enclosed area. These were numbered by Taylor based on site and position within the site.

They laid this on top of the site after Doc pronounced it closed to gain a representative layout of subsurface masses. Forensics arrived and took pictures of the layout of the machine. After Doc finished, they developed a complete pictorial history for entry into evidence. Swares only said something or someone else was down there. He moved on to the next site to repeat the process all over again. The overall area had filled in with several departments and sundry personal. People were setting up a command tent, others shoveled sand, and still, others unloaded miles of electric wire for lighting. After Swares processed the third grave, he came back to sit next to Jack and said, I am sad to uncover all this, but someone needs to do it. I am glad it's us, Jack. Thank you for letting me help. They shook and smiled. Jack understood all what Buddy had said.

Later, they both stood by the ever-present catering van, and Buddy said, you know, we need to bring in the big guns. My little toy can provide only an image of present content, but my Baby can do so much more. We'll need to calibrate, Baby. Do you know any place we have permission to scan an organized grave setting pre-measured and soil density recorded, such as a cemetery? Jack leaned over and joked, "I'd give you a kiss, but I don't aspire to be the talk of the town." They smile as conspirators do.

Back to work, a long night. Which was for all present. Word had spread throughout the department and the street. A crowd gathered, and speculation flourished. A mob burial ground, an old burial site for duelers, and a place for the disposal of malarial victims from the 1920s. Thursday

Next morning saw the infamous three back of the lab, rolling a box truck out into the dry sunlight. Inside sat Baby.

A total station hybrid. Which is multifunctional using thermal, digital, and LiDAR (Light Detection and Ranging) technology at its core and there are different modes of operation. It will coordinate ground penetrating radar wave signals to reflect as colored layers in nanoseconds within an amplitude of the combined signals, giving a more precise, detailed image in its most simplified form. Jack and Tay both say, we'll take your word for it.

The truck drove out and turned toward the cemetery. They arrived at the grave site exactly at 9:30 am and unloaded both machines. Doctor Swares quickly went to work and turned on the Mole, reviewing Jack's wife's grave for images and points of interest, showing much dismay at all he was receiving. By 10:15 am, Monsignor Chase arrived and demanded to know what we were doing? The guards, standing guard over the procedures, jumped to explain. They have permission. From whom? Chase shouted. From you, sir ah Father or Monsignor. Excuse me. Let me see that. The priest turned on Jack next; all the while, Buddy kept moving. I was told shouted Chase. Jack, in a calm voice, politely asked. Who told you that? The Bishop and Chief Swanson came as his reply. Sorry, that information is incorrect. I'll see about that. Stop that man now, pointing to Doctor Swares as he grabbed his cell phone. The guards yelled STOP to Buddy. Both Jack and Taylor pulled out their handcuffs and said, please turn around, put your hands behind your back. We are arresting you for interfering in a police investigation. The wind and all else stopped. The monsignor looked at Jack with fire in his eyes and motioned the guards to stand down for now. He heard a voice over his phone. Olson here. To which a pious priest yelled, get your ass down here now, and hung up. We'll see about this. All of you are in a world of trouble, he said while throwing glares of hate and fire toward all three. Buddy declared, this damn machine can't penetrate correctly and moved it over on top of Rachel's grave. Monsignor complained, but Jack said quietly, that is my daughter and kneeled by her grave to pray. Buddy worked feverishly on Vivian's grave to get the correct calibration performed as he kept grumbling. The sound of a siren was heard after 45 minutes, followed by a car screeching to a halt with flashing lights. The car had hardly stopped, with lights and sirens still shrilly working. Olson jumped out and began screaming. The Monsignor Chase interrupted his screams. Shouting louder, What the hell do you think you are doing with all this stupid noise, lights, and siren? Please go back and shut everything off. Olson looked like a chastised young boy as he returned to do as they had scolded him to do. On his return, Taylor spoke. He does not want to wake the dead. Olson turned purple and, in a stifled voice, asked, why are you here? Doctor Swares looked straight at Olson and spoke.

The top priority from Superintendent Kirby is to have me recalibrate my toy. Pointing to the machine on Rachel's grave and setting calibration on the Baby. It needs to be done, before proceeding with Rock Creek today. This is the only spot to verify. We have permission from the nearest relative and Jack was kind enough to oblige. We don't know this guy's problem, and he never explained. Just yelled. Jack spoke up and said, Call Kirby or follow us over. He and many people are waiting for us to dig. Why not come over.

Olson's purple face subsided, but the monsignors recolored, as Olson said Ok, I'll meet you over there. Buddy had turned off his machines and packed up, so Jack turned his back to help his two friends. They left the graves with a final knee from all and a silent prayer of love.

Around one-thirty, they arrived at Rock Creek to see a gathering at the first spot. They were doing final preparations for forensics to allow the removal of the body. As the three men unloaded the Mole and Baby, voices in prayer arose from the workers, the assembled and the curious crowd by announcing a body resurfacing.

The three amigos stood by the coffee truck and sipped the hot brew while going over the morning events. Buddy felt delighted by all they had accomplished. Also, the cherry on top was when Tay told Olson not to wake the dead. I almost fell over laughing, glad I was on my hands and knees then. Jack asked, what about my images? Good got better. Poor resonance on your daughter, but your wife was great. I will get them analyzed as soon as possible. But this here thing is the highest priority and will be first up with all the big shots clamoring for results.

I know you'll do your best and thanks for everything. It's fine, we are partners like the three amigos. Tay quips, did they not all die in the end? Both Jack and Buddy called NO in unison. Kirby walked up and said, if you will not come to me, I'll have to come to you. Sorry, boss, just resting. They then spill everything about the day. Laughing about the funny, agonizing over problems and issues uncovered. Buddy took Baby and trolled the rest of the sites. Final tally was six bodies left to be identified. More lights and tents were being set up, and another deli truck arrived. It was to be another long night. Jack, Taylor, and the doctor finished loading the machines and left together around 3:45 am. Jack hit his pillow at 4:30ish.

Jack ambled into the office and went directly up to see Josh. Josh looked up and said morning, or should I say afternoon. Jack replies I can't tell anymore. Both chuckled, and Josh began. The shit really hit the fan while you were diligently doing your job. At least, that's what I told the Chief of Police. Olson complained to Swanson, who complained to the chief. I was called in, and with all three of us, I laid out the scenario. The chief was ecstatic. The department looks successful, and today's poll shows morale soaring. Our area of Metro has the highest number of case resolution in the department. VIP status for all.

My first training officer told me, the higher you fly, the more the fall hurts!

Jack was glad. Josh was safe, and we could get on with investigating without interference, at least for now.

Back at his office, he went through his messages. One was from Olson telling him what a decent job he had done. Some other calls to return, one from Swares and finally from Sam. Jack grabbed the phone and dialed Sam. Hi Jack, are you awake yet? Yes, he responded, how did you know? Josh called me earlier to check on our RSVPs. Oh, I forgot; that was his contrite reply. I straightened it out. We are all set. Thanks, and would you like to go to dinner tomorrow night?

Yes, and can you get your doctor friend to join us? Jack hardly paused and said, this smells like a setup.

But I want everybody to be as happy as I am. He is a workaholic; I know how that is. It will burn him out. Please, Jack, force him at gunpoint if need be. Jack only said, where? Sam chuckled and said, Casa Royale, love you, be there at 7 pm. and hung up. How do I get myself into these situations? The better question is, how do I get myself out? Jack bit the bullet and saw the doctor.

Swares, as usual, was working and looked up as Jack walked in. Jack walked in and interrupted Buddy just as he was about to speak. He explained his need to attend a dinner with Sam and her friend tomorrow night at 7 pm. Ok, was Buddy's reply. Jack looked quizzed idly as Buddy explained where the process was. He laid out a directional approach to be taken for each body and notified records department to hustle up and make a return of all evidence and files concerning each body as identified. No Jason Cole yet.

Chapter 13:
Searching for Gold

Next night saw Jack and Buddy entering the Casa Royale at exactly 7 pm. The host greeted them, and Jack said, my party is already here, Samantha Billings. Yes, of course, right this way, leading them past diners, all happily sipping cocktails and reviewing the menu. Jack noticed the ladies sitting at a corner table, waving. Buddy's eyes lit up, and a big smile appeared. After being introduced, the boys took a seat. Small talk began to make everyone comfortable.

"Since I work here as a party planner, I can answer questions and make menu recommendations," Jennie explained after cocktails were ordered. "Great," said Jack, I see some items of unknown origin that I may like, but my system may not. Jennie prompted, tell us the likes and dislikes of your system, and Sam and I will fill in the menu for you. The server brought the cocktails, and we made a toast to an evening. A discussion followed around the food, and Sam says, what does your body like?

Jack looks at Sam and says, everything I see. Sam retorts, I mean to eat.

Jack chokes, and all laugh. Seriously. So, Jack discusses items on the menu with Jennie. Sam ordered while Buddy and Jennie leaned into each other to decide his order. Finishing his choice, Buddy casually asks Jennie, you want? Jennie looked directly at him and spoke. I want to find a good man. One who will appreciate me, not just for my body, but for my mind too! Jack chokes on his drink, and Sam becomes a statue. Buddy smiles and says, Great, I want a good wife who will appreciate me not just for my mind but for my body, too. Jennie hesitates, gives a sly smile, and replies, well, I have not seen your body yet. Silence reigned until Buddy smiled and said, I am not that kind of guy. Everyone laughed, and the party began. Jack looked at Sam and said, Who knew?

Conversations continued throughout the meal, beginning with Buddy explaining his dedication to exercise but not for bodybuilding. He believes that exercise and nutritional values can lead to an extension of life and its quality. She asks him how it formed his hypothesis and is surprised by his doctor status. Sam chimes in with an explanation. Working at the police department lab can lead to stereotype jesting and wisecracking. So, he does not use a real name. That silliness, be proud of your accomplishments and name. Buddy, breathing deeply, tells his tale of woe concerning his name. My name is Doctor Bodusto Swares, and when I started at the department. My name tag only said Swares. If I used my first name, it would be shortened to Buddy, anyway. You can call me Buddy anytime. Certainly not. If I may, can I call you Bo? Buddy asks, like a ghost, yes, it's personnel between us.

Anytime, was his reply. Jennie told her tale. She worked to put herself through George Washington University in Biomedical Engineering and was in her last year. She was looking for a research residency. The conversation centered on medical issues and medicine, with Sam joining in. The three went deep into discussing the morals of research and the probing of the human mind and spirit. Finally, Jennie, looking at Jack, says, sorry, poor Jack has been left out of our discussion.

No, said Jack. I am enjoying every bit. I am learning so much and enjoying watching Sam have knowledgeable parties to partake in a spirited conversation like this. Sam comes back, No, Jack, but Swares interrupts to state, Jack, I have learned more from you in a month than 8 years of grad school. You know, a reality we can't even imagine. All nods. Your advice is valuable to life itself.

Sam says, Jack, you amaze me every day we are together. We are a page of academia; you are a complete book of life.

Jack looks at them and smiles. I don’t want any sorrow or misgiving. I said what I said to clarify. I am totally satisfied with my friends' brilliance and with my own. I am glad we are all together. Now, what is for dessert? The laughter continued until the dessert cart arrived. Final decision was six desserts for sharing. Jack, I hate you, Jennie concurred, and Buddy sat patting his belly with a smug smile on his face. They all got up to leave, and Buddy placed his hand out to shake Jennie's.

She looked at it and said, Oh Bo, we are way past that and kissed him with a firm hug. The old lady at the side table clapped and said: good for you. You two are made for each other. We enjoyed watching all four of you talking and having fun. No cell phones or any other crap. Just enjoying each other. Congratulations. At the door, they agreed to attend next Thursday's reception for Josh and Estelle's anniversary. As the couples departed in separate directions, the men rehash the night's festivities. Jack called Buddy Don Juan and recanted his almost choking to death many times a successful night, and both retire to blissful dreams of their ladies and future nights like this.

Sunday found Jack and Sam having breakfast at a Morgan Circle bookstore, known for its successful omelets and coffee, plus tons of reading materials. They had discussed going to church, but Jack felt more comfortable going to the cemetery of both their loved ones to talk to God or whoever was available. After glancing through the local paper, he said, as usual, that they write in broad strokes. A minor fact, a little assumption, and a lot of crap. They drove to his family's graves first while listening to the music of religion, as Sam calls it. Jack spoke to Vivian and Rachel. Introducing Sam and announcing their relationship as a growing friendship. They said prayers, separately and together, while kneeling at each site, including Jessies.

They then went to her father's grave and, with the radio playing walked up to stand and talk under the enormous tree overlooking, as if in protection, of the graves.

Sam questioned, why didn't he keep the radio on at his family's site? Too much anger and uncertainty are still associated with it still. Jack spread the blanket as Sam spoke to her dad. She sat on the blanket and listened, but only the birds, bees, and wind answered. They are all at service, said Jack. My dad probably sleeping late.

They settled back, and Sam said Jennie liked Buddy a lot. She originally went out with a bunch of losers who wanted to paw and climb all over her. Don't talk, just spread your legs. A hole. Finally, like me, she decided to pursue a career and later a man. She's worked hard studying at work, on a bus, and anywhere else she could. She's a smart girl and knows what she wants. Like you! Said Jack. Don't mock me, was her reply. Jack spoke up to tell Sam he knew of her past from the file and Josh. None of it mattered other than it strengthened her, and she was more determined not just to survive but to prosper and become the noble person she was. Damn you, there you go again with the melting. They laughed. Jack spoke of Buddy's instant affection for Jennie. Her straightforwardness and honest talk melted him. It was something unfamiliar to him from other women he had dated. He, too, gave up the dating merry-go-round and focused on a career and his body, I guess. Laughter filled the area. A voice complained, settle down with the noise, kitten. I am trying to sleep. Dad, Sam cried, you are awake! Am now came a reply. This is not like a phone; it requires a lot of work to implore. Hi Jack. Glad to see you. I have some words for you later. So, this day continued in a family conversation. Some gossip, some advice to Kitten and a passage of love between them.

The moment has come for me to say goodbye. But before I go, Mathew pulls Jack to the side to deliver a message from a close friend of yours. Don't believe everything you see and cross over the bridge. Thank Lucifer for me. Love her, and he was gone. Drive back was muted as each reviewed the day's events. A kiss and a powerful hug, followed by a longer kiss, and the day was over.

Next morning, Jack met Tay, and they went to the lab and saw Buddy.

Buddy had a partial list of victims and several boxes of evidence for them to process. More to come later today was his only statement.

As the detectives left, Buddy called Jack aside to ask what Sam had said about Jennie. Jack responded you are in the race. Run faster. Damn you, came Buddy's reply with a giant smile across his face. I'll check your photos at lunch. See you later. Down the hall to catch Tay and help carry the evidence.

They sat and read the list of victims:

First was a 36-year-old woman, presumed murdered in her home. They found blood along with trace evidence; a violent struggle had ensued. Husband presented signs of a fight and laceration and is suspected - kept under observation. Name: Rosalie Griffin.

Second was a man robbed and beaten at his storefront pawn shop. Cameras were smashed upon entry and no recognition ID. Blood was all over the floor, and the contaminated evidence unknown. Name – Jacob Schiltz.

Third was a young girl of 12 years, kidnapped. Ransom demanded, not picked up family ties Name- Margeret Daevos.

Fourth was a man of an unknown age of foreign descent dressed in business attire.

Fifth Sixth Seventh Eighth Ninth. Taylor finished the list and said, Hell of a way to start the week.

After cutting the tape on each box, Jack gave the first one to Tay and kept the next one to view himself.

After two hours, a forensics report came into the lab, and Buddy dropped it off. Jack, I am going to lunch at the cafeteria if you need me, was his only comment.

Tay and Jack poured over every word and diagram in each section and made copious notes. They went for coffee and sat in their car to discuss developments and questions. If the husband had a fight with the wife, why was there no blood evidence found on her body or clothes and why none at the house? Although he bled from the fight, there was no evidence of blood found on her body or clothes. They found other evidence on her clothes and detected traces of skin under her fingernails. Someone else did the job. We need to pressure the husband to discover all he is not telling. The old man showed trace amounts under his fingernails and on the body. We need to run that through the database. They went to see the husband.

They knocked and showed their badges to the man who answered. Jack asked, Are you Mr. Griffin? Yes, can I help you?

We are sorry to report that Rosalie Griffin's body has been recovered. Griffin fell to the floor. Sobbing, he said, they told me nobody would find her. Jack asked, Who told you, as he went down to one knee next to the man.

A woman came out of the kitchen and demanded to know what was going on. Tay told her of Rosalie's discovery and asked her name. She said Juanita, Rosalie was my sister. Jack helped the man to his feet and suggested they all sit down in the living room and hear their story. I don't know everything, but my sister came across the border from Mexico to marry Ricky, and a year later, she ran away. Taylor looks at Ricky and says, that's not what happened, was it? Ricky, still crying, shook his head no. Jack said, tell us the entire story, or we will arrest the both of you. So, Ricky began. He only had half the money required to pay the smugglers to get Rosalie across the border. They took that and made a loan to him for the rest. The interest was too high. No matter the amount was not enough, and the interest caused his debt to get higher. Finally, two men caught him outside his workplace and demanded the full amount. They beat him and wanted the money. I said I have no money, but they would not listen. They threw him in the back of the car and came to his house. Rosalie answered, and they beat her. She grabbed a knife in the kitchen to stab one, and the mean one just kept punching her until she stopped breathing. They threatened to say I had done it and I would spend the rest of my life in jail, and they had friends there. He beat me again and left with Rosalie's body, telling me to say she ran away. One man kept coming back to collect any money I had.

Do you know their names? No, who did you originally pay? Some blonde-haired man. He said his name was Jack Spock or Speck or something, and he was a police officer, so he would know everything. Ok, said Jack, don't tell anyone about this, and just keep on with your life for now. We'll handle this. Taylor asked if that other guy still came around. No, he stopped about 5 or 6 months ago.

As they walked back to the car, Tay said, Holy Shit, does anything not come easy anymore? They rode back to the precinct, each thinking the possibility of Olson being the imposter. If he was, then how widespread is this operation? Can it involve the bishop and a congressional representative?

Jack settles it by telling Tay to get all blood and trace evidence run through the combined databases of (DIVS), (CODIS) and (NDIS).

Jack walks into his office to see his desk phone blinking, a message. He hits the button and hears Buddy saying to see him ASAP. Jack hustles down to the lab, where he finds Buddy crouched over his light table. Buddy, you called. At the call of his name, Buddy did a startled jump and turned towards Jack. This shit is real, he said. Jack responded you heard from Tay. Damn right and more. Look at this; it was Buddy's retort. I have pulled more pictures, and one grave has two bodies. Jack leaned over and noticed several dark masses in one image.

It gets worse, said Jack. Buddy nods and motions Jack over to another table, looking at this blurry image of a smaller mass undiscernible to identify. Jack, this is from Rachel's grave, said Buddy, hard to tell. It could be her or a doll. The signature variables produce no definite. I should send it to get another opinion and analysis. A Micro Spectrum may enhance some detail and allow other analyses to be performed. Jack said, You are the expert. Disappointed as he was, he knew enough to wait for the end before turning a page.

Jack had a sudden thought. Can we go back and walk over that bridge and search that area also, just a few of us? Sounds good to me, for any specific reason or a spiritual feeling. O, Ok said Jack, I'll set something up. And walked back upstairs to see if Josh was available. He was. Hi Jack, Josh greeted, have a seat. Are you ready for Thursday? Yes, we are told, Jack. And Sam is looking forward to seeing Estelle and you. Sure, that was Josh's reply; they'll have a lot to talk about. Estelle is dying to get the scoop on Sam and you. Every day, she asks if Jack has popped the question. When are they getting engaged? Where are they going on a honeymoon? I am going crazy with her, and there is not any mention of our own anniversary. What gives? Jack looks squarely and says, seems like she's setting you up big time. If you don’t come through, you will be roadkill. I know says Josh, Jack retorts, what can I do for you, Josh? Only if your party is good. If not, you were on your own.

We are going back out to Rock Creek to search the other side of the bridge, said Jack. Any reason came back, Josh. Just a hunch, the other side is closer to the road and more readily accessible to cover, was Jack's response. Ok, let me know when.

When Jack reached his desk, his phone blared. Jack heard, Buddy here, I need your help immediately.

Jack was getting his exercise in and wondered if Buddy was trying to hook Jack on his theory to extend life. What do you need asked Jack? I have got a big problem said Buddy and went on to explain That Jennie had called, and she was so ecstatic to have gotten an A on her final exam that in Buddy's enthusiasm, he told her he was going to take her out to dinner tomorrow night. Success was her answer. Where are we going? I said it would be a surprise. I have been saving for a special occasion and someone special to celebrate with. I have got another date with her. Jack, looking puzzled, said, Happy for you both, What's the problem? Buddy comes back to earth and says, No special place. Help me! Jack sits down and thinks, why do I always get in these situations? Let me think for a minute. I believe the special place you want is near the redeveloped side by the water. They repurposed an old bordello into a high-class restaurant, but they left most of the interior unchanged. Successful atmosphere and food. How did you like it, asked Buddy? I never ate there. I was called to an assault of a woman and was inside and talked to the people. Jack, a bordello where a woman was assaulted is the best you can do, was Buddy's lament. No, it is highly rated. Some guy wanted to date this chick and wanted to get her heated, he thought the old photographs of naked women from the 1920s and 30s, along with the red wallpaper pictographs of naked bodies in various poses, would do the trick. It did because, after dinner, they had sex in the car in the parking lot. When done, the lady looked at him and said, I normally get at least fifty bucks for that, but since you paid for dinner, I'll call it even.

My God, she'll hate me, came Buddy's reply. No, trust me, it is unique and perfect for a romantic night of celebration. Buddy sat down in his chair with his head in his hand.

Ok, I'll try it. The day ended with Jack trying to cheer his friend up.

Next morning was a madhouse as several returns had come into the lab and were being processed, it would take a few hours until it was ready for Jack and Tay.

Tay asked, how about some poker to while away the day, so off they went? They arrived at Samuels around 10:30 am and got right to business. They brought the boys up to speed on all the current evidence and knowledge. This took at least an hour and floored the boys. Can this reach the bishop and a congressional representative? Raymond questioned the possibility of Olson being involved in a smuggling ring, the Assistant Chief Swanson too. It boggled their minds and needed stronger refreshments.

They filled everyone's glasses and then raised a toast to the success of their efforts. They also prayed for God's help if they failed. Jack says, "Amen".

They then set about systematically laying out the evidence and sorting to which cases the relevance was most noticeable and pertinent. They reviewed and took comments and suggestions to heart. They learned to look for leads in certain places known to be frequented by suspects or associates of suspects. Taylor noted they were returning to Rock Creek to do further research for more bodies or evidence and could use some help. Several yelled DAY TRIP and stood up. Jack pointed out that they had been retired for too long. They all laughed and said it would be the most fun in years, and it made them feel alive and useful again. The day ended with Tay and Jack returning to their office and the boys mapping out a search quadrant across the bridge in Rock Creek.

The office was dark, and Jack and Tay entered through the side door directly into the downstairs area by the office. On Jack's desk was an envelope with several reports analyzed by forensics and reviewed by Buddy. I wrote his comments inside the sealed envelope. Buddy wrote Victim

#1 was covered in blood splatter and skin traces that returned to one David Blaine and another associate, Chunky Aristarch. Blaine shows deceased in our files, and still not received an answer from BOLO.

Jack, surprise number two, David Blaine and Chunky Aristarch show DNA and trace evidence all over the old man's body. Poor guy.

More reports in the morning, still on for RC search tomorrow at 11 am. Off to dinner.

Jack and Tay sat back and spoke in worried terms. Is this all interconnected, and why does it also connect to my attack? Tay says, Jack, the old case you were working on, what was that about? Jack sat back in numb silence. Tay continued because he saw the effect on Jack. Who took over that case after your attack? I don’t know. I'll talk to Josh in the morning, said Jack.

Olson took over for you after the attack, and shortly after, I was promoted to superintendent. Olson filled my slot until his actual promotion came through. The case was then transferred to Ralph Hanson, a new detective from PSA 403.

Is there an issue? Jack brought up the question to apprise

Josh, but no more.

He met the boys out beside the bridge at 11:00 am, and they sat down and reviewed the grid line and pattern. Several park police came up and asked, what are you doing here? Jack and Tay took the lead and displayed their badges by showing authority and informed them of their intentions to traverse the wooded area across the Riley Bridge. The lead officer said I thought you were done. Do you have a warrant? Taylor reached into his file and pulled out the warrant from last Wednesday to show. Lead Officer said gruffly, this was for last week. Taylor said, see that allowed area stated, an area surrounding the Riley Bridge for half a mile. Are we searching within that area? Yes, we got our orders. Do you want to have your boss call and disturb Superintendent Josh Kirby for his input? Both Jack and Josh rolled their eyes, and the lead officer said, no, if you need any help, just call and they scrambled away. Bushes says that it is nice to have friends in high places, and they all chuckle and spread out to new perimeters. Halfway up a hill about thirty meters above the bridge was a gully caused by erosion, a sign of a disturbed surface layer and a cavity exposed in subsurface strata. Marked on the map to be scanned, forty meters left of the first site was another depression, and a slightly larger one was fifteen meters downslope from that, all marked and notated on their map. Jack called to get Buddy's machine over, but chaos was the word Buddy used for today, Friday. Jack said Ok, and they all went to Bread Furst for a late lunch.

Jack goes directly home to get some much-needed sleep. However, he is startled awake at 11: 30 pm when the phone rings, which he ignores. He goes to the bathroom, and on his way back to bed, it rings again. He picks it up and says, Jack here. Detective John Renton here, Jack, I really need your help. Jack struggles to remember Detective Renton, and when it finally dawns on him. He replies, sorry, I was sound asleep, and now I need my coffee to wake up.

Renton describes his predicament concisely, and Jack fumbles to get a pencil to jot down the address he is at, so he agrees to come over. John had said this was significant for Jack to be involved in. Jack quickly dressed, filled a thermos cup with yesterday's coffee, and nuked on his way out the door. Jack took a sip.

And his eyes popped, and he was awake. URGH. Renton had told him an informant of his gets his drugs from a legislative aide who moonlights as a dealer. The aide and the informant were partying a little too much, and the aide had OD'd. He was called to come over quick. He gave an EpiPen injection, and the aide recovered. He did not want to go to the hospital out of fear of discovery. John knows of Jack's case involving Capitol Hill and thinks this person could provide some insight or information to help Jack. This process of thought took up the time to get to the Kennedy Center Apartments. The informant was waiting for Jack to ring him in. Jack asked, what's your name, after a slight hesitation, the man said, Everett. Ok, Everett shows me the way. No words were spoken on the elevator ride to the third floor until the apartment door opened. Jack, said John, I am glad you are here. They sat on the couch next to the man, asleep on the floor. John started; I think this guy can be squeezed big time. He works for a senator as a legislative aide and interacts with everyone from the chief of staff down to receptionists, as well as supplying many of them. That may help, says Jack. Renton holds up his hand and turns to Everett to say go back downstairs and wait for the doctor I called. When he left, Detective Renton got to the good stuff. This dealer receives the information on drug delivery and pickups over the radio. He just answered my questions because he believed me to be the doctor that saved his life. I asked him about deliveries to find out the quantity of the drugs taken, and he obliged. He said to not tell anyone; it was too dangerous. John divulged that the religious station would play certain hymns and chants at specific times and different frequencies, which he monitored to get his information. We can own him, he is more afraid of discovery by his family, his bosses, and the suppliers than of us. You need to find out all he knows. We must protect him and my informant.

Jack agrees! The doctor entered through the open door and was warmly greeted by John, as if they are friends. John then proceeded to explain the situation, but only gave a partial explanation. He mentioned the sensitivity and delicacy to all involved. John returns to the kitchen table and told Jack the doctor knows the score and has helped me in the past. Sleep was out of the question as a long night unfolded. It is overrated. The doctor works on his patient and remains at a respected distance as the two detectives interrogate the informant and later leaves after administrating the patient's recovery. The informant had already left to go home, knowing his dealer was alive and safe to party another day. They sat down next to the patient, who they had helped place in his own bed. Small talk began and slowly evolved into a complete interrogation of all he knew. He was a smart kid who was hooked on a habit in college and promoted to a dealer to support that habit. Most of his clients, as he referred to them, had developed a habit in college and continued to use it as the stress of work increased. His information kept Jack and John continuously writing in their notebooks and recording on their cell phones for later review. The doctor had left a message at the senator's office explaining his absence for the next two days because of the flu. The aide went off to sleep, and the detectives left as daylight flirted with the windowpanes.

Jack came into a very crowded office on Thursday around noon. Boxes of evidence and files were piled on the desks, the floor, and the file cabinets themselves. Taylor was buried behind a desk walled in by boxes.

I was up all night. Let us grab a cup of coffee for lunch at the deli across the street, which was code to Tay that he had news for outside discussion only. They walked over to the deli while Tay filled Jack in on current events, as he knew them. They ordered coffee and a sandwich each and sat at an outside table. The drought continued, so another warm and sunny day invited them.

Jack explained the reason he was up all night and gave background on John Renton. Tay said, yeah, I heard some guys talking about him. Olson has a continued bug up his ass against him. Why do you have any idea? queried Jack. Some think that John is gay and too close to those people. I could not care, but there is still bias in some jerks. Olson has made a quest to completely get rid of him from the department. Poor guy can't catch a break. Olson has him on a second warning for shit stuff. You and I would not even be under reprimand. Jack sits thinking for a while, and finally, he says, Tay, we are overloaded with all the cases in our office. Would you mind if we went to Josh for some help? Taylor laughed out loud. I was wondering when you had come up with that. Jack smiled and said up with what? They finished and returned to find Josh had left. His party tonight; has too much to do.

Jack picked up Samantha on time and was impressed, as usual. You look gorgeous, babe, and kissed her. Feeling on top of the world, he strolled in with the most beautiful lady on his arm. Jack noticed the many guys' appreciative looks until he realized all eyes were on Sam. The two whistles he heard only fed into his growing jealousy. He took her shawl off her shoulders, placed it on the back of her chair and went to get drinks. He quickly came back as two Romeos approached. We should mingle together as he held on to her arm, and they approached the bar area. Jack spotted Buddy and Jennie and waved them over. The evening had begun. Later, sitting at their table, Jennie excitedly told Sam about the high-quality restaurant that Bo had taken her to the previous evening. They had such an exciting time. The atmosphere is out of this world. It is exactly like you would imagine a 1920 bordello should look. Because that was what it was. Jennie went on about the naked statues, both men, and women. Sam asked, anatomically correct, Jennie nodded.

They giggled like schoolgirls, and Jennie went on about the red velvet pictograph wallpaper of naked figures in poses and actual photos of multi-sexual content. Sam turned to Jack and said, why don't you come up with such interesting places. Jack frowned and said, successful job, Bo! Bo then said Jennie jumped up to say, look at that picture, it is between a woman and a horse! No, I did not jump. They all laughed. Bo then told of the two ladies from the next table. Bo went on. One elderly lady got up and, with her spectacle in her hand, leaned into the picture for a closer look and shuffled back to sit down. Whereby she leaned towards her friend and said aloud, don't worry Ethel, it's not you. Ethel responded, You Bitch, and they both convulsed in laughter.

Both couples did the same. Clearly enjoying their time together.

The night continued with Josh being called upon to make a speech about his wonderful wife and happy marriage. Estelle rose to give her version of what a wonderful life of a cop's wife. The pain of worry every time they leave the house. The dread at a doorbell rings. When he worked on the night shift, she told him not to call and wake her. She could not sleep anyway, but if the phone rang late at night, she could not stop shaking for the rest of the night. These are the real things a wife of a cop must endure. But to be married to Josh makes everything else not so important.

However, the toilet seat must be down, the shoes wiped off, and put the milk back into the refrigerator. If not, I am going to kill him myself. Josh grabbed her and kissed and hugged her for a long time. Many eyes were teary, and men used napkins to their noses.

Everyone had an exciting time, and the evening seemed to fly by. Sam was home at 12 and Jack by 1 am. Sleep was a welcome treat.

Next day, Jack left a message for Josh who had not come in yet to set a meet, and he told Josh, he was going to Rock Creek to research most of the day. Tay and Jack met Buddy and his machine at the bridge along with the boys. They were overjoyed to take part in action again. Buddy began getting the machine ready as the boys, and Tay cleared the brush and rocks away from each site to be scanned. Jack had to help the Mole climb the slope to reach the first site.

The Mole slowly went back and forth over the gully, sometimes needing help to reach into corners, until finally, Buddy was satisfied with the results. A coffee van had come, and all sat and drank to relieve muscle aches. Raymond said what all were thinking, I don't remember hurting like this during my workdays. Several groaned, and others laughed.

Price, you pay for living this long, said Bill. Twenty minutes later, Buddy announced, a mass of a body on its left side.

They then tackled the higher site, which also produced a viable scan. Since the next site was downslope, each man gratefully helped push the Mole downhill.

This site scanned a larger mass, such as a large trunk or barrel. It would require having a backhoe to excavate it and pull it up. Jack offered to take all to dinner because it was after 5 pm. But the boys had supper waiting, and the wife's, enough said. They all shook hands and ended a tiring but enjoyable day. On the way back, Josh called and told Jack to meet him at Casa Royale for drinks while he settled for last night. They drove directly to the restaurant, where Josh saw them enter. He said, two of you, I'll wait to finish writing my check then. Both men said thank you. Josh smiles and asks them," What's up?" They sat and described the events of the last two days, starting with their discoveries made at Rock Creek. More bodies and another day trip are added expenses to the budget. Taylor told us about the larger find and Buddy's assessment of what will be needed to get it out. Josh says the budget will be shot for this year and next. I wish I was back on patrol, at least I was in control of my area. That's not all. We are of the rate of cases to be closed, said Tay. Josh made a wry look and responded; no way I can allow more labor. No Way!

Jack had held back just for this reason. Josh, there's something else.

Jack comes clean about his late-night meeting with Detective Renton and all that had expired. Jesus was all Josh could say. Jack said Renton had brought this all to Jack and was involved. He should be brought over, somehow, to help ease the workload and allow the use of his contacts. Josh tries to create a method to have Olson loan Renton to them. Jack lowers the boom by saying, No, can do, sir. Olson has a severe hard-on against John Renton, plus Josh interrupts to say, I'll talk to Olson. Tay breaks in to explain Olson is a biased SOB who believes Renton is gay, and he wants him off the force. Jack continues to provide further details as to Olson's involvement in everything, down to the murder of Howard Martin and others. This clinches Josh, who says, ok, I'll get the paperwork in order, but nail that bastard and close these cases expeditiously and quietly. Jack spoke of a solution to move Renton over to the Cold Unit under Josh to keep Olson in the dark and out of the loop. Josh had a better idea. I'll try something better and let you know on Monday.

If this goes as high as both of you think, I will only be able to protect you for a little while. Oh well, said Taylor, I was retired once already. I don't mean retired, but all of us may need to learn to swim with the fish. Instead of eating, drinks were ordered. Over drinks, Jack asked if Josh believed the current search warrant would be the other side of the bridge and any other site surrounding it. Josh replied, I'll call the attorney to see, and if not, we'll amend the warrant.

Monday was set as the next day to go back to the bridge.

Chapter 14: A Friend in Need

Jack called Sam and set a date for Sunday. They talked for over an hour.

Jack spoke to Detective Renton to explain the new situation and to have him meet Josh on Monday morning as soon as he came in.

Sunday was another fine day, and Sam looked magnificent to Jack. He asked, what do you want to do? Sam had an outline of items. She mentioned going to the bordello for dinner. Jack quickly responded that it was closed on Sunday. How convenient, came her reply. She asked about going to Rock Creek to see where he had been spending so much time. So off they went to walk the trails and cross the bridge. A lovely walk, romantic and muted. After two hours, Sam saw a food vendor and offered to buy lunch. Jack quipped, lavish as we are today. Sam stuck out her tongue. Sitting at the picnic table, Jack spoke of the death this place had seen, not just now, but through the centuries and if the spirits haunt or just see all the enjoyment that fills this space. Sam leans close and whispers, I sense their presence and an acceptance of its current use for a restful, beautiful refuge from the chaos of life.

After eating, Sam says, I want to go to the Capitol Rotunda to visit the "Meet your Legislator" display today.

Ok, so off they go downtown. Jack parks the car, and they climb the impressive steps to the Capitol and pass a guard to follow the signs directing visitors. The first level is dominated by statues of past dignitaries, and they take the stairs up to the second level to pass each station that had been set up with bios and papers of accomplishments of that legislator. Some stations had actual aides or receptionists to discuss the concerns of constituents. The next level had committee members' stations from congressional committees. Halfway around the huge Rotunda was the station of Congressional Representative Catcher, and his receptionist was on duty. She called Mr. Spec, hello, it is so nice to see you. Jack introduced Samantha, and they talked about the congressman. Sam spoke about his bio and the fact of his loss of a wife and child in childbirth. The receptionist's name was Sandy, and she told of the agonizing pain everyone felt and the trauma going forward. The congressman was devastated for two years until he met his new wife, Sarah. Saying that she pointed to an easel and a picture. The family of the congressman was shown; he, his wife, and a daughter. Jack froze and stiffened. Sam took his arm and continued talking to Sandy. Is that their daughter? Yes, said Sandy. I thought I heard somewhere that she could not bear children, commented Sam. Oh, she can't. They adopted, was the reply. Really, how lucky for them. They tried for a year but were not picked. The bishop called and told them he had found a small girl in the Catholic hospital. Her parents had died in a tragic car accident, and she had been severely injured. It was a while before the highway patrol discovered the car down a ditch and, with the child still having signs of life, rushed.

They saved her life but were forced to amputate her left leg, as you can see in the picture. She lost any memory of the tragedy and had suffered trauma. The bishop helped the process and the new parents have been dedicated to her recovery and love her as a gift from God. Jack heard all this and came out of his trance. He only said it was time to go. Sam thanked Sandy and hoped to see her again. The walk outside was with no conversation. Jack, are you ok, you are white as a ghost. Jack's face was a mask of emotions, from hate to despair. To kill was too little, and to consume his enemies, which now number more than yesterday, wasn't enough. The beauty of the day was now shrouded in darkness, terror, and memories of voices screaming, "Daddy, help me".

Sam drove to her place and nursed Jack over this spell. He hardly ate the dinner; she prepared nor spoke much. He was locked in his mind and a breakthrough was for another time. She set up the couch, and he went to sleep.

A sleep of drifting lost in space without consciousness or belief in anything.

A deep baritone voice penetrated from his soul to a clueless mind. Jack, I am here. Rest, and we will talk. This happened for a purpose, which you'll soon know. Rachel is in a safe place and loved. If you continue, you will find your answers and peace.

Jack's body seemed to relax, and Sam saw a peace overtake him. His sleep was full of rest, and she knew it was

time to go to bed. Tomorrow will bring hope and new realizations.

Sam was right. Jack was open about his reaction and its cause. The girl in the picture was Rachel. She did not just look like her. She was her, his daughter, alive and without any recollections of the attack. She, like him, had survived. Her little leg was too small, and frostbite had destroyed it. She is alive, and he does not know what to do about it. She believes in her adoptive parents and appears happy. He must be careful to not cause her any harm. Her mind may still be fragile.

Sam agrees and suggests he give it some time, and she will research, to find a way forward.

Jack arrived at the office to find Olson waiting. Olson let out a stream of expletives about Jack stealing one of his men. Jack says, whoa, I have not stolen anyone. If you are talking about Detective Renton, Josh felt he was the best man to transfer over because of his low seniority. Don't come in swearing and using that tone to me. I remember the days I taught you, and you did not listen. Cut the crap! Olson stormed out the door. Taylor and Renton stood aside in the hall. Olson stopped and told Tay to watch his back because this fag won't back you up. Renton grabbed ahold of Tay's arm to prevent him from action. Jack said, you heard. Tay, said yeah, Josh says he'll meet us at Rock Creek later to fill all of us in.

They went together up to the bridge. There, they met Swares and helped map out the area to scan with the Baby.

Soon after, the humming and whirring of the Baby signaled the search was on. Baby was heavier than the Mole, so the boys had to help push to cross difficult terrain. The first grave portrayed a body folded in half as if just dumped from a shoulder. It was not deep, as this was a hurry- up job. Detective John Renton took off his jacket and dug. The others pushed Baby to the second grave. A small child-like mass presented, also not too deep. Finally, down to the larger site. Buddy had a lot of trouble getting any type of definitive readings. Whatever it was, it gave an extremely large signature.

The size caused much concern for Buddy, especially because it seemed to taper off the deeper, he read. He looked at Jack and Tay and said, not a body for sure. Lopsided metallic. I just don't know. We'll need a big backhoe and a truck to get it out and move it. Just then, Josh arrived. How is it going? he said. John called. I have got something, and everyone hustled over to help. The body was Jason Chase. Josh called forensics as the others placed a tarp over the open grave. They walked in silence down the slope to the coffee van to await the crowd. Josh explained the new setup to include Detective Renton in the squad. He had gotten approval, based on the successful results so far, to form this squad to review all cases stalled or cold by other detectives. Jack will be a new squad leader, with the potential to be lieutenant, and up to three members will be allowed. They are to serve directly under me, with complete authority granted by the chief of the department. Jack, you, and your people have impressed the commissioners with a little leftover for me. They all laughed, and Jack bought the coffee.

Buddy spoke to tell Josh about their finds and sought a backhoe and truck. Josh asked if he was sure, it wasn't an elephant or a car. No either. The triangular shape has me confused. After a while, Josh left and the boys went back up the hill and dug in the second ground. Soon, forensics arrived and took over. Buddy remained and studied the third object and made sure it was handled delicately.

The rest of the day was devoted to reorganizing the files among all three and set protocols. Jack said he was going to lunch, anybody else. Tay declined, and John said sure. They went to Nick's to eat and talk. John opened by saying thanks for his escape. Jack said an escape leads to an unknown. Welcome to the unknown. John laughed. I appreciate your sticking up for me to Olson and Kirby. Your ass is way out there. Don't worry about my ass, just watch your own. My life has been in turmoil for months. I don’t know if my feelings are real or just politically correct. I have lots of friends who are gay or close to it. I am simply confused. Some I have known since grade school and love them like brothers. I can't tell the difference between a brother and a potential lover. My father passed on when I was little, and I had no male influence except friends. Some friends became brothers. I stayed at their houses. My mother worked long and hard to support us and prepare me for college. I ate most dinners at neighbors and was treated as a family member.

Lately I have become confused as to brothers or lovers. One, especially, is gay and remarkably close to me. I love him but as a brother or what? Compound that is his sister, a beautiful woman and newly divorced, by a sister or something else? See, I am confused. Jack said, You want ketchup for your fries? Both smiled, and Jack said I am not competent to give marital advice. All I can say is brotherly and sisterly love is closer to the love of your mother. Great love, respect, and obedience, but for a mate. That love is of devotion, protection, and if lucky, can be felt deep in your soul. You become their soulmate, which is far beyond just a mate. John Renton thought and told Jack; it had never been explained like that. Is that what having a father is all about? Jack said it should be.

They returned to find chaos in the garage. Buddy had gotten an enormous machine to extricate his thing and hauled it on a flatbed back to the shoppe. The mud and dirt had been saved by forensics to dissect and he had hosed it off, saving the water used by the recycling carwash, available for cleansing patrol cars. He planned to evaluate the water for evidence. Buddy was alone. Everyone had abandoned him. Jack asked, what the hell happened? Buddy said in a faint voice, The thing had glowed red and vibrated, after the water poured on it. I turned off the water immediately, and the water seemed to vaporize or be absorbed into a skin encasement. Jack and John stepped back and looked at Buddy. I am not crazy was Buddy's reply. Me, if anyone can relate to that, said Jack and Renton nodded ascent. What do we do with it, asked John?

Buddy looked at both and answered, examine it, and be careful.

A long night wait for all.

Outside of the thing, it or him, the business had to be done. So, Jack and John left Buddy locked away in his lab to follow the evidence. First was a review of what they knew about Jason and see what Tay was up too.

Tay was working on the case of Margret Daevos, the third body discovered. Her family insisted that none of them had anything to do with her disappearance. She did not come home on the bus from school and that was all they knew. Father

Barnes had been called immediately upon her lateness, and he came right over to provide sustenance and prayer in support. He had given a statement to the police. It was in the file. Except it was not. Jack looked at Taylor and said I know that guy. Pull him up. What school was she going to? All good questions, but Jack felt he already knew. The facts were soon clear. Taylor said, Olson was the officer on the scene. He took the statements. Jack had made the connection already and said, I'll be late tomorrow. I must see the bishop.

They continued with their review.

First was a 36-year-old woman, presumed murdered in her home. Blood was found along with trace evidence; a violent struggle had ensued. Husband presented signs of a fight and lacerations and is a suspect - kept under observation. Name – Rosalie Griffin.

Second was a man robbed and beaten at his storefront pawn shoppe. Cameras smashed upon entry, and no recognition. Blood all over the floor, evidence contaminated unknown. Name – Jacob Schiltz.

Third was a young girl of 12 years, kidnapped. Ransom Demanded, not picked up, family ties Name - Margeret Daevos

Fourth was a man of an unknown age of foreign descent was dressed in business attire.

Fifth- unknown Sixth- unknown Seventh- unknown Eighth- unknown, Nineth- unknown

The day ended without progress and a need to develop leads in the cases. The forensics reports were due tomorrow, as well as returns from BOLOs. So, they called it a day. Renton was going in search of his snitch; Taylor had a dinner date, and Jack wanted to call Sam.

Jack arrived at the diocesan office early the next day and requested an audience with his excellency immediately. It was police business. A half-hour later, the bishop came into the waiting chamber and greeted Jack. What's this matter with police business? Jack replied, Father Barnes, a pedophile, and murderer. The bishop stopped and said, that is a horrible accusation to make, even if he is dead. Jack stepped closer. Do you remember all the priests under your authority or just the ones involved in sinister events? The bishop sat down behind his enormous desk as if it were a barrier to the truth. He replied, what are you inferring?

Too much! Was Jack's comment. He continued to say; I saw my Rachel with the Catchers on Sunday, and I want to know why you did it?

Sit down was the response.

The bishop explained the circumstances as they had unfolded. The attack happened, and all four of you were dead, except Rachel came back after several days in the hospital. You were still dead or dead. The hospital treated her, and I looked over her progress. She almost died several times. The congressional representative and his wife were desperate to find a child, and I am friends with them. The adoption agency would not consider taking on the case of Rachel because of her lost leg. I approached the Catchers and took them to the hospital. They both were heartbroken and fell in love with Rachel. They immediately wanted to care for and adopt her, so I planned for them.

They are devoted to her, and she is safe, loved, and happy in her ignorance of the tragedy endured. I hope you will respect the confidence given and avoid any further pain to Rachel. As for Father Barnes, he was a priest and a servant of God for most of his career like many priests, the constant stress from congregants seeking answers to questions with no answers build up and can affect the brain and the mind. This happened to Father Barnes. Somewhere along his path, he decided God needed him as an avenging angel. His warped mind heard God describe those children as too loved and protected by their parents in place of loving God. The parents needed to be punished for the loss of their children. You solved that case; I needed to step in. He would not have survived in prison, torture, beatings, and worse would have happened. He did a lot of good and deserved better. I kept him as a prisoner in his body until he died. His penance was to live with his sins and take them to God. Jack asked if it was all right for him to play God and not his priests. The bishop responds to Jack with a question, how often does he play God in his job? Has he shot or killed anyone? Who judges him. When was his last confession?

Jack looked at the bishop and spoke. Too long. Jack walked toward the door. But turned and queried him. Who do you go to for confession? Bishop Frys says. To God, directly to God!

Jack returned to his office, where Tay and Renton were matching DNA reports to the open files.

First was a 36-year-old woman, presumed murdered in her home. They found blood along with trace evidence; a violent struggle had ensued. Husband presented signs of a fight and laceration and is suspected- kept under observation. Name - Rosalie Griffin. DNA report states that the blood evidence was not a match to her husband, as was the skin and blood evidence for the husband's trace. Both matched the samples of one, David Blaine - Deceased.

They returned to interview the husband again.

The second was a man robbed and beaten at his storefront pawn shoppe. Cameras smashed upon entry, and no recognition ID. Blood all over the floor, evidence contaminated unknown. Name – Jacob Schiltz Blood evidence not conclusive, but saliva tests on the clothes of the deceased were positive for a David Blaine- deceased- had prior arrests for extortion and assault.

Third was a young girl of 12 years, kidnapped. Ransom Demanded, not picked up, family ties. Name- Margeret Daevos Evidence does not match any on file. Case to be closed by the death of perpetrator Father Barnes.

Fourth was a man of an unknown age of foreign descent and dressed in business attire. Newly arrived from a European country, clothes are of a make from Portugal or Spain. Aviation fuel found in his treads indicates a private flight on a possible Lear King jet.

Fifth Was an old man, not reported missing, SS, Medicare, or pension fraud- died of natural causes. DNA- no match on record- filed in database.

They decided to BOLO all three services and city and district welfare agencies, as well as voter records for absentee.

Sixth Wife reported missing and thought to have run off with the neighbor; see combined file.

Seventh- husband reported missing and thought to have run off with neighbor.

Combined report both buried in one grave - DNA shows enough evidence of deception to indicate a high probability of double homicide to defraud state and local regulation and laws and Federal crimes. Suggest a meeting for direct coordination of data and warrants. DNA confirms 1st Male and second female are brother and sister. BOLO shows possible, not first-time scams.

Eighth Jason Cole-Awaiting results.

Nineth Bartholomew Jinx -Awaiting results.

Copy of BOLO was attached, and Detective John Renton is taking the lead on those. Taylor will follow up on victims Five and Eight.

While Jack takes the lead on Victim 4 and 1.

They go to their own desks and make calls to start their investigations.

Jack sets up an appointment with Mr. Griffin for the next day and sends BOLO to all airports in the New York to DC corridor to identify all private flights incoming to the USA from Europe over the last 4 years with passenger lists of five or fewer.

Jack left his two mates to continue and went to see

Dr. Swares at the lab.

Jack enters to the sound of chanting. Buddy is standing in front of the thing and speaking in various languages, from ancient Greek to Latin and Hebrew, all to no avail.

Chapter 15:
A Friend Indeed

Hi Buddy, says Jack. Buddy turns and says I am fine, but Tubby here is not talkative at all. Jack starts a discussion about Vibrational Frequencies intertwined with radio waves of the lower frequencies. Currents of energy are adaptive to the 'Solfeggio Frequencies', which were used in Gregorian chants to communicate with other apostles and between monasteries to spread the word of God during the early years of Christian repression. The special tones of Solfeggio are used to unite a man with his maker. They did this by undoing all the conditions and conditioning that separate from the source, be it physical, mental, or spiritual. The 'Solfeggio Frequencies' were so effective that they undermined the power of the Vatican, so they were conveniently "lost" and went into oblivion for a lengthy time.

The 'Solfeggio Frequencies' contain the six pure tonal notes that were once used to make up the ancient musical scale until they were altered by the Catholic Church and Pope Gregory I (better known as "Gregory the successful"), who served from 590 to 604 AD. The Church claims they have "lost" 152 of these amazing ancient Gregorian chants, but more than likely, someone has purposely locked them away in the bowels of the Vatican archives. Adolph Hitler demanded them from Pope Pius XII during the second World War. This was a reason, given why the Pope received blame impartially for the Holocaust, he would not give in to Hitler's extortion attempts.

UT – 396 Hz – Liberating Guilt and Fear

RE – 417 Hz – Undoing Situations and Facilitating Change

MI – 528 Hz – Transformation and Miracles DNA Repair– and derives from the phrase

"MI-ra gestorum," in Latin meaning "miracle."

This is the exact frequency used by genetic biochemists to repair broken DNA – the genetic blueprint upon which life is based.

FA – 639 Hz – Connecting/Relationships

SOL – 741 Hz – Awakening Intuition

LA – 852 Hz – Returning to Spiritual Order

Sound is a vibration of air, while vibrations in the energetic field are primal and affect everything because, as the physics and metaphysics agree, absolutely everything, including humanity, is vibrating energy.

The two discuss options to generate any redaction necessary to create communication with Tubby, as Buddy calls the thing. The chief item is to introduce a correspondence of the six notes on the Solfeggio which can give a vibrational tone to notes. This can create a syllabic message. This will allow a pre-programmed computer to translate the vibrational electromagnetic sound frequencies into a conversational language. Buddy had studied coding of frequencies at university and understood the concepts Jack was trying to explain.

Dr. Swares calmly said, I'll work on this. Jack replies, let me know when you produce something.

Jack arrives back at the office to meet a last time with Renton and receives news. Chucky's body had been found by an angler in Bear Creek just off Mustang Park on Ban Brook Reservoir, next to Rock Creek Park. Only a short distance away from our burial site.

Renton discloses he met his snitch last night and gathered further details of Olson's activities. Swanson directly controlled Olson, and he did all the dirty work for him, including hiring outside muscle. I asked him if he could find out anything about the identity of that muscle. He would try, but he additionally said, the bishop had Jason Cole on a short lease within the congressional caucus and aides, a spy for him. The bishop especially desired any information from within Congressional Representative's Catcher's office and family.

His BOLO yielded a response regarding the brother and sister scammers.

They sold the two houses after a sham remarriage between them, filed insurance claims, and applied for and received new passports and documents for filing and receiving insurance checks and funds held in banks. This all amounted to a million dollars. The couple fled to Mexico and disappeared. Renton filed BOLOs to Honduras, Mexico, and Guatemala to seek any relations living there.

Things are moving fast, and as usual, answers will often lead to further questions as a trial develops. Each question is a step along the path to secure a conclusive answer.

Top questions are, what is the bishop doing and why? Next, what is Swanson doing and why? Third, how do the combined deaths fit into the puzzle or do they?

Jack swore, mainly because he did not have the current information to discuss with the bishop. The day was late, and he called Sam to ask her to meet him for supper at the Casa Royale. She agreed.

Around eight o'clock, they met and got their favorite spot. Sam was eager to tell him of her fresh revelations. She began by revealing that she was researching the vibrational aspects of his investigation. People have been using Sanskrit chanting mantras for centuries to generate energy, and the key element that makes the mantra powerful is its vibrational qualities. It is supposed to reduce the mind to a manifest level, which allows you to feel what you are beyond just the manifest level. This ability to hear and feel silence is the heart of the mantra. It creates the ability to tap into the actual vibrational language of the cosmos.

When you were in your state of non-existence, you only received stimuli from the cosmic environment and through the divine language, you talked to God and divinity. Somehow, you keep this exceptional gift and can receive it. Can you send it also? Jack was stunned. We have sought guidance and received responses from your father. I really have not tried. God is busy, and if he wants me, he contacts me. Sam says that's logical. Let us order, I am starved.

Sam, looking at the menu, states that silence in YOGA is not just the absence of speaking, it also is the absence of thinking. This state of inner silence creates a feeling of unity with all, part of the cosmos.

During supper, Sam explains her research further.

As a doctor, she has studied the brain anatomically and physiologically but had missed a simple conceptual item. The brain is an advanced computer, or more logically put. A computer is a limited version of a brain. It acts the same but is far less advanced. A computer communicates and operates using binary codes, which comprise ones(on) and zeros(off). A simple system of combinations to help computers to create dialog, among other important things. A central processor and counterparts process the binary code combinations into understandable representations that are unlimited in potential.

The mind is the central processing unit, and the brain is the counterpart working in conjunction to control all aspects, both involuntary and voluntary, within the body. Frequency is a cyclic pattern of secular waves flashing on and off. The process of energy contracting toward a neutral point is vibration, and expanding from the neutral point is called oscillation. The combination of these two actions determines frequency rates and the patterns of secular waves flashing on or off, which creates energy patterns to be processed by our consciousness and DNA to generate our external reality. Frequency and vibration play particularly important roles in creating the material structures of matter and are essential to the existence of life.

Jack sits back and asks; do you want coffee and dessert? "Don't ridicule me," Sam replied. I am not really, you are too beautiful and smart for that said Jack.

This is way ahead of my pay grade, and I am just a simple cop. Sam replies, no cop is simple. I want to help you in any way I can. I want you to know I believe in you and all you are doing. I have a better understanding of somewhat of all you are going through. Jack smiled. He said I appreciate your efforts and your knowledge. It helps me to comprehend the explanations from Buddy and the divine without appearing an idiot. Thanks.

They spoke of the development of the bishop, the congressman, and Rachel. Jack told of the bishop's tale of how Rachel had survived and come to the current situation. Sam asked Jack the million-dollar question, what are you going to do about it? Jack did not know and worried about Rachel and any reaction to whatever he could do.

I have also done a lot of research in my medical journals to discover the extent of your phenomena, and it is not unusual for a near-death experience (NDE) to be an experience of an atypical state of consciousness that is induced by the neuropsychological consequences of a passage near death. Far from being a psychologically traumatic event, these experiences never cause flashbacks and can even eliminate the fear of death. These situations are well documented and researched to enhance the patient's return to a normal life.

There are six different main patterns of NDE, but there are many individual outliers.

Out of body, often felt by cardiac arrest survivors; next is a through the tunnel, whereby survivors pass through a cylindrical form into an ethereal light. Some experience an arrival at heaven's gate with an indescribable feeling of love. The University of Liege found many had close encounters with past loved ones or spiritual beings. While at the heavenly gateway, some are given a choice to return to earth or continue beyond.

Your experience is not dissimilar to others but has some unrecorded aspects.

Jack, correct me if I am incorrect, but you were not given any choice, you did not go through a tunnel or go to heavenly gates. In all my research of the medical and university documents and papers, no one has ever floated in the universe, nor have they sat down to discuss a problem with the divinity, much less have recurring discussions with them and other spirits. You are truly a unique case and not crazy. You can slip into this state of meditative suspense, much the same as a YOGA seventh stage, which is called dhyana or 'meditation.' Dhyana signifies that stage when the mind, calm, and Y receptive, loses itself in the light (or in some other divine attribute) and finds its ego-consciousness dissolving in that light. If one is communicating with AUM, the sound vibration is experienced by the entire body. The soul marvels in the realization: 'This is what I am! It is not a physical body but a blissful manifestation of AUM, the mantra of the vibrational language realized by the ancient rishis and monks to communicate with all things cosmic.

Sam smiled at Jack and spoke. People say lovers only talk about sex, what is wrong with us. Jack replied, we should correct that now. Dinner was over, and they left.

Jack arrived late at the office the next morning. He had overslept. Taylor was waiting for him to see Mr. Griffin, and he had a picture of Captain Olson standing with the Assistant Superintendent Swanson to see if Griffin could recognize either.

They arrived at Mr. Griffin's residence and rang the bell. After a brief wait, Juanita, Rosalie's sister, answered the door. Taylor asked to see Mr. Griffin. Her response was that the police already came to arrest him. Jack asked, why? And she replied, They said for murdering his wife. Both asked the names of the detectives, and Juanita said, I don't know. They were in uniform and took him away in a patrol car about an hour ago. They thanked her and left. Taylor called Renton and told him to get down to processing and stay with Griffin. Jack called Josh to explain the status and the need to secure Griffin as a material witness ASAP. Renton called back from processing and said that Mr. Griffin had resisted arrest and had been taken to the hospital. They turned around and, with lights and sirens raced to the emergency room. They entered and immediately sought his location. Exam Room 8 was the reply from the front desk as they both ran down the hall. They pulled back the curtain to find a doctor and nurse talking on the speakerphone to somebody. Jack quickly asked to whom they were speaking too. And the nurse responded, your captain. Jack said sternly, Hang Up. We are here to protect Mr. Griffin as a material witness in our investigation, and his health is to be a priority. Do you understand? They nodded, and Jack went on. No one is to be allowed to see this patient without direct permission from Supervisor Josh Kirby or myself, Detective Jack Spec. What is his prognosis, doctor?

Doctor Jervis is my name, and this is supervising floor nurse Liz Krutter. This patient has been beaten severely and received multiple lacerations and contusions, causing rib and other internal damage. We were just discussing scheduling X-rays, bloodwork, and a CAT scan to start. Great, can we talk to him yet? asked Tay. Not yet. He is sedated, and I would like to keep him that way till I see the results of testing, then. Jack says ok, but one of us must be at his side throughout the testing.

Taylor speaks up to claim the first shift.

Jack goes to get coffee at the cafeteria and meets Renton on the way back. Sorry, I did not get you any. John says, ok, I'll live with it. How is everybody? Alive is the best, right now, replied Jack They sat in the emergency room outside Exam 8, waiting for their return, and John Renton opened a file he had been carrying under his arm and said, Several items came in this morning while you two were out.

An answer to your BOLO came from Philadelphia Airport Terminal P, which provides data on a private flight in at 8:10 am on March 9 last year and left 2 days later for Vancouver, Canada with only one passenger. A man named Franchot Tulieux of Marseille, France. He worked for the Ruisseau

Company, also owned the jet. He was 64 years old and walked with a cane. His pertinent information is included, and it has been sent to forensics for testing. The next bit of news came from the coroner's report on Chunky's DNA testing against case samples, and they were a match to both Victim One, Rosalie Griffin and Victim Two, Jacob Sabitz. The last was a request from Jack regarding the licensee's operation of the equipment at the radio tower for the religious station. It listed an electrical engineer Rodigo Callez, as the holder of the Commercial Radio Operator license for that location. He does not sound like a priest to me. I also have a word out for my snitch to call me.

Around 9 pm, Josh and his wife stopped by the hospital on their way back home from dinner. They sit in the cafeteria while Jack and Taylor leave Renton to guard Mr. Griffin and come to meet them. Josh has news of his own and is eager to discover all that occurred on this day. The boys say hi boss! In unison and continue to greet Mrs. Kirby. Josh begins by saying that nobody has seen Olson since this morning, and Josh issued a watch and report back call for his whereabouts.

The top brass is frantic and has a complete blackout on any information given to anyone.

Jack provides details from his BOLOs and the church radio station. It was being used to facilitate smuggling of illegals and drug operations. Numbers were issued monthly with a list of music, and each day, a different location would correspond to a song and its number for the day. This would indicate the day's delivery or pickup of both smugglers and dealers. Very sophisticated process with checkoffs and alternates based on rhythmic tones to adjust schedules. Today's thinking is that Olson was a mid-level organizer, following Swanson's directions and those above. Josh asked, any ideas on who calls the shots and please don't say the bishop. I hope not, but anything is possible said Jack. There seems to be a connection to the graveyard we discovered and several victims. The latest could be a victim, Franchot Tulieu, who flew in and disappeared immediately. He arrived on a jet owned by a French company called "Ruisseau". We are trying to connect them to another company called Arroyo.

Wait a minute! Came from Josh's wife, and she went on with in Spanish Arroyo translates to the same as Ruisseau. Each means a stream of light or particles of intergalactic matter or rays. Often used to describe the aura or circular light shone around the divine as a sign of holiness. Damn! Said Josh. I can't believe it can really go that high. Josh's wife placed a hand on Josh's arm and said, you can't stop. The truth is too important.

The enormity is settling in on each one. Josh breaks the silence to say, well, at least we have someone highly connected. Looking at Jack, he asks if he can seek guidance?

Renton called to say that the doctor gave permission for Griffin to answer some questions. Jack looked at Josh and said, I'll try. Saying goodbye, he and Taylor went back upstairs.

The doctor was present, and the nurse, as requested functioned as witnesses if needed. Jack spoke softly and reassuringly to quell any fears Mr. Griffin had. They spoke of their protection of him and why it was needed. If not, those responsible would continue to silence him and all he knew. Mr. Griffin agreed to provide a recorded statement, with Renton transcribing as best as he could. They proceeded to ask questions of voluntary statements and showed Mr. Griffin a picture of Olson and Swanson for identification. He pointed out Olson as the imposter cop named Jack Spec but was unsure if Swanson was the other party left in the cruiser. He gave a full list of accounting as to payments made to Olson and the claims made against himself for future arrests and subsequent violence in prison. The doctor and the nurse went on the record as present and verified all statements, as well as signing Renton's transmittal. Josh had sent over a trusted patrolman to stand the night watch and a relief officer for the shift. They made copies of the written record in the hospital offices and gave copies to each present.

Jack went home to seek a celestial meeting but to no avail. Probably because his mind was filled with the previous days, and he couldn't try meditation or even a restful sleep. The arrival at the office was chaotic, as suspicions and fear permeated the very building. Olson was still unaccounted for, and search perimeters have been increased. Jack and the others settled into Josh's office to go over the statements witnessed last night and ensure procedures had been followed. No errors would be allowed, as this would reach the upper levels of the department and the mayor's office. Griffin was to be released later today and moved to a safe house guarded by the Justice Department until a court resolution had occurred, where he and his sister-in-law would be placed into the Witness Program as an added precaution. Josh announced the issuance of warrants against Olson and John Doe.

Several prosecutors were present to ask and answer questions to verify all aspects of the investigation, as Josh had prepared them for. It was noon time before they finished, and Josh offered to take them all to lunch, but Jack told Josh that Buddy had left at least ten emails or calls to see him. So off he went to the lab.

Buddy was waiting for him and quickly asked, where the hell have you been? No one knows, is it a big secret or what? Jack smiles and says OR what is the correct answer? What do you have for me? Buddy turns to point to Tubby and says, He speaks! I think. I have tracked the notes that cause any reaction and at similar frequencies to solicit any positive response, and I got one, a question. It was garbled but still seemed coherent. It asked me, who was I? I answered Jack Spec, and it replied to verify. I did not know what to do, so after several minutes, Tubby went berserk and glowed red, green yellow and made screeching noises before shutting down. I am afraid to try again. Jack said, calm down and start over. We'll need some music. Buddy said, no way. That station has been off all day. The only notes are what I copied and made to communicate with Tubby. Set it up was all Jack said. Buddy generated his copies of sound at 528hz and added some vibrational movements to it. Jack sat in a desk chair and tried to remain relaxed while Buddy fiddled with resonating the sounds in attempting to reach the higher plane of consciousness, and Jack focused only on his inner self. Suddenly, a voice came through clearly, Luc's voice. Hello Jack, I am here to introduce you to friends of mine in need of your help and to verify that you are the only one capable of helping them. Can you understand and will you assist them? Yes, was Jack's comment. Luc spoke to something else and came back to ask, why do you address them as Tubby? Jack spoke about the endearment structure of the term, and no offense was intended. They like the term and your endearment. I will have instructions conducted to make communications between you two more accessible and channel them through to you. Expect them to contact you directly soon. The bishop is slightly misguided but still lacks evil capacity. The music returned anew.

Buddy was sitting on the floor in shock at what he had witnessed. Jack, you can talk to the divine. Jack laughed and helped Buddy to his feet, and said, Let's keep this between us, please. Keep trying to follow up on your research.

Buddy just stood there as Jack left, still not fully comprehending all that had transpired.

Taylor had just gone out to visit some old friends and would be back late. Renton was about to go meet his snitch and gather some new data sheets. Jack sat at his desk, and after some time in thought, he called Sam. Sam was glad he had called and told him about all she had learned from him, and he had opened her mind to a whole new world. I am thinking more and understanding more of the world around me.

You have reinvigorated my life and captured my love. I love you, Jack Spec, and I hope to deserve your love back. I am so happy to discover you are not crazy because I would be, too, by loving you so much. Have a meeting, will call tonight. Love you, Jack. She hung up before he could even respond.

Later that night, Captain Olson was sitting in his car in lower Georgetown, talking.

To a man named Rodigo Callez, Olson said we need to get on that radio to schedule a pickup to smuggle us out of the country before the Janitor gets to us. I know, but the cops have shut it down. Olson says, I don't care, just get it done somehow. We are running out of time. You were supposed to arrange everything, so you should have been on top of all of it. How did you lose control? Suddenly, a knock on the window, and an old beggar leaned against the car with his hand out for money. Go away yelled Olson. Please, Sir, I am starving. Olson pushed the button, lowering his window, and he noticed the small gun too late. One shot into the head, and Olson slumped over, only restrained by his seatbelt. Rodigo was also restrained and could not release his belt. Finally, the door opened, and he jumped out, but the old man quickly got around the car and shot Rodigo in the back of his head. The man picked up his cane and calmly walked, whistling a tune, away. The night was again muted and dark, as a grave.

The phone rang in Jack's apartment. Just as he was shaving, Jack here was his initial response. Josh here came back a voice. Olson's body was discovered early in lower Georgetown with one shot to the head, and Rodigo Callez lay next to the car, door open, and one shot to the back of his head. It was an execution; the boy was dressed as a priest. Hell is about to explode. See you at the station ASAP and hung up.

Jack stood there covered in shaving cream and thought, shit did not hit the fan, it is falling from the sky!

Chapter 16: Conversational Tones Among Friends

He stomped on the gas to rush to the precinct. The parking area was full, as an all-hands call had been issued. He parked in front of the garage service doors and went in through the lab's side door. Buddy was nowhere to be seen, and Tubby was humming a tune. Jack soon reached his office, and Tay and John were sipping cold coffee and pouring over their files to find anything they might have missed. Taylor spoke first. The forensics boys are at the station going over every inch, and another team pulls his car over to Buddy. Jack's phone rang. Jack here, Buddy replied to get his car from in front of the garage, ASAP. Jack hurried returned to the garage and found Buddy with the double doors fully open. Buddy said pull it in next to your new friends. There is not anywhere else.

Jack asked, was there any response from Tubby? Buddy said, you'll be the first to know. Jack went back upstairs to attend a briefing by the bigwigs. Josh stood off to the side, away from Swanson, who stared stoically forward as if in a trance. The mayor was sitting in the front row, as was most of her administration. The Police Chief and two members of the police commission stood behind the pedestal. The informational officer was outlining a general situational assessment of events and trying to gloss over some details. He commended the Department for its diligence, hard work, and thoroughness in this investigation and promised a swift conclusion soon. It was a dog and pony show for the troops and the brass. No mention of the brutal attack on the star witness nor his false arrest was made. The reporters present jumped to ask their cookie-cutter questions and polish the apples. Someone should have asked the simple questions like, how did this happen? How was a patrolman promoted to a corrupt captain, and who gave cover? Who are those brutal patrolmen that beat Mr. Griffin, and what will happen to them. No, the reporter's job is to create stories to sell papers and keep in good graces with those who allow them to be included in the next briefing. Jack thought of a day when the people dictated the truth in the news, which is what they thirst for.

Jack returned to his office in disgust and looked over the coroner's report on Chunky's death. Seeking any piece of evidence to connect his death to the death of Mr. Franchot Tulieu. Reading the report was tedious because of the style of this coroner. Suddenly, Jack sat up and reread the middle section. It spoke of a skin section with melanoma cells and of a different doctored DNA reading. Screw this guy's style. He good and hypervigilant. Bingo was Jack's praise. He called over to speak to the coroner who did the report to find out where on the body this evidence was found. The coroner stated it was on the rope around the head and torso plastic wrapping and on the wrists, where they had been tied and around the ankles.assailant. Little things mean a lot. He quickly asked if the report on Mr. Franchot Tulieu was complete and if he would check for any similarities.

While Jack hung on, his other phone rang, and he picked it up to say Jack here. It was the congressman's secretary informing him of a cancellation this afternoon if he still wanted to see the congressman. Yes, was Jack's reply, and the time was set at 4:14. As he replaced the receiver, the coroner came back online to summarize the completed report. Mr. Tulieu had been strangled, and the assailant had worn gloves. However, the strength of the strangulation showed a marked strength in the left thumbprint and in the array of the remaining prints. This would indicate a left- handed person. Skin samples from the victim's fingernails provided enough particuli to assess the blood and skin, showing melanoma present and DNA inclusion. Great news, Jack thanked the doctor for his diligence and asked for the report to be sent ASAP.

Jack drove over to the capitol parking lot and found a space because of the lateness of the day. He arrived on time and prepared. He was directed into the congressman's office to see the chief of staff and the congressional representative waiting on him.

The congressional representative walks around his desk to stretch out his hand in welcome and says, I am glad to finally meet you, and I researched your background. I am sorry for your loss, and I can feel your pain. I lost my wife in childbirth and my baby daughter. It was not as you suffered, but I hurt for a long time. Please sit down and tell me; what I can do for you. I know of your pain and sorrow, began Jack and I don't wish to add to it, but I am investigating several murders and need to follow up on several similarities between your adopted daughter's parents' deaths and the deaths I am examining. Reginald jumps up to say that there is no way an inquiry into the girl's adoption, or any questioning would be allowed. Jack slowly looked at him and said, I lost my children, so it is unthinkable to think I would put any other child through a painful inquisition. I came to speak to the congressional representative to avoid any undue publicity or suffering to anyone. I am sorry if you think that is my intention, sir. No, I don't, responded the congressman. I did some research and discovered that your father was a highly decorated Vietnam veteran. Yeah, I heard! Came Jack's retort. The congressional representative asks, Are you not proud of him?

Yes, I am proud, but he was not. He often told me that before Vietnam, he was a little boy playing as a soldier in defense of his country, but during his time in the country, he and his buddies became just frightened little boys fighting to escape the quicksand hell in which they were trapped. Grabbing any vine or chance to survive. After NAM, they were all just lost boys, many too lost to go on, and some lost all hope.

Yes, I am immensely proud of him, Sir.

The office was silent for several minutes until the congressional representative said I did not mean to reopen old wounds, and I am sorry. What do you specifically want to know? Reggie, please make a list to allow us to get all we can for the detective. I have a list already prepared for you, was Jack's reply. Jack then turned to look squarely at Reginald Dwyer and asked, exactly, how long have you worked for the congressional representative? Why? Was the reply. If it was long enough, you may have some pertinent information to add or help the congressional representative recall details he may not remember. If you can't assist the process, why are you here? I am sure you are too important to waste time. Congressional Representative Catcher rises to the bait and tells Reggie to come back later. Reginald goes to the door and says, I'll be right outside if you need me. Jack says he is sorry to upset Reggie, but the congressional representative waves his hand and says, Reggie's good at what he does, but can be a pain.

Now, what do you really want, Jack, and call me Tom?

Jack looked into the eyes, staring back at him, and began. I have discussed everything with the bishop, and he has urged me not to inflict pain or problems on Rachel. I have a father's respect for our daughter, and I am grateful to have her in a safe and loving environment with you. I want to set your mind at ease, and I will do anything to help you and your family, but I want to know any details about the strange activity coming out of your office. If anything affects you, it will cause Rachel pain. Congressional Representative Catcher, or Tom, sighs and begins his story. He was devastated after losing his wife and baby; he did not even want to live. Reggie came to him on a reference from the bishop, and the two of them got him through the next years until he met his future wife, Grace. She provided reasons to live and a chance to recover some to have children. A visit to an OB doctor resulted in unwelcome news. A rape as a young girl had left her unable to conceive. The adoption services refused to oversee our case, saying we were too old and busy to get a young child. Suddenly, Bishop Frys called me to discuss a delicate matter. The paper had been full of the attack and killing of your family. James Frye was an old family friend to trust. He told me of your daughter's survival and the extreme danger she would be in if anyone discovered she was still alive. He spoke of her trauma and injuries but that she was a beautiful child from a wonderful family in need of help. Please meet her and contemplate. You are her safest spot. Grace and I, knowing her whole family were dead, or so we thought, we went to her hospital bed. She was so pitiful, all bandaged and a leg in a cast still, that we sat by her side all night, and come morning, we both were in love with our daughter. A year plus of therapy and speech training has brought her back to all of us. My wife and I have been so worried since we found out you are alive and what the future would hold?

Jack states, tell your wife how much I appreciate her love and care shown to our Rachel and have no interest in causing trouble. If you need any legal documents to prove my intentions, please have them drawn up for me to sign? The only thing I ask is if she finds out somehow, I should not let her think I did not want her. I love her and know what is best for her. If we meet somewhere, just introduce me as a past member of your security detail and a friend. Tom stands and puts out his hand and says, you are!

Now, what the hell is this about doing out of my office? Jack settles back and begins. It started with the death of a congressional aide and has snowballed from there to include members of the PD, a captain, and others up to the bishop's office and to yours and other members of the Hill unknown. The congressman was floored. He avoided obvious questions and spoke to the heart of the issue. What can I do to help? First, tell no one, not even Reggie. Remember your daughter is an unwitting pawn to these guys, and if you are implicated, they will try to kill your family. So be careful. He saw the sobering effect on Tom's face and went on. Do you know anything about ARROYO or dealing with this office? Yes, it was some time ago, but they sought government transmission documents to import and export products from mid-eastern countries. Reggie oversaw it. I'll ask him, said Tom.

No way! came back, Jack's reply. He had the aide arrested for looking through those exact documents, and within 4 hours of that arrest, the poor guy was killed and dumped. Who can I trust, asked Tom? Welcome to the bigger leagues, only you can decide. But keep the circle tiny; it's not just your life that depends on it. I did not learn that the first go around. Don’t actively search for anything, just keep your eyes and ears wide open and register strange items in your mind. I'll be available for you. Keep your family safe were Jack's last words.

Jack drives back to his office, feeling slightly better about Rachel's well-being. He believed that Tom and Grace loved her and would protect her. The congressman was smart and not an average politician. He understood all that was at stake and could be trusted. His cell rang. It was Samuel, and he wanted to meet tomorrow at 3 pm in our coffee shop. Ok, he said and drove into the parking lot by the garage. He went in and was at once accosted by Buddy, who said we have got problems.

They stepped through the big door, and Buddy threw out his arm, pointing to Tubby, who was gone.

What the hell happened? asked Jack. Your FBI guy, or whoever he is, was Buddy's reply; and he and a bunch of armed guys came in and wanted you. When you were not here, he just said Ok and gave me a bunch of papers that said he was to take possession of all artifacts seized from Rock Creek Park not directly relevant to the official murder investigation. He also claimed that they had cordoned off the area across the bridge, and we could not cross the federal lines under federal laws. They used a big rig and a power lift to load Tubby on and just drove away and said not to find them because you can't. Damn, was Jack's comment. What else did he say? Nothing, but he will, was Buddy's comment and smile.

What did you do? said Jack. Doctor Swares does not like the way they treated us or our friend, Tubby. So, I made copies of everything and sounds, which made and even created a triangular footprint. Mr. Bigshot will call you and leave a path to Tubby. We can even send messages through his cell service if we want. Both laughed, and Jack said, if I ever said you were smart, I'll change it too brilliant?

They went back to working on the notes and frequencies Buddy had been studying in preparation for a future call.

Jack tells Buddy about the connection between the company, Ruisseau, and the named affiliate, ARROYO, on the documents left by Jason Cole.

Both words have the same translation of streams or rays of light: flood of intergalactic matter or rays. They are often associated with the aura of a circle of light around a divinity or God. A message must be in there somewhere. As Buddy went about recalculating frequencies and oscillations to generate greater resonance, Jack slipped out to see how Taylor and Renton were getting on with their cases.

As Jack entered the office, Tay asked, have you talked with Samuel yet?

No, said Jack, we meet tomorrow at 3 pm at the coffee shop. Want to come. Sure, was Tay's response. Jack looked over to John Renton, who said, I talked to my snitch, and he had lots to say. The bishop was worried about some shady dealing going on at the congressman's office, especially with Reggie, whom the bishop had known for a lengthy time, in fact, he mentored him as a boy and got his first job, which ended suddenly, and the bishop got him into the service, to avoid something worse. Years later, he regained the bishop's trust and got referred to Congressional Representative Catcher for employment. All prior records are sealed.

Mr. Bartholomew Jinx was a dealer and had a long record of violent tendencies. He worked with various cartels around the world and was lost in a failed coup in Africa. No further data is available. Renton also had information about Rondigo and Olson. The two were using the radio as a front for a cartel to run a smuggling operation to include drugs and non-legal aliens. The cartel was run out of France and used a fictitious name of Barranca.

The phone rang. It was Buddy, come down.

Jack left, telling John to check on its translation into French and English.

Buddy was eager for two reasons. First was a call from Mr. Bill. I told him to hold on, and I would get you back here. He said, no, I'll call back in fifteen. He did not say 15 hours or 15 minutes. I like him less every time. Also, I could generate some distorted sounds as words, smiling happily and proudly of himself. The phone rang ominously, and Jack picked it up to say, Jack here. This is Bill, and I have this thing. I know, was Jack's response. What are you going to do with it? Whatever I want. Sorry, said Jack, but Tubby may have something else on his mind. All the while this dialog was happening, Buddy was busily typing and generating a connection, and the chanting was like squawking in the background. I don't care about Tubby's feelings or yours, said Bill and you are not to find where we are. Buddy hands Jack a note. Jack slams the door on Bill. I just must ask Tubby. Thanks! You are in Bladensburg on Baltimore Ave off Route

1. The phone went dead. Jack held out the phone and looked at Buddy, who was rolling on the floor, laughing. As he stopped rolling, he said, if only I could have had the video to see his face. They both laughed again. He really is a rude person, was Jack's comment as he sat down to wait for the phone to ring again. Buddy went back to his computer, saying he still had a direct connection with Tubby.

He is sending it to you. The phone rings, and Jack walks away.

After a while, it rings again, and this time, Jack picks it up to say, Jack here.

Bill is yelling because the thing is humming and whining loudly in the background. Bill asks, what did you say to it? Tell me now. He is unhappy with you and your antics. Calm down. I will talk to Tubby and see what he wants. I don't care, was Bill's comment. Jack said, ok, throw a small bucket of water on him to get him to listen to you. And Jack hung up. Jack, said Buddy, which will not be good. A short while later, the phone rings. Jack says, Jack here, but Bill was screaming, you bastard, turn him off before he kills us all. Jack says, what happened? You know as well as I do. He roared and turned unusual colors, and suddenly he just sucked all the water up. What is he or it? My men are all hiding behind the desks and the files. You used too much water; I told you a small bucket, was Jack's reply. Put your phone on speaker and hold it in your hand near Tubby, so I can communicate. I am not going near him, came Bill's answer. Jack smiles and says, you better. You wanted him, and you got him. They hear Bill climbing out of his hiding place and shuffling to Tubby, and Bill says, good boy calm down. Ok, Jack, talk. Buddy is rolling in laughter. Jack gestures to him to get to the console, but a voice comes over the speaker. Hello Jack Spec. Hello, and who are you, was Jack's response? Why I am Tubby, and I am glad to meet you at last.

Buddy is just sitting on the floor in shock. Jack asks, are you alright, Tubby? What do you need. I need you! Luc said you could help. We need to meet to discuss my issues directly, was the response. Please be calm, but I will need time to get to you, said Jack. That will be fine. I have waited over a thousand years, so a few more will not matter to me. But others may be less patient. Can I talk later? Jack said, yes, I am always close by. Just leave a message, and I will get back to you quickly.

Tubby asks, is it quickly a year? No, much less, said Jack. We'll talk soon. Tubby says, look forward to it. We like your melodies. It goes muted and returns to its natural color. Bill stutters and slurs his words as he says, this is unbelievable, I stood next to an alien, and you calmly spoke with each other. Yes, we did, and if you behave, he will as well. Call me if you need me and hangs up. The phone rang again, and Jack said, Jack here. Bill starts with we need to meet. Can you? No! interrupts Jack, come here tomorrow morning at 10 am and hangs up. Buddy, still on the floor, claps loudly and showers praise on Jack. Wait till I tell the girls about this. You deserve an Oscar or something for that performance. Jack just says, go back to work and leaves.

Jack returns to the office. Taylor is at his desk writing notes to his file. Jack, I have got an update on Victim 5. Forensics' dental report has confirmed his dental work, placing him as Russian from around Leningrad because of the style and filling metals used in his teeth. He was now around 80 years old.

My BOLO revealed at least nine males that could meet that criterion in the DC Metro area receiving some benefits and SS payments, nothing related to pensions. Great, responded Jack. Tomorrow morning, I'll start canvassing suspects, said Tay.

Jack agreed and told Tay of his appointment at the lab and set the time to meet with Samuel at 3 pm.

Chapter 17: Love Can Be Complicated

Jack called Sam to invite her for dinner tonight to tell her about meeting with Catcher. She was happy to hear from him and had news. Jack was to pick her up at 8 pm. As he hung up the phone, he noticed a memo from Renton and picked it up. Barranca translates into an opening, gap, stream bedcap, stream bed, fumes caused by fire, gully, or a formation caused by erosion from water. Jack found the irony in the translations and references. Its usage predates Latin and has origins from Iberia throughout Southern France and Spain.

Jack drives home to shower and change all the while his mind is thinking. But it is like watching a slide presentation-first, the note, and the different options it stands for and how to fit each into the puzzle. Next is Catcher. I can't believe he is dishonest and still a loving father to another man's daughter. Reggie was the focus of the bishop, but what was he looking for, protecting my daughter or Reggie or himself? What was he told? Remember, God's words. Good questions deserve answers. What is a good question?

Jack's thoughts, though in a whirl, focused on Samantha. Promptly at 8 pm, he rang Sam's bell, and she opened the door, looking radiant, as usual. Beautiful was all he could say. She kissed him, and off they went.

They went to their comfortable place, Casa Royale, and were warmly greeted by a young hostess. She told them that Jennie was not in yet but was expected. They were shown to their table, ordered cocktails, and reviewed the menu. Jack offered suggestions, and Sam reminded him of her favorite dish. Jack agreed it was the best and ordered two. He then spoke about his meeting with the congressional representative and the evolution of the conversation, especially being careful to provide a verbatim recitation of the dialog between him and Tom, as he now referred to the congressman. The congressional representative wants Jack to come to the house to meet Rachel in comfortable, familiar surroundings and with his wife present. He'll set it up. Sam looked skeptical and asked if he believed the congressional representative or if it was a setup. Jack was convinced that Tom was very sincere and loved Rachel and his wife more than anything. The reality was he seemed genuinely shocked to hear of any inappropriate activity conducted by his office. He trusted his Chief of Staff, Reggie Dwyer, and was concerned about some of his goings-on. I reminded him of the risk to our daughter and the need to keep everything we had discussed secret. I believe him, and I trust his intentions. He was sincerely glad to hear my suggestions about Rachel and her future within his family.

Sam was still worried but felt better. She could be in danger, as he and his wife could be. I know and recommend that he call me, for any reason, for help.

Suddenly, Jennie appeared and sat down. She was laughing at them, holding hands, and looking like lovers. Is marriage on the table, she asked? Sam looked startled and repeated the question back to her. Buddy and you, are you? He is anxious but is waiting till my graduation. To change the conversation, she spoke about Buddy telling of Jack's Oscar performance with a government official and an alien. To hear Buddy tell it, Jack's performance was hilarious and stunned by this government creep. What happened, Jack? Hold it, Jennie said, let me tell it because you will not do justice to it as Buddy did. So, Jennie began with the creep coming into the lab and just removing Tubby. He lorded it over Buddy and functioned as a bigshot of major proportions. He was very demonstrative and made demands over everything. He demanded Jack not try to follow or inquire into Tubby's location. Jack said to Buddy not to worry; this guy named Bill would call him. Sure enough, he did to gloat. Buddy, said Jack, and I had prepared, and after Bill called, Jack talked directly to Tubby and blew Bill's mind and created some chaos at that location. Buddy could not tell how Jack did it and intimated it was a national security secret. But Buddy was rolling with laughter and could hardly talk.

Sam looked at Jack. He said you heard Buddy.

Jennie had to go to her first appointment and left. Jack at once spoke up to ask Sam about her studies. Despite a frown, she began. I am still confused about your suppositions on vibrations generating energy output. I have read a lot to corroborate it, but this energy of the world is a part of God's creational process and is a way out there for me. I realize people have used different terms at select times, such as "the force be with you" to indicate an energy field that connects all things. But the view of energy emanating from the mind and body is beyond my current academic level. That, combined with the notion of a vibrational conversion into mega energy of the cosmos generating a creative process from God, cannot be assimilated into my academic brain.

As a doctor and a scientist, my thought process has been limited to focusing on all that I was taught in academia, but now there is so much more available. I realize that thinking extends academia, and that is the most important lesson. I thank you for showing me that. The most important lesson started in first grade, a simple thought process, and expanded until fifth grade. Then, an upgrade to logical thought should occur. Each subsequent grade level must expand on a logical thought process. In High School, this process should have been developed to generate questions, with gradual step-ups to instill an inquisitional mind fostering opportunities to research already accepted thoughts and principles. This is the advanced logical thought process of the world.

I am enthused to advance my thought process and educational levels to investigate the unknown without preconceptions, fears, or knowledge. You brought me to this level, and I can never repay you or forgive you. If you don't spend the rest of your life with me. Please marry me, Jack. I love you so much.

Jack was too startled to respond. Sam looked shattered at his silence. Sam, about to shed tears, said I am sorry. I should not have put you on the spot like that and picked up her glass of water to drink. It just overwhelmed me, and I burst out with it.

Jack reached across the table to take her hand, which was clenching her napkin. I am the one to be sorry, said Jack. The server arrived to clear their plates. Jack ordered coffee for both. Jack says, Sam, let me explain and listen clearly. I love you and want to marry you. But my life depends on a jury beyond this world. Each visit to the heavens may be my last. They judge me till they find out how my problem came about and can fix it. They keep replying; each time I ask, the jury is still out. I can't create a future with you if it can end tomorrow. I can't create that pain and sorrow for you. I am sorry, and I should not have allowed this to continue; it is all my fault and my weakness. I love you.

Jack, I did not know, and if it is a day or a lifetime, I want to spend it with you. Keep doing what you are doing. They must be happy with your progress, and we'll just keep along. ok, my love. I can wait till they make up their minds. My prayers go to God also, maybe not to the Devil, but he'll listen in. The coffee came, and they smiled and drank. They left as lovers.

The following day, Jack came whistling into the laboratory at 9:45 am to meet Bill and see what he wanted. Buddy was there with a big smile.

And immediately asked for the details of last night's dinner. It seems as if Jennie had squealed on his date, and Buddy was to report back. Jack was more interested in what the terminal was flashing and if anything had come in or sounded. Before Buddy could answer, the door opened, and Bill walked in, his governmental stride indicating his importance. Good morning, was all he said. Jack noticed a reluctance to shake hands or implore any niceties, so he went directly to the key question. What do you want? Bill looked at him and said you. I want you to come to my secure place and work under my direction. I will contact my superiors and yours to force you if you resist my demands. Buddy looked stunned and worried. Jack smiled and replied, I already said I was busy and I would come over as soon as I finish my current case. Bill looked furious and said your funeral. Jack said, look, I am not trying to create problems, but I am on a special assignment collaborating with members of Congress on a highly secret project involving many high-placed individuals. If you even speak of this, you will be further out than even Tubby has been. I don't want to pull rank, but my guys go to the top and will not like any intrusions by an underling. Bill blanched, and all color drained from his face. He stuttered and apologized for his actions. He reiterated his request to have Jack come to assist him whenever he could and hoped Jack a speedy resolution to his investigation. He left without acknowledging Buddy. Jack turned back and asked if they had received any further contacts from Tubby. Nothing. Jack said thanks and went upstairs to meet Taylor and John.

As Jack entered the office, Renton and Taylor were deep in conversation over a stack of papers. Tay turns around and says, Jack. We are glad you came back. John says we have a big problem. Jack joins the trio and starts the briefing. Taylor begins with a questionnaire sent to agencies that give benefits to older adults citizens within the Metro, DC, area. I have a list of about fifty seniors who might not be missed and who were part of a massive fraud scheme. Renton opens a file to disclose a scenario of just how the operation could be run. Seniors can be targeted at senior centers, welfare offices, or clinics—many potential locations exchange personal data.

A strict criterion is required. Not gender-specific, but no relationships local or relatives living. They must live alone and use as many benefits as possible. Partially abandoned buildings in need of repair are also a prerequisite to facilitate an excuse for why they move away. Before proceeding, they would rent a post office box to receive mail and establish a legitimate address for checks, ballots, and other nefarious reasons. They may force them into old retirement facilities or eliminate them if a senior balks. Jack sits back with disgust.

Taylor speaks up to say, that's not all, Jack. We went to the listed addresses of some names on this list and discovered empty derelict properties. We entered to check them out and discovered several skeletons around the premises and in the basement, next to the furnace. We checked inside it and found evidence of more bones and skeletal remains burned. We need warrants to search correctly and more people. Immediately, Jack reached for his phone and called Kirby to explain the issues and the need to proceed. He placed his team in charge of this process and left to meet Samuel at the coffee shop.

A short 10-minute drive took 30 minutes in 4 o'clock DC traffic. Jack found a place to park and saw Samuel at his corner seat facing the doorway, looking very melancholy. Hello, what is the matter? Do you look troubled? Samuel said, yes, I am very disgusted. I must tell you; how sorry I am to withhold evidence from you. I knew you had, was Jack's response, and I knew you had reasons to do it. Also, you will eventually trust me enough to hand it over. Don't worry; I would have done the same. Trust must be earned to be valuable. I did not know you, but I liked what I saw and should have known better. Samuel replied, here is a packet of notes and a small black notebook that was the possession of Mr. Martin. I held it back because the notebook is like a diary with appointments and discussions. Many were with Bishop Frys, also with Reginald Dwyer, discussing several confidential issues and plans. This guy was a spy for both. I felt compelled to protect the bishop, but I needed to provide you with everything after Olson died. I am sorry, and would you still trust me? I will help in any way you ask. Jack smiled at his friend and said, yes, you can, as well as the other guys. Samuel grinned and said, you bet. Since the last time, they have become bored and grumpy, at least according to their wives.

Jack explains the recent developments in the older man's missing case and all the others, including the current perceived scenario. Jack explains the need to trace down each person on the list Taylor has and verify they exist and are well. If not, just document what you discover and call Tay at the office. He also told Samuel about John Renton; a man assigned to Jack's team. They finished their coffee and each left.

Jack stopped back at the office to see Kirby. He walked in and said hi to Josh. Josh gave him an evil stare and said, just the problem I was looking for. Please sit down and bring me up to date on what has gone on in the last hour. Each hour brings me more work, so let me have it. Sorry, boss, said Jack, but things move fast in DC. Josh says, Yeah, but do they have to move so damn quick in my building? Has Tay got to you yet? Was Jack's question. Yes, he has, and the warrants should be ready tomorrow by noon. I also have ten cadets to help go through the building, assist with forensics tag, and transport the remains to the morgue. Jack says, great; I also will need more space in the garage for Buddy to work. Sure, you want my desk too.

Jack says, and Buddy needs more room to process all the radio equipment from the radio station. If possible, he must set it up properly to transmit waves or trace down the smugglers and dealers. That is above my pay grade, but he thinks he can. I asked, see what you can arrange. Is there a bigger building he could use or something. I could give you the morgue but wait. You are already filling it up. Thanks, boss! Jack drives slowly home to have time to sort everything out in his mind. Josh was right; things were going too fast. He tried to call Sam, but he had to talk to her answering machine, so personal to say I love you to a device.

Jack grabbed a hamburger, and some beer to eat at home and made himself comfortable on his couch to read through the papers and notebook Samuel had given him. Many revelations sprung from the pages on the bishop's concern regarding Reggie and Tom Catchers working together. The bishop knew Tom had been raised in a protected household with staff and love and trust to support him. While Reggie had been on the opposite spectrum, an abusive father, and an alcoholic mother with a sister who committed suicide because of her father's rape? Bishop Frys knew all this and wanted to save Reggie but had his doubts. Some traits and wounds went too deep and festered for too long. The bishop was especially wary of Reggie being around Rachel, and he had warned her mother, Sarah, to be observant. Tom was a trusting soul and needed proof to fault Reggie. This was the reason for spying. Other pages spoke of a sinister meeting between Reggie and Olson with Swanson present. They worked with a firm Reggie had been involved with back in France and Spain called Barranca or something like that. A conglomerate or cartel controlled that firm; it was not discernable yet. The bishop wanted further information on them and pushed Jason and Howard for specific letters and forms to prove suspect dealings. Jason had made notes on the middle page of the book. Bishop has a past with Reggie, a boy, and his mentor.

Something stronger here. Bishop has some secret about this cartel or company. He was the one to send Reggie to escape problems and get Reggie involved with their operation in southern France; Reggie talked when drinking.

Jack had several beers and was dozing when he heard voices that differed from the usual. They were indistinguishable and far away. He understood, but all was a vague echo, as if in a vault. He awoke in a sweat and had to go to the bathroom.

He had trouble going back to sleep and lay in bed thinking of many things of little value and others of huge significance. Finally, he fell asleep at 4 am to awake at 6 am. Groggily, he took a shower and dressed; he had toast and coffee before going out the door. A nagging thought persisted in running through his mind, all things have imperfections, but God created self-correction over existence.

Jack arrived early to find Buddy wrestling with many cases and boxes of equipment that had just come. Hello, said Buddy, just in time to help bring this shit in. Jack looked at the serious cases and asked, What the hell is it? Buddy replies, your bright idea to bring all the crap from the radio station to me for set up and to find the why, how, and where of the smuggling and drug dealings. Jack and Buddy huffed and puffed their way inside the lab and set it up according to Buddy's directions. After a couple of hours, Renton came in to announce they were going over to pick up the warrants and meet forensic people onsite to begin recovery of remains and any evidence of DNA or whatever to support a case.

Jack acknowledged their efforts and asked if Samuel had been in contact. Renton said yes. And his people will meet us on-site and divide the list between them for actual visits wherever possible. They'll call you later. I'll stop over after this guy lets me go, was Jack's response. In the next hour, the machinery lit up and hummed. Buddy had expected this, but Jack was overwhelmed by their success at just humming. Soon, the panels and consoles were warmed up and ready to broadcast, but Buddy was concerned because they did not have any legal license to broadcast. Jack asked whether we could just send out frequencies or waves to space. Buddy thought and said, I can contact Tubby.

Another 30 minutes later, the humming caused a vibrational element, shown on an oscillating unit, and a lower order of oscillation. Modulation adjustment followed, and noise came out. Buddy jumped in success.

That was it. Jack checked with Taylor, who said Samuel had called in to say the first two spots were a bust. Both places were torn down, and one was under construction, and nobody recognized any names. They were going to another site a little farther out but would let us know. Josh calls Jack to tell him the news about rearranging the garage area to incorporate some space for an overflow morgue storage facility. If Jack can stop finding bodies lying all over the place, there may be some extra area for his needs. Jack tells Josh, I am trying, but they keep finding me. I know, replies Josh, you are doing a wonderful job. We'll run out of cold cases for you to check. Not likely, was Jack's reply. Talk later; I am about to meet forensics at the apartment building to get an update.

Jack left soon after to meet everyone at the building site. In the meantime, Taylor's phone rings, and he answers. The voice at the other end was Samuel, in a very agitated state. We need help here as soon as possible, that old farmhouse. Number 7 on your list was occupied, but now only bodies are left. We looked through the windows, and some were in beds, and a woman was lying before the door. As if trying to escape. We called the locals and emergency services, and they were on the way. Randy thinks everyone has been dead for a while. He says it looks as if some vomited before death, as if sick or poisoned. Call Hazmat and have them ready to activate, called Randy from the background. We'll stay outside and keep anyone else out. Hurry out here. Taylor grabbed his cell and speed-dialed Jack.

Jack received Tay's call, got the new address, turned on his lights and siren, and sped away. After 40 minutes of weaving in and out of Route 395 traffic, He drove up to witness an organized chaos scene, as a truck marked 'Morgue" rushed down the street and another pulled into the vacated space to be loaded with two black body bags. Waiting was another truck alongside two more forensics vehicles, with gear scattered all around it. People in cadet uniforms were scurrying back and forth to the open doors of the structured wreck. Taylor was sitting in his car on his radio with Superintendent Kirby, providing a situational briefing and additional requirements. The current staff will be required to be quarantined, and a hazmat force will be needed to set up a perimeter until the doctors discover how deadly this potential crisis might be. Army personnel may need to be called in. A yellow tape barrier was tied from trees to stakes to restrain anyone from passing. County workers set up a spotlight system to continue a daylight setting with the electric truck already connected to their grid. Jack's phone rang, and he picked up to answer Taylor, who was standing alongside his car. Hi Jack, Tay said, It's not good. We are stuck here for however long it takes. They know it is deadly but don't know if it is still active. They don't even know what it is. They will start epidemic procedures to manage basic requirements, like feeding and housing us indefinitely until we show signs of something or discover a diagnosis. I have got a hazmat suit and will go back inside to keep searching for any evidence. Talk later! Jack walked back to his car, hopeful but worried for his partner.

On the drive back to the office, he called Samuel's wife to inquire about Randy's condition, and she had arrived at the hospital just before he had. She told Jack that they had not entered the premises and were low-risk patients but would still be held for precautionary purposes until a final diagnosis. They are in an incubation chamber, stated Samuel's wife. Jack hung up, feeling that she would soon change from a concerned state to one of wifely agitation at all of them. Poor Samuel, he was not to be bored for a while.

Neither would Jack. His phone was ringing, and he answered, Jack here. Hello Jack, this is Tom Catcher, and my family and I would like to invite you and a companion if you'd like to come for dinner a week from this Sunday. My wife and I have talked with Rachel, and she is eager to meet you. We have explained to Rachel how we met years ago and that you, like her, lost your family to a tragedy and were in a coma for a few years. I told her I owe you my whole life, and my family would not exist without you. So, she wants to meet you to thank you for saving me for her. She still has issues of speech, some sight issues, and scars, but she is a beautiful person. Please come! Jack appreciates his efforts and would love to go. Thank you so much. Tom will send directions to his house.

Jack hangs up with some apprehension, but a chance of seeing Rachel and a renewal is too good to pass up.

Jack picks up the cell phone to call Sam, but it rings in his hand. Jack, here is his response to Buddy. Buddy excitedly tells Jack about some DC engineers who measured and assessed the cost of changing parts of the lab and the garage for a morgue facility. Jack tells Buddy,

Buddy was standing at the door, waiting for Jack. As Jack pulled up, Buddy started speaking before Jack's car door opened. Hold on, said Jack. I did not know they would be here so quickly; when have these guys ever come so fast? My chair has been without a wheel for over six months. There were two of them, and they measured every inch of the place. They were trying to reduce their estimates to convert into a morgue. I told them, no way. We needed this space, and it was only to share with them temporarily. I gave them my suggestions on what to save. Leave the doors and just caulk, put insulated curtains over the doors, and install an outside AC compressor to cool and an additional heater on the roof. They were happy and said I cut their budget by 60%.

Jack laughed and asked if Buddy was also a building contractor. Jack followed with, after today's tally. I would not be surprised if they came back early tomorrow with a crew and machinery. What happened, says Buddy? Jack explains all the day's events and tells him to be quiet about it. No, sense starting a panic if we don't have to.

Jack grabs a phone to call Josh, but he is not in, so he returns to his office. He makes a mental note to tell Sam to stay home for a few days and not go out without a mask. On his desk is a reminder to go immediately to the mayor's office.

Out he went and double-timed it over to the mayor. He was quickly granted entrance into the mayor's conference room, and it was crowded with all the agency's bigwigs. He approached Josh, who had waved him over and whispered. What the hell is happening?

Before Josh could answer, the mayor spoke up. She said, Is this your detective? Yes, came Josh's reply, and he uncovers this ring of senior abusers and fraudsters on a grand scale. He will explain and provide answers to your questions. Go ahead, Jack, tell them what you told me. Jack spoke in briefing terms, and most were attentive and stunned at the callousness' and broadness of the crime. Jack explained that this is the tip of the iceberg, and it will involve contractors buying some derelict properties under the market to rehab or develop for profit. The demand for Medicare cards is tremendous, from doctors' fraud to citizens. The banks may also have employees washing funds and checks to cash. Wait, do you know all this, or just guessing, asked the mayor. Jack looked at her and said that nothing is definite until an investigation is complete, but from what I know and my experience, this is less smoke and a raging fire. Older adults are the most at risk in all society, primarily geared to abuse and kill older adults. The next hour was dedicated to talking about creating a task force to show they mean business.

Josh and Jack left in disgust, knowing more talk than action is the way of politics.

Jack drove home to a dinner of eggs and beans, all that was left in the refrigerator. It filled him, and he went back to reading the diary and having a beer alone. God, he missed Sam. He could not wait to call when her class was over.

An hour later, Jack rang Sam and left a message to call him. Soon after, the phone rang, and it was Sam, Hi she said, I have missed you and have news for you.

Jack replied that he also was lonely and had news for her. Well, since I forgot to tell you my information the other night, I should go first, so Jack said, go for it. Your talking points about vibrational frequencies struck a chord in me. Wait, replied Jack, what I struck in you, But I thought it was a G chord. Sam exacerbated comes back, I am just going to hang up. Jack replies No, don't, I am sorry, ignore me and go on. Sam spoke about having several discussions with her students about vibrational wave frequency's controversial impact on a brain and generated a lot of interest from them, so I assigned a project to choose some impactful topic on a brain, not just human, but any brain. The response was tremendous, with many professing their desire to focus on how windmills affect the brain. So far, I have received a prospectus on animal, fish, human, airwaves, and underwater effects to infra and sonar wave frequency damage of counter effects. This is so exciting.

I have always wanted to do research, and this response has uncovered enough research data on the effects of Windmill Farms emitting vibe frequencies at levels that may cause brain damage to all species. Throughout Europe, most countries are sharing data about abnormal clusters of afflictions to the brains of multiple specifics and lymphoma, plus certain other maladies. Enough to warrant further research, so I have applied for a research grant. Great was Jack's response.

Are you sure this is a clever idea for you to pursue? Jack, somebody needs to do it, and I can provide insight into the brain and its effects and why. This research is required to answer questions raised by citizens living near or around these wind farms and the industries dependent on the oceans to survive; WOW, was Jack's comment. Congratulations.

Jack then asked if it was time to tell her about his news. Sure, said Sam, laughing.

Jack told her of the invite to Congressman Catcher's house for dinner the next Sunday night and the incredible explanation given to Rachel by Tom and his wife, Grace.

They are so gracious to give their time and Rachels to make him welcome into their home and include him in their lives. Jack also talks about the events leading up to and including finding many senior-aged bodies. Some were murdered and almost died from some illnesses. Just left to die alone without comfort, proper medical treatment, or nutrition, a true crime for which someone should pay. Sam had many questions about this, but Jack could not give answers to many of them yet. They discussed the callousness and cruelty to some people, and finally, they spoke of Tubby and how Buddy has become so attached to him. For the next hour, they just talked as many lovers wanted to.

The next morning, Taylor came back, having been cleared of any illness, to return to work for the next three days. All three men devoted the morning to going over all potential evidence to find any evidence to place them in a direction to discover those responsible. Around 10:30 am, the coroner's report came in and provided a name and address for the woman caregiver, and Renton out to that address to check on it.

A man answered and failed to recognize the name given. He claimed to live by himself. Detective Renton asked about a suspicious smell permeating from inside the house. The man said it was work clothes. He works at a slaughterhouse, and that smell requires him to boil his clothes to get rid of the stench and then use the washing machine to finish. Jack looked at John and then handed over a card, saying, please call this number if you think of anything to help us. The man said, ok and closes the door. Jack stops turning around and says, I am so sorry, I must have given you the wrong card. That one is for my laundry; please take this one, handed it over, and took the other back by his fingertips. Walking down the stairs together, Jack heard the door reopen, turned in time to see the man pointing a gun. A flash, and sound of it firing, falling, and blackness.

Chapter 18: Vibrations Lead the Way

Josh picked up the ringing phone, and all he heard was an officer down reported and gave an address. Sitting at Jack's desk, Josh looked across at Taylor and asked if we had anyone at this address. Jack and John are there now. Both jumped and ran to Josh's car as he once again slipped into the recall of his nightmare. He has never forgotten that horrible night and many months of fear and depression over all the news. The race was against time, and time seemed to win. The tires screeched to a halt. Tay and Josh jumped out and raced the final way to where Jack stretched on gurney, prepared to go to the hospital. Josh quickly yelled, how's Jack, to no one in particular? Renton, next to Josh, says he'll be ok. I am the one-shot. Josh says, oh, thank God. John looks at Taylor, who says, glad you'll live, but not as important as Jack. Josh swings around with a grim face, which breaks into a broad smile, and he leans over to tell Renton how glad he is alright. We'll clear this up and meet you at the hospital.

Taylor takes charge of setting a procedural order to follow with an officer shooting and a death. Forensics soon came and said, does anyone other than the two of you end up with bodies? Are you exhausting us?

Two hours later, they arrived at the hospital and sat in a room waiting for Renton to come out of recovery and Jack to return from CAT scans. Josh asks Tay how he is after the ordeal he went through. The events had allowed no pleasantries between these two. Both laughed and wondered if things would ever slow down. Not in DC was the reply. Renton came in first with a lovely young lady holding his hand and an aide with a tray load of food. John looked at the two men and said, what? I am starving; a wounded man needs his nourishment. Pardon me, but this lady is Sandra Hopkins, a close friend for a lengthy time. She seems to care about my health, so please tell her that detectives get shot all the time and it is not a big deal. Tay calls out, nurse, please order this man a CAT scan also! Josh tells Sandra not to worry, and most detectives learn to duck. Teach him to duck. She smiles and says, call me Sandy, and every day, I'll throw something at him. Both men tell her, good girl! Jack soon comes in, and the talk turns to business. Jack mentions that everything was normal when they arrived. They spoke to the individual who answered the door, and he said the name was not familiar. I gave him a card; Renton interrupted by saying Jack pulled a switch by giving him a card to get his fingerprint. Then, he acted like it was the wrong card and carefully took it back while replacing it. I smelled something awful, like death and mold. He claimed it was work clothes from a slaughterhouse, and he was cleaning them. We said goodbye and walked down the stairs. I smelled a rat, besides what he said, so I turned to tell Jack halfway down the steps. I glimpsed him, opening the door with a gun, and shoved Jack. He fell, I was hit in my leg, and I shot him and fell down the steps on top of Jack. Somewhere along the way, Jack hit his head and was knocked unconscious. Taylor speaks up: a center kill shot. Good job. Jack speaks up with, now I know. The doctor told me my head had hit several times as I fell as if someone had fallen on top of me on the staircase.

Renton apologizes. Everyone laughs in relief. Samantha greets everyone, telling Sandy how glad she is to meet her and how lucky John is to have such a lovely friend. Sandy says I have been telling him that since the third grade, but he was always stubborn. The girls gravitated to one side to talk and left the men to finish their business of firming up and checking for any mistakes. After an hour, both patients received medicine to help sleep and relieve pain. The nurse instructed the visitors that visiting hours were now over, and they had to leave.

Both men were released late Saturday afternoon and told to rest. Sandy and Sam were there to take them home and put them to bed for the night. Both ladies were to stay the night, inform the doctors of any issues, and ensure both men received their proper medications. Sam made dinner and set Jack up on his bed to relax and read. She settled in on the couch to watch TV and read some research. She liked to read while a TV spoke low in the background. It relaxed her somehow.

Jack continued to read and reread Martin's notebook and notes from Cole and the bishop. Some things fit perfectly, and many others were disjointed. And made little sense. It was as if the writer knew much more than he was saying and left out pertinent parts for the reader to conjecture about. Jack reread those parts repeatedly until his eyes and head hurt; he then shut off the light to seek sleep.

The next morning, Jack awoke to the smell of eggs, bacon, toast, and coffee. Today's coffee, not last night. He dressed and came out to kiss Sam and hungrily devour her cooking. After his second cup, he asked her what she had spent the night doing. Worrying about you, what else would I do? When we get married, I want you to stop all the heroics and let the young guys take all the risks. Jack smiled and said, have you got it all out of your system? Yes, came the reply. You are getting up there and need to slow down. Jack looked at her and asked for his cane. She grimaced and cleared the dishes. I called out today, and Josh gave you the day off. So, what do you want to do?

Since it was raining, they stayed indoors and rested or cuddled, as Jack suggested.

Sam said, “Rest was what the doctor ordered, and that is what you'll do.”

As Jack read the paper, Sam browsed some of her students' papers and questions to research. She finally says, here's one. Jackson asks if vibrational frequencies or waves can reactivate the brains of dead or unconscious people to discern potential prior activity or memories. Julie asks if they can generate buying patterns or impulses. This is good. Professor Manning wants to inquire if vibrational frequencies can intertwine with other waves to generate energy and propel aircraft, spacecraft, or even vehicles cheaply. They seem to travel at tremendous speeds and distances through the cosmos, so why not spaceships, or can they create warp speed or time wormholes? We know they exist, but what creates them?

They all are interested and have questions galore. Some are basic, and others are overly complicated. Another professor asked about the gravitational effect generated by the vibrational frequencies wavering in circular series and conducting electrical currents that will absorb pressure pulsation.

Another asks about a study done in early 2020 that sought to duplicate a preexisting study done in 1981 using a nine-note Ionian scale that showed after 18 months that cancer cells lost their structural integrity and exploded. The report showed "cancer cells cannot maintain their structure when specific sound wave frequencies attack the cytoplasmic and nuclear membranes. When the vibratory rate increases, the cells cannot adapt or stabilize themselves and die by disintegrating and exploding." Other studies, including the latest in 2020, have produced opinions and medical suggestions that ultrasound can destroy cancer cells while leaving adjacent cells intact and unaffected.

Today's modern use of vibrational medicine is an attempt to use vibrations to put a body's frequencies back into rightful balance to recreate its original relationship.

Here is my question: If vibrational medicine is, in fact, based on the fundamental biology and quantum physics principles upon which the universe is constructed, then what might be possible? What powers might vibrational medicine hold?

Jack looks at her and says, you better get started on your research quick. Sam responds that you had better ask God and whoever to answer some of these questions and help me generate some answers. Can any of this be possible? She asks. Jack just asks if it is possible to die and be alive. Is it possible to talk to God or, worse, a thing called Tubby from a million miles away? Yes, anything is possible, and any problem can be solved if people just think for themselves and the rest of us, was Jack's response.

The rain continued all day and into the night, with Jack seeking answers to fill in the blanks in his cases and Sam seeking questions to sort out and develop agreeable solutions for her students. Their excitement was high, and she wanted to feed off it to foster greater enthusiasm to study harder. She was very motivated to become involved in researching the many interactions of the brain and the vibrations associated internally and externally with the world. Around 5 o'clock, Jack said, I will provide dinner for you tonight. Sam asked with what and how? Jack says, I can manage it and goes into the kitchen. Sam shrugged and returned to reading. An hour later, the doorbell rang, and Jack answered and gave the delivery man money and took a large bag into the kitchen. Sam shook her head and smiled.

After dinner and dishes had been done, Sam gave Jack a hug and a kiss and asked if he would be alright if she left. Naturally, he said no. My brain hurts. Sam kissed his head and said, you'll be fine. He said not without you and kissed her again.

After she left, he sat down and thought about Sam and his relationship and where he hoped it would end.

The next day was Monday and the start of another week. After all that stands out from last week, Jack stood in his shower and mused on what else could happen over the next week. He hopes it will slow down but does not think it will.

Jack gets in to find that John and Tay have already gone out to meet Samuel and look over a neighborhood that Samuel's team thought to be a potential hotspot for these new creeps. Jack looks over his messages and finds little of importance now and visits Buddy. He enters the lab to find Buddy seated at the table with Jennie and Sam, discussing her questions deeply in medical terms. Sam stood up and spoke. Long time no see! Jack smiled and asked, why didn't you tell me last night you were coming? Jennifer said, would you have baked us a cake? While smiling and then standing to say hello and kiss Jack.

Jack grabbed a cup of coffee and sat down to listen. Sam speaks to what Buddy was saying: go ahead, tell us. Buddy starts with part of the overall process of vibrational frequencies, which is the energy created and the gravitational effect of spreading bodily fluids throughout the human body. It has long been theorized that this is the catalyst to a functioning cardiac system. The flow further creates energy, which helps maintain a balance of energy and water in the internal organs and motivates output to the systemic functions of our body. This balance is often talked about, but few understand the essential nature of its maintenance. Everything is independent of this balance. Ever notice how thoughts will attract like thoughts and correct those that are unfavorable?

Jennie agreed and talked about how the vibrational circular dichroism extends circular dichroism from electronic to vibrational transitions in molecules. This has opened a new way to forecast and measure molecular development. Jack finishes the coffee and stands to leave. This is fascinating, but I need to go back to work. Good luck and have fun. He is about to leave when Jennie asks him to stay awhile. She has something on her mind to ask Sam and Buddy and wants Jack to have some input. She asks Sam about the research grant and how it is coming. Sam tells her they are in the final stages of writing up a proposal for me to sign. Jennie boldly asks if there is a place for a biomedical engineer to use traditional engineering expertise to analyze and solve problems in biology and medicine, providing an overall enhancement and applying advanced technology to the complex problems in working with living systems as they arise.

Sam thinks and says, you might be on to something. Do you know of anyone? Jennie smiles and replies, I'll think about that. Buddy buts in to ask, what does this mean to me? Both ladies explain the time commitment and intensity involved and the potential pressure on a couple. Buddy has no issues and thinks it will be a significant career move. Well, that leaves Jack, and he looks at Jennie and says, no problem, I'll still love Jen. Sam makes a face, and all we need now is the proposal.

Jack's phone rings, and he answers as he goes out the door. Jack walks in on Randy, Samuel, Tay, and John, who are sitting in the office waiting for him. Hi team, was Jack's greeting, and he continued with, what's up with this hot lead? Randy responds that no one has said anything about a hot tip. This cluster of older homes is the same company gaining all, rehabbing them all. Samuel spouts off to state; they turn the three bedrooms into studio apartments to triple the number of units and get elder housing loans and rent subsidies. Jack looks at them and asks, what is wrong with that? It sounds like good business. Tay speaks up to provide context and reasoning to start an inquiry. The first item is the chief partner of the enterprise is a foreign national named Mr. Franchot Tulieu, now deceased in our morgue awaiting cremation and a return flight to southern France. His family has requested this and is going to spread his ashes over their beloved ancestral lands.

The second item is his prior connection to the Ruisseau's Company, which is somehow related to the conglomerate called Aurroyos. Taylor looks around the room and says the world is getting smaller or crazier. Samuel responds, both. Can all of this be interconnected, or are we seeking connections where they are not? Jack replies we need to recheck everything from scratch and make sure that all the pieces fit before going further. Each man agrees and grabs a folder to start research. Jack issues advice to each of them, checking out everything about the plane and that company. We want to know who flew the aircraft and anyone else on it. Renton acknowledges that I am on it and will investigate the guy's family, business operations, and other partners and directors. Samuel will go over all medical records and coroners' reports. Randy has a relative living in the south of France to inquire about local news or gossip; she is great at gossip, he said, smiling. Tay will coordinate everything.

Jack's phone rings, and it is Bill, bitching about Tubby's antics. He makes loud noises all night, and his guards and staff can't perform their duties. Every night, the lights blow out, and the air conditioning unit does not work correctly. The thermostat does whatever it wants and then shuts off. Jack calmly asks, Bill, why are you blaming Tubby? It's him; he's driving us crazy. Please open your phone and go near so that I can talk. Bill does as he.

Tubby states that they all want it too hot for him. At night, they all go to sleep and enjoy their temperature. I need a much cooler space, and they put all the lights directly on me to watch my every movement. The enormous lights emit a large amount of energy, heat, and weird vibrational sounds. So, I shut the light off for good and hummed myself to cover their awful sounds.

I understand, Tubby, and will tell Bill to make changes. Tubby responds with ok, but if he stalls, I am out of here. Bill grabs his phone back to his ear to tell Jack; I can't believe you will let him dictate terms and threaten to leave. It took a crane and an enormous truck to get him here; he is not going anywhere. Bill, don't tempt us; make the changes. He is your guest and free to leave. Sure, and Bill hung up.

He feels like a kindergarten teacher with two small brats. Seeking some respite, he goes to see Buddy and explains his conversation with Tubby and Bill. Jack enters and looks around at the cleanliness of the expanded space. Buddy starts with the morgue and does not need the additional space. They were deadheading the system. If they blamed their backup and slow response time on a crowded space, they were looking for lots of overtime; instead, they were asked for volunteers to staff this substation. Suddenly, space was found, and the place became a more sterile environment. So, we are the beneficiaries. We need to think about what to fill it up with before Josh comes down and decides for us. Jack laughs and remarks on Buddy being cynical. Buddy suddenly gets serious and asks Jack if he thought Tubby could address him. After a moment, though, Jack agrees that is possible since he talks to me as well. What makes you think he is?

Last night, I was sleeping deeply and having a dream when suddenly his voice broke in and spoke to me as if he could see my dream and gave me historical data. The dream was about an article I read yesterday, exploring the myths and conjunctions regarding the Great Pyramid builders in Egypt. Tubby recited technical data about where the stones had come from, and it had been built a thousand years before the Egyptians were a civilization. The greater Nile basin was flooded, and the sandstone was cut stone-milled in a quarry on the west bank of the Nile, slid onto barges, and floated into place. The base stones were sunk into flooded basements, and it began from there. This civilization was more advanced than we are today. There were eight sides, and each stone was cut to strategically placed angles. The inner core framework is what we see today. Originally, other limestone was cut to actual proportions and laid out and encased in the whole structure.

This civilization advancement included a redirect tool to intensify the sun's rays into an effective cutting tool and drill boreholes into granite blocks and limestone. They additionally developed a process to use tools to polish the limestone encasement in place.

This is the basis for the legend of "The Jewel of The Nile" because of the huge reflective nature of this structure. Today, even without the encasement, it can be seen from far away, even in Israel. He told me that in 1303Ad, a giant earthquake loosened the layers, and many were stolen or taken down to use in other structures. They had become hazardous to worshipers and caravans passing through.

I was frozen in place and cold. I told him I was afraid and would not remember most of what he said. He laughed, and it was ok. We will talk again and disappeared.

I can't believe my dream happened and have doubted my sanity.

Jack laughs and tells Buddy, I have been there and still had doubts sometimes, like this morning. I should call Sam and have a session with her, said Buddy.

Jack smiled and said, can't hurt, as he left to return upstairs.

Jack returns to the pen which they referred to as the office. Renton had left to pick something up and would be back soon. Taylor says Josh called and wants you to call him as soon as possible. Jack sat down and made the call: Hi, boss. Josh talked for a few minutes and then hung up. Jack looked around and remarked that the Fed would take over Medicare, Social Security, and voter fraud cases. They have an additional twenty cases to add to ours, so Brass wants to have them do the work. The chief and the boss both congratulate us on breaking this case. Taylor says we were good enough to uncover this scandal but not good enough to manage politics. Same old, same old. Renton returns, and Jack tells him the news. Renton says, what else is new? I have some good news to give; he continues by pulling out a small picture of two young men standing in front of a house. He explains this was found in a concealed slot in the victim's empty wallet; on the back of the picture is a scribbled date and the names of Franchot and Renoir. It looks as if these two were brothers.

Renton hands over the picture for all to look at; anything jumps out at you. Jack looks up and jerks his head around, but Renton says, yup, they are identical twins before Jack can speak. Besides that, Renoir took over the family empire after his brother's death and moved himself into the mansion house with the wife and kid of his dead brother. Tay said, too much of a coincidence. That is not all; my friend, Mr. Renior, was the pilot of the jet. Holy shit, came several replies. Jack tells Renton, fantastic job! Does anyone know if identical twins will also have identical DNA? They all nod no. Jack goes back to Buddy, telling everyone to tidy up their notes and case files to hand over to the Feds.

Jack enters to find Buddy bent over his bench, fiddling with some dials to adjust. Wait, Buddy, can identical twins each share the same DNA? Yes, the reply was that they share the same fertilized egg, which divides in the womb, so each can have an identical genetic code. Other physical events can occur in the womb to alter state. For example, one can be in such a way over the top of the other, causing shorter stature development, or one gets more nourishment, so one may be born with more fat cell development and consequently may weigh more throughout their life. Why do you ask?

Jack explains the newest discoveries. Jack asks Buddy, why are you so down?

Buddy describes an incident that happened at the local coffee shop this morning. People were discussing the greater capabilities of a modern computer than the human brain; my barista turned to me for the correct answer because of my computer background. Even though I did not know the others, she plugged me in as an expert, and they had a bet for some free coffee. So, cornered, I explained that the average human brain uses a handful of energy produced by the body, about less than 10% typically. To match the speed and functionality of the brain, you would need several supercomputers direct wired to Megawatts generating power stations to approximate a comparison. So, the answer is no comparison; the brain wins. One big guy stands up to challenge me; he thinks I am a showoff and self-righteous. My girl gets me my coffee and says that the other guy is a hole and to forget him. I am always worried about that. Is that the way I come off? Jack smiles and says, Buddy, there are A-Holes, jealous of people who studied and became educated. Never try to hide your real self, especially from idiots. Remember: education does not stop at the school's exit doors; it starts. This jerk jumped and threw his books away the day he left school. Millions of people never realized their true potential and left a loss in the world.

Buddy takes over the conversation by saying thanks; it is, as my father always told me, that education is the key to life, and most lose it too early to appreciate it and not end in regret. Jack says your father was a smart man. Buddy were required to enter the workforce to help support the family. His sister and three brothers went to college, but he was too late. He was self-taught and never stopped learning. He would sit by a fire in the evening to tell me wondrous tales of others. He once told me a story of Hedy Lamar, the movie star, and Howard Hughes, the first billionaire. The studio set them up for a dinner date to entice him into directing a picture with her. At the halfway point of dinner, she got mad. All he had done was talk on the phone and moan about a big problem with getting biplanes to fly as single wings. After telling him off, she grabbed the waiter's pencil and flipped over the menu. She drew a picture of a bird and a fish and asked what they had in common.

Howard, in exasperation, didn't know. She drew lines and explained. Birds have feathers to stabilize their wings, and the tail also has feathers to control flight. The fish had the same issues with resistance, and its gills and tail equalized everything.

Put flaps in the wings and side panels with stabilizers for control; next time you want a date, call yourself. Grabbing her coat, she left.

A week later, he called and pleaded for a date. She went. He gave her a complete laboratory at his factory. She created many inventions that are the basis for modern technological models we use today, like cell phone apparatus and radio technology. She was a proponent of vibrational development, and with all her patents given in the Second World War, she should have become the richest woman in the world. What happened? Jack asked. The government confiscated all the documents and usage under war acts as highly classified and never released them until after her death and with restrictions. The industrial complex won again, as the connected appeared to profit the most, and many patents are still classified. The rumor always was she developed a prototype for a vibrational engine to propel about anything at no cost. This was the reason Howard Hughes and she had to hide out of sight for the rest of their lives.

What a remarkable story, it should be made into a movie, said Jack. Buddy said, can't, my dad was always a successful storyteller and always true. He told me not to forget that a beautiful woman is a jewel, A smart woman is a diamond, and a woman that is both is a diamond with emerald clusters; never lose her.

I have found my diamond with emerald clusters, and I will ask her to marry me. Jack looks at Buddy and says, I did not realize you were that close; how many dates have you been on? Buddy says, double the two of you.

Jack rctorts we have been busy. If you are too busy now, what will happen later? My father always said marriage is the biggest thrill of your life, like the best job ever. You can love both but get your thrill from the marriage and not the job. Don't repeat the same mistake as before.

As Jack walked out, Buddy said that Sam was coming over in the morning to check him out.

The following day, as Jack was driving into the parking lot at work, he saw Buddy waving frantically and pointing to an open parking spot. Jack was no sooner out of his car before Buddy grabbed his arm while yelling. We got into big trouble; we got into big trouble repeatedly. Calm down was all Jack could say. They entered the side door into the lab, and Buddy still dragged Jack through the doorway into the garage area and pointed to the trouble. Jack was dumbfounded to see Tubby on the floor in a comfortable position. Jack only asked if he was comfortable on the floor. Tubby just said, I was buried upside-down underground for over a hundred years, or so you say. So, this is much better.

Buddy still had a grip on Jack's arm to help him stand. Ok, Buddy, you are breaking my arm, was Jack's response, and he looked at Tubby to ask what happened.

Well, Bill is stubborn and needs to be the boss. He stalls on anything we ask him to do. Why do you always refer to the two of us as one? We are, Tubby exclaims! Tubby tells Jack to sit down first.

Buddy grabs two chairs while mumbling. This is going to be good.

In the first encounter, I told you I had been waiting a thousand years to meet you. I guessed!

I meant I had accumulated a specific type of genetic code to keep its purity. So, your family tree, which has thousands of branches, has been followed since its inception.

I had to maintain every member of my ancestry and monitor specific aspects to arrive at this moment and with this purity. Did you notice my loss of weight? I have shed the myriad branches of your tree and received a reduction in girth. See me in a few months. The door burst in with a whirlwind of people led by Bill. He is shouting to arrest all of them for stealing government property. Suddenly, a loud noise like an explosion, and bodies went flying in all directions, except Jack and Buddy.

Soon, all had assayed that they were unhurt and stood; some were even shocked to realize their weapons had disappeared. What happened was the question each asked. Jack looked around to find Bill and said, hi Bill, what do you need? Bill was still in shock and needed a chair to steady himself. Buddy gave his chair and went to get another. Bill finally came back into focus and demanded to know why Jack had abducted Tubby. Jack laughed and told Bill that we were just as surprised to find him sitting in our garage as we were to see him gone. It was your fault; I warned you, as did Tubby. He tells it as it is, so listen next time. Now, tell me what happened. Bill started, and when we arrived, everything was as usual. The alarms were set, and guards were all outside at their posts. We entered to find staff asleep in bunks, but inside guards were also sleeping at their posts. Tubby was not there. No evidence of how he got out or where he went. No footprints or anything to suggest a large vehicle had taken him.

We can't understand how you did it. Jack looks at Bill to impress him. We did not do it. He left on his own.

Showed up. Buddy spoke up to say, I have a theory. Jack nods to go ahead. Buddy says this may sound crazy, but Tubby uses vibrational wave sounds to reduce his molecular structure to attach to vibrational sound waves and direct them to another location and reconfigure his structure to the original at this new location. No damage to anything in between and no evidence.

Bill stutters, asking why he stayed buried for so long if he can do that. Jack speaks to say he was where he aspired to be. Why did he remain there?

Jack looks at Tubby and asks, why?

Tubby answers with the knowledge; I can only tell you, everyone else must leave immediately. Bill yells NO, I am not going; my orders are to watch the interaction between the both of you and listen carefully to all discussions. So, I am staying. Everyone else leaves now. After they all go, including Buddy and Bill adjusts his chair back, still in earshot. Jack looks at Tubby and says, why? Tubby breaks into Jack's thoughts to inform Jack to think of what he wants to say and let his thoughts reply.

So starts a commentary on what Tubby requires in his mission while Bill strains to listen. First, there is a massive reduction in vibrational wave emissions. This has resulted in an imbalance in life's existence. Vibrational activity has been disrupted, causing increased volcanic and earthquake movements or realignments within all climatic events. This has been represented in the human body by novel diseases, pandemics, and diseased epidemic abnormalities. Climate is not the problem but is a symptom. Consider the earth as a body; the whole body is not diseased, just a smaller part that affects the whole. Man believes everything is up to them to correct, but how can they fix something that they don't even understand how it works? They are fumbling in the dark: all ideas but no accurate knowledge.

Suddenly, Bill realizes that Jack's head is nodding, but his lips have never moved. Bill jumps off his chair and yells, Damn you two. It's thought transference and runs to intercede. A large flash of light, and Bill is seen lying on the cold concrete floor.

Jack looks at Bill laying there and asks if he hurt him. No, says Tubby, just a repellant shield, and now he is in the presence of the angels for a corrective session.

Bill awakes to float on a cold marble slab surrounded by a chorus chanting. A greater experience awaits him than ever could be imagined. A change of life is about to begin.

It will be as if another lifetime has passed for Bill, but he returns shortly to see the two looking at him, lying as he was. He stands and strolls towards Jack, who puts out his hand for Bill to shake and says, how are you? Bill replies, excellent, better than great. It's like a whole new body. I feel more energized and balanced. And he looks to Tubby to ask, Am I brainwashed? Tubby responds, no, just a body wash. Please sit and join our conversation.

Tubby again builds on the vibrational foundation already expounded. The inadequacy of vibrational waves is the root cause of earth's changes.

Everything we are, see, and touch is just clusters of molecular dust glued together by vibrational waves, and if they are disrupted, then all changes, even us.

Bill speaks up to say, what do you mean by us? Homo Sapiens today will be the last of the species. They are changing as we sit here and have been over the last century. In a century or two, they will need to change totally or will destroy themselves. It is frightening but true. Jack asks, how are we changing today? The brains are getting more prominent with the skulls, and the body changes gradually. For example, newborns primarily will not develop wisdom teeth as a way for the body to regain extra space for the additional mass. Another change has been discovered in about 33 percent of older dead senior bodies, showing a third medium artery in the forearm. The supposition is that the third artery carries increased blood flow to feed the needs of a significantly increased body with new requirements of bodily functionality. In a shocked voice, Bill asks, Like an extra arm or two or head, what? Jack seems calmer and responds with greater brain activity to start. Another change is that over the last 50 years, the human average temperature has decreased to 97.9 from 98.6 because of changes in their metabolism. The forecast is to continue by an average of 0.05 degrees °F every ten years, indicating a much healthier environment. One problem with all this is that a culturally based environmental change is also co-occurring. This will develop cultural and chemical changes.

Sexual and conversant intercourse will be affected. Taller men will become more attractive to women of all heights than shorter men, and there will be many other cultural changes. Bill acknowledged all this and asked if this meant half of all people or more would not survive after the next century. No. Darwin's theory of, "Only the Strong Will Survive" was misinterpreted to facilitate the politics or desires of those with special agendas. It does not consider any physicality, brainpower, or many other personal and cultural attributes. Humans, to survive, will need to embrace changes and not fight them. Civilizations that sought a fight were destroyed. Check history. People are subtly changing before our eyes, and change must be accepted. Eventually, all will not be diverse but will become the same. This is the ultimate correction to Adam and Eve's sin. If people perform time-proven examples of human interactions, the level of vibrational wave frequencies will be rebalanced along with the stabilization of earth's patterns.

Humans have considerable input in correcting some parts and can assist nature's reclamation process in securing the natural balance. There is a complete plan to help procedurally and strategically with accepting and reinvigorating the balance of life.

The conversation continued over the next few hours, with Tubby laying out the first part of the plan designed from beyond. He would not clarify if it is divine or cosmos, except to convey God's words that the smallest to the biggest life form in the cosmos includes all and depends on all.

The day was late, and Jack went home to let Bill receive the initial information he had missed.

Jack calls Sam to give her the rundown of the day's events and asks about her day. Sam quickly responds to her class load and the sequence of following details to research more data regarding the potential of vibrational treatments to the body and the mind. The many treatment plans to seek repairs on different body parts for physical and mental ailments are astonishing. She continues to describe some of the more well-known; the potential is too great even to contemplate. She needs to discuss some with Tubby. Jack says to come on in tomorrow and chat with him; he has not stopped all day. I can't wait until after my 9:30 class is over, so you can then take me to lunch. Jack said, ok, and a feeling of love carried the rest of the conversation.

The following day, Jack walked into the lab to see Buddy exiting and closing the garage door. He tells Buddy hello and asks how our friend is. Buddy replied, OUT, and when I approached him, his voice stated, I am out and will contact you when I return. Buddy stops to look at Jack and asks, did you sleep here last night? There is a blanket and cushion in the big chair. No, it was not me. Jack continues; it was Bill. I left him here talking to Tubby, and they were friendly.

Cute, Jack. I get it; Tubby was chummy! Let us get some coffee and talk. They sat down, and Buddy began by saying that I was in a quandary about my career and needed a competent friend to help guide me. Considering all you have gone through; I can't think of anyone more competent than you. Jack knows this is serious, so he treats it as Buddy deserves. How can I help? Buddy starts. I have been unhappy for a while, and if you, Sam, and Jennie had not come into my life, I would have left a long time ago. I am stir-crazy in this job. My education screams to explore and do some meaningful work to benefit humanity and create a legacy of why I was here. Fiddling with these toys is far beneath my skills and bores my mind. Until Tubby showed up, the world was crushing me, and now with Jennie and everything else, the world has become the potential to be all I ever wanted. I am stifled and buried here. Can I explore?

Jack sits back and tells Buddy; you don't need my permission to go. Your future needs you to become your future.

Jack, I am asking you to include me with Bill and Tubby in whatever is coming. I did not realize all this until I was left out yesterday in the meeting with Tubby. The more I sat out here, the more I thought about my situation and what meant the most to me. A future with a wife. She is eager about joining Sam's trip, and you and Bill just leaving me as the odd one out. I don't want that. Please ask Tubby if I can be included. Glad we spoke because I did not realize you felt like this, but I can understand your reasoning. I will talk to Tubby. Speaking of him, he is back.

Chapter 19: Vibrations To Live and Beyond

The two go into the garage and greet Tubby. Where have you been? Bill stayed all night learning, as he said. We discussed vibrational activity throughout the universe, especially on earth. Most of the night was spent explaining the discoveries of vibrational and radio frequencies and their interaction with infrasound waves and low or high frequencies and current applications. He was impressed with many other items.

Buddy was also impressed, and he asked a simple question. Why is vibrational wave data so important? The importance to NASA and space is that every planet contains a vibrational history of that planet implanted within it.

With the right combination of sophistication and technology, this will be an open textbook of all consequential structural, cultural, and environmental phenomena to decipher each planet's sense.

Use Mars as an example. NASA understands the potential to develop Mars. They use probes, Voyager, and the current Mars Rover as an escape spot if earth is destroyed. Rover, through pictorial evidence, has shown that flowing water, as in rivers, lakes, and oceans, existed.

Digging deep into the soil produced microbes of growth. All this means is that life can be a viable environment on Mars. Today, on Mars, the Rover is conducting experiments to determine exact vibrational frequencies. They need these to preset these vibrational waves to penetrate the atmosphere. Mars's atmosphere, because of some cataclysmic event disrupting those waves, caused an atmospheric change. Today's atmosphere contains the heaviest forms of isotopes of hydrogen, carbon, argon, sulfur, and nitrogen. All of which distorted the original environment. The belief is to change the frequencies with radio waves to regenerate original properties and reinvigorate the environment.

This is the most uncomplicated way to explain.

Just then, Sam and Jennie come in. Jack introduces them to Tubby. He also explains why they and Buddy participate in this meeting and asks each to provide Tubby with a biographical snapshot to prove their potential in the project.

Tubby chimes up to say he forgot one item he and Bill had discussed. Bill expressed dismay when we spoke about LRAD technology and its usage when weaponized. He became concerned and discussed smuggling and whether LRAD could be broken down into separate small parts and reassembled elsewhere.

Jack's ears perked up, and his mind flew into overdrive. Please amuse the ladies, as I am sure they will you. I'll be back later, Sam and everyone. Bye. Out the door, he left.

He rushed into the office to find Renton on his computer and Tay on the phone. Jack sat down and opened his laptop to share files and search for his past cases. Ten minutes later, he found the right one and opened it, reviewing it and sending file copies to both others. Soon, the others finished checking his file. They looked at him; Jack said, this is my case from 15 weeks before my attack. When I initially returned to work, I reviewed all my old files and could not find any connections. This may be the one. There was a robbery at the customs storage facility. The two normal agents on duty came down with cramps and diarrhea and could go to the hospital. Only a janitor was left in another part of the building. This guy ate his lunch from home, so he was ok. The others ordered in and thought they caught food poisoning. Sometime overnight, the cameras went down, and a robbery occurred. Two huge crates had been opened, and smaller boxes were removed from each crate. It went unsolved. I questioned everyone and searched the entire facility myself, spending days and nights. The owner of the stolen property raised the roof, and the brass lowered the boom on me. Even Josh felt the heat.

Review all the documents taken by that aide, Jason Cole, especially the invoices, if you have time. I want to know everything that was in those crates and precisely what was in the stolen boxes. John, trace down all details on the manufacturers and shippers, the ports shipped from and to, and the routes here and abroad. These are the guys responsible for my family's deaths.

They all went to work, doing their job.

Meanwhile, back at the lab, Tubby has continued to be questioned by all three and answers each with a complete explanation while leaving much to their thought process to plan better questions to further their inquisitive minds. He explains why he does this. Thought is a catalyst of energy, a vibrational requirement for earth's survival and the cosmos to expand. We all must worry about the structure of the earth breaking down. Air and water are most crucial to formation. We can see the remnants of a vibrant Mars, and we can prevent earth from repeating that demise and continued existence of life here and elsewhere. The kernel of life is a part of God's creative process. The human species can generate greater vibrational energy than anything else through their thought processes, emotions, and activities, resulting in a multiple expansion of power, unlike the leaves blowing and moving in the wind or trees, which is a one-dimensional generative process. This lop-sided event is caused by a considerable reduction in human endeavors of thinking and moving.

People stay indoors to work and play. Interaction between crowds can generate an energy cycle equal to several dozen megawatt generators alone. Every drop in vibrational frequency further degrades energy basis and axial containment.

Billions and trillions of dollars are being spent to solve a wrong problem.

All governments can't save earth; only earth can and all its inhabitants together.

Bill enters Jack's office with some important news.

He has wangled the federal file on a customs robbery a couple of years ago, and several aspects relate to current events. He believes LRAD may have been smuggled into the country in disassembled parts and then reassembled and sold to rich people to ward off unwanted neighbors, squatters, or protesters.

One buyer set this upon his property to force the homeless away from his neighborhood with the help of his neighbors. Some people suffered damage to the eardrums and brain caused by their lack of training and high frequencies. I have those notes being copied. This guy who bought this stuff claims to have bought it by contacting a priest or somebody like that or higher up here in DC.

Two angles to proceed in this case. Jack calls the bishop and asks for a confession.

He and Bill return to the lab and join the group. The conversation gets around to Tubby asking Sam about her research grant into vibrational control's impact on the brain and the mind. Bill's ears perked up, and he jumped in to inquire if they were discussing LRAD equipment. Sam says Jennie was speaking to Tubby, and she had a lot to say, so you should talk to her later. Bill nodded. Buddy spoke up to invite Bill to dinner after eating and discussing; ok with you, Jack. Fine, Jack said. and sat back to think and let the voices flow excitingly by all. His thoughts were on the meeting with the bishop in the morning.

Jack enters the bishop's sanctuary at his appointed time and sinks into a large, cushioned chair to await his excellency. The bishop arrived in his confessional garb and sat opposite Jack. Morning and blesses Jack. Jack blessed himself in response. Bless me, Father, for I have sinned. Have you ever sinned, Bishop? The bishop looked perplexed and said, I have, Jack. Everyone sins. Jack, is this a confession or an interrogation? Confession and interrogation said, Jack, and goes on, who oversaw the radio station? Bishop responds Monsignor Chase, your old friend. He manages all the facilities of the diocese.

Jack sighs and says, we'll need to speak with him. The Bishop responds with a question. Why? Jack says the engineer at your radio station was wearing an authentic priest outfit, purchased by this diocese when murdered.

Jack kneeled on one knee in respect and continued. I have done a lot of dreadful things; some were sins, and others were not ethical or moral. I have lied and been deceitful to those I love and friends, and the weight has grown greater each time. Does absolution reduce the weight? Bishop says Jack, my religion forbids me to disclose what is said in the confessional. Speak your mind and cleanse your heart.

Jack begins; Bless me, Father, for I am a sinner. I am continually forced to lie and cover up to protect those I love. The details are well known by your Grace, having been involved from the beginning. But an accounting must be done! I know about AURROYO and all involved, looking straight into the bishop's face for a reaction.

Sorry, was that your missal that fell? Said Jack, looking to the floor.

The bishop responds slowly, you are right, Jack. This is too dangerous to speak openly about.

Under the authority invested in me by God, I absolve you of your sins, and for your penance, say a Hail Mary for your sins, and Our Father for mine. God bless, Jack.

In Nomine Patris, et Filii, et Spiritus Sancti, Amen

The bishop turned slowly and, with shoulders hunched over, struggled to walk from his sanctuary back to the real world. Jack again asks the bishop, to whom do you confess? 'Directly to God" was his answer.

Jack goes to work with a heavy heart for the man he just left. That man has a lot to think over and to decide.

Jack arrives back at his office to find Taylor and John, who are reviewing files again. Jack tells them about the news from the bishop. Our old friend, Monsignor Chase, is the higher priest. He oversees the radio station and all other diocesan facilities, including storage warehouses. He quickly could appropriate a total priest garb and hide smuggled radio parts or other items. Jack also turns over most of Samuel's reports and notes. Follow up on these leads and whatever you have. I am going to stay with the bishop. He still knows a lot more than he is saying. Also, see Bill about all he was telling me about Aurroyo and the twin brothers. I am going to see Buddy and the congressional representative to see what else I can discover.

Jack goes downstairs to the lab. Buddy and Jennie are there with Sam.

Boy, I am so happy to see you, Jack tells Sam as he hugs and kisses her and holds her hand. She can feel his concerns but sets them aside to offer good news and cheer him up. My grant has been approved and expanded, including a co- grantor, Johns-Hopkins Medical Research Unit. Sam explains that this allows for several research assistants, including employment and a scholarship to 1 Junior and 1 Senior, plus a Doctoral Fellowship. I have already spoken with Jennie here, and she wants to seek the doctoral position grant. Isn't this great? Jack asks, what has Tubby said about all this? Jennie says that he is all for it and is already searching for another place, conducing to serve as a working lab. He is already telling Bill what will be required. Jack looks around just to say, Thank God, it's Friday!

Jennie goes off with Buddy to sit and make notes while Jack takes Sam by the hand and leads her into the garage. They look at Tubby, and Sam shakes her head to say, I swear, he is smiling, even without a mouth. Jack laughs and tells her of his morning confession and the sorrow it wrought. The poor man looks broken, and I am not sure he was at fault. He trusted many people to help others. They abused his trust, and now, he will be held accountable for their sins. The end will soon be here, and he knows it. God forgive him. Sam hugged Jack and said some good words on the bishop's behalf to God or the Devil, whoever would manage this issue.

Tubby speaks, remember, Jack, all of God's creations has an inherent corrective process to atone for their sins. Even Jesus was too trusting, and God forgave him and welcomed him into his home and bosom for eternity. God is generous and forgiving in the way a father may be forgiven to a prodigal son.

The human creative process is ongoing and continues to display its fallacies. This is also part of his plan to conjure up the vision of each fallacy for corrective adjustment on the way to perfection for all.

Sam looks at Tubby and says, are you getting thinner? Jack and Sam share a laugh of relief. Tubby exclaims, Thanks for noticing; Jack is helping. Bill tells Jack he was upstairs with John and Taylor and provides all he has for their use. Bill also has some potential sites and talks about his agency's provisional support besides the grant. Sam asks, what are the provisions?

Bill says the grant needs to be signed off by grantors, and they provided a signed copy to my agency. There are no other provisions except my participation throughout the term of the grant. Jack speaks up to ask, just what will they provide? A site and two million a year and access to NASA engineers for support and any required security requested by you. A scheduled inspection once a year to meet medical practices.

They will also need an annual budget and permission to audit if required. Jack says, sounds good. Excellent job, Bill.

Tubby wants to go over some needs for a new site. Bill turns and goes over to Tubby and sits down.

Sam quickly says. Jack, we need to check all this out. I don’t want to jeopardize my grant and leave bureaucrats to monopolize my project. How will we protect ourselves?

Jack smiles and replies, we have a secret weapon, Tubby, and he trumps bureaucrats every day. Both go over to sit with Buddy and Jennie to tell them Bill's news and discuss ways to ensure the project remains theirs. After an hour, they had decided on all the details and on everything Tubby had requested, except a 20-million-dollar radio telescope. Besides not knowing about time, Tubby does not understand about money.

They all decide to view all the potential sites to determine how to proceed and develop a pro forma budget for the grantors.

Sunday will remain a rest day and for preparation to go for dinner at the congressman's house.

Chapter 20
TRAP

Sunday morning, Jack rolls over to awaken Sam and kiss her. After an hour of romancing each other, Sam pushes Jack away to say; I am starving. Where are you taking me for breakfast? She says I could get used to this, and I reply, so can I! They laughed and took a shower together, and another hour came and went before Jack took Sam for lunch. After meandering up and down Riverwalk, they returned to her apartment for Sam to get spruced up for dinner and drove to the congressman's home; as he drove down the lane, searching for the right address, he commented on the difficulty of finding an address number. Sam said they want seclusion and not sightseers.

Jack notices a big black car searching the other side for numbers and says, I am not the only one lost. Jack finds the driveway and enters, rolling up to a beautiful home with a swing set in the back. As they exited the car with Jack holding the car door for Sam, he looked up to see the exact vehicle slowly passing and the driver staring up the drive at them. Apprehension and danger flow through his body.

Jack turns as he hears the door opening, and Tom, his wife Sarah, and Rachel stand on the front porch smiling in welcome. Rachel walks up to Jack, puts her hand in welcome, and states,

May I welcome you to our home? Jack bends in the middle, taking her hand and barely touching it with his lips; congratulations, this is a lovely home. Rachel is thrilled and giggles. Jack introduces Sam, and all enter for cocktails and snacks. Tom explains Rachel helped prepare all the snacks; she is becoming quite adept in the kitchen. Sarah shows them around the house and grounds. Sam remarks on how beautiful everything is, and the style is impeccable.

They arrive in the parlor and sit down as drinks are prepared. Rachel comes around carrying a platter of finger sandwiches made up of cucumber or some egg salad or tuna salad, plus scones and fruit tarts. She tells Jack the fruit is for him.

She returns to sit on the settee next to Jack.

Jack starts the conversation by telling Rachel that they both have a lot in common. They tell each other about losing a family and spending a lot of time in hospitals. They spoke of learning to walk and even talk again. Rachel tells Jack a funny story about trying to mispronounce some words, and they laugh together and cry at levels of the pain of relearning to walk and fall and their constant sorrow. Rachel speaks to how everyone tells her all this has strengthened her, but she does not feel stronger. Jack explains they mean a strength to be better prepared for anything life can include. He says you are such a lovely girl. Rachel touches her facial scars and says, thank you, but I know! Heartbreaking, Jack tells her; some of the most beautiful faces hide the fact that an ugly person is inside that body, not like her. Scars are on the skin, but it is everything inside the skin that is real and wonderful. Rachel reaches out, takes Jack's hand, and speaks. My dad was right; you are a wonderful man. Jack hears sniffling and looks to see Sarah and Sam with tissues to their noses and Tom with watery eyes. Jack asks for another fruit tart, a custard one. But, the server announces, dinner is served. Rachel takes Jack by the hand, and he grabs a custard tart with the other. Rachel giggles and leads the way.

As they start dinner, Sarah asks Sam what type of doctor she is. Sam discusses her specialty and her plans to pursue research. Tom asks, what will you be researching? Sam discusses her desire to research the effect of vibrational frequencies on the brain and the surrounding environment, especially Windmill Farms. Tom says I would have thought that would be well covered by now.

Sam sneaks a glance at Jack, who smiles and nods. So, she jumps in with most applications on filing to build, presenting a glossy report full of supporting data dealing with vibrational frequency levels but never addressing a myriad of problems. As Sarah asks, the earth, like the body, comprises 70% water, an excellent conductor of radio and vibrational frequency waves. The greater the distance traveled, the greater the increase in frequency in water and the effects. The regulated maximum hertz is often exceeded to the detriment of all lives. Wind farms continually run 24 hours, with peak saturation rates exceeded all night in the wind and vibrational damage. This sounds dangerous to people. Are there no studies done? Asks Sarah.

Yes, many have been ignored by the industry and, sorry to say, government regulations. Tom says, wait, it is a heavily regulated industry and constantly reports to agencies and Congress. Sam says yes, and industry people have written most of the regulations. Look, some well-known problems are that the marine industry is being destroyed worldwide, where wind farms are allowed. Cape Cod's economy has suffered a 60% loss because of failing clam beds and lobster mutations all along the eastern coast of Maine to New Jersey. Beaches have disruptions because of frequent shark sightings and the beaching of dolphins and whales. All marine life is suffering brain damage caused by a mix of vibrational and radio waves intertwining and confusing mammals. They seek the shallowest water with its decreased frequencies to escape, and many get trapped or just expire. Check the numbers, both economic, and mortality.

People are frightened to go in the water, and tourism is suffering. The number of brain-damaged individuals living on or near Cape Cod is skyrocketing and around the

Chesapeake Bay. Many western states have pending legislation and studies regarding mutation in cattle, horses, and crops because of death in campers and those living near these wind farms. Another aspect is an extreme loss of hearing caused by the sounds emitted by the blades and squealing gears overtime every day. The ground is also a conductor, although not as great as water. The ground carries the waves a shorter distance but at an increased level, robbing the soil of needed nutrients and chemicals, creating a desert area. Something well documented in other countries. Australia reports the death of trees and susceptibility in all plant life and vegetative growth. Many options exist, even non-vibrating windmills or blades, but government subsidies make current models slightly more economical, and grants are also contributing factors. Tom is impressed and shocked to hear all this and wants to know more about her research, the grant, and her efforts. She is interested in the effects on brains, people's life moods, and environmental impacts.

Sam speaks to the co-grantors, GW Memorial, and John Hopkins. She tells of Jennie's involvement as a Bio-Medical engineer and a doctoral applicant to be a research assistant if approved by JH to use her traditional engineering expertise to analyze and solve problems in biology and medicine, providing an overall enhancement of health care in a coordinated effort with engineers, physicians, and scientists to provide interdisciplinary insight into medical and biological problems to focus on the advances that improve human health and health care at all levels, especially brain cognition.

Rachel is getting fussy and bored, so Jack tells everyone that if they will excuse the two of them, they need to get some fresh air on the swing set, and off the two go. Rachel says as they go outside, I knew you were getting as bored as I was. We'll let the adults talk, ok. Sure, ok, said Jack. They walked and talked about her swings and how much she liked them. Could he push her? Jack was in real heaven!

Inside, Sarah, and Tom agreed to help and take part in any support Sam required. Sarah asks about JH and tells Sam that both she and Tom are alumni and are on the board at JH. They met and dated while at JH, but Jack was two years ahead and graduated to go into the service. I graduated and went to grad school, where I met my first husband. Unfortunately, he died in a plane crash. I attended JH board meetings and eventually reignited with Tom, as he was also a widower. We married and continued with a happy life.

Tom, smiling at his wife, asks Sam if they can make some calls to ensure Jennie is approved and to smooth the process. Sam agrees and asks Tom to investigate the waiver exemptions discovered in the bill granting the subsidies to current windmill farms. Tom does not have a problem and quickly agrees.

Suddenly, the phone rings and a server brings in more coffee and sets down the tray to answer. She listens and cries; she turns to hand the phone to the congressman. He listens for several minutes and sits as the voice continues and on. Tom's eyes were heavy with tears, and his hands and voice shook as he said goodbye and thanks. He looked at the two women and said the bishop had been discovered dead in the church.

Jack and Rachel are having a wonderful time playing and running around in a game of tag. The time is long before they return, but Jack is not ready to see the end of this day. He looks at the house to see Sam coming toward them, and her expression is of concern and repression. Hi babe, what is the matter? All ok, she says in a muffled voice, time to go in. Your mom wants to get you changed for bed. Give Jack and me a kiss goodbye, and we will see you soon. Rachel could feel something, but she complied, giving Jack an extra special kiss and hug.

Jack almost stumbled on their way to the car as he listened to Sam's narration of the phone call. Sam drove home since Jack was clearly disturbed and needed time to collect his thoughts. Jack had trouble reconciling his views to what he knew of the man. The bishop, above all else, was a deeply religious man, and Jack did not consider suicide a viable alternative to facing life's problems. By the time Sam had reached her house, Jack had decided. He told Sam to pack a suitcase and be prepared to stay with him for at least a week until things sort themselves out. He believed the bishop was murdered and made to look like a suicide. The killer was out there, and he believed he might know who that was. He was placing her in protective custody status. He searched her apartment and kept watch as she packed, and Jack was on high alert. As they got in his car, Sam proclaimed she did not think the protection was needed. Jack looked at her and said, if you believe this is protection, wait until our wedding day?

They reached Jack's home, and he repeated his precautionary activities. Jack put her into bed after checking the windows and locking the door on his way to the living room. Jack laid his gun and extra clips on the coffee table in easy reach and stretched out on the couch, knowing sleep was not in the cards tonight.

Jack lay all night alert for any sounds and stressed at his inability to envision the right questions to give him the answers he needs to protect his loved ones.

Jack suddenly sat up; that's it, it is his loved ones. The killer will want to attack the most accessible target first. He led to an answer Jack dreaded. He planned plans over the following hours until daylight came up, as did Jack. Jack woke Bill up and told him to be at the lab by 8:30 am while explaining the reasoning. His next call was to Renton, requesting his presence. Last, he spoke to Taylor to provide different instructions. Sam woke soon after and took a shower as Jack scrambled some eggs and bacon. Coffee was just being poured into the cups with the meal already served when she sat down. Jack, what has you so spooked? Jack replies to Sam with all his thoughts about the killer's next move. Sam asked, why does this person hate you so much? Not hate. I am a loose end to eliminate and bring me to him. He needs leverage, and that is you. I have arranged protection for you while I am chasing him today. Don't worry; you will be safe.

Jack pulls into a parking space right next to the labs entrance door and escorts Sam inside. Bill is waiting inside at the table, with several steaming cups of coffee, along with Buddy and Tubby. Bill acknowledges Jack with an all-set, and Tubby's voice rings out to welcome Sam; he is glad to see her. Buddy comes back in the open garage door to greet Sam. She turns to Jack to say; this is my protection detail. Jack laughs and says, Bill is here to not let Tubby kill anyone that threatens you. Bill will kill them as he will be easier to explain than Tubby, and Buddy is here to help Renton restrain Tubby if they attack you. Tubby responds with, that's right, don't worry, we got this.

Sam laughs and kisses Jack, Buddy, and Bill and throws a kiss in Tubby's direction. Jack leaves her in excellent hands and goes upstairs to the office. There, Renton awaits Jack for instructions. First, Jack calls a meeting with the caucus and will be free in 30 minutes; Jack asks for an immediate callback. He lays out a plan for Renton and gives details of what Jack expects to occur.

Jack called the congressional representative again and was told he was walking back now but would meet Reggie Dwyer for a luncheon meeting with a constituent. Jack tells the receptionist not to do anything until he talks to me. The girl stops in mid-sentence to tell the congressional representative that Jack is on the phone. Tom picks up and says hello when Jack stops him and asks him to go into his office and lock the door to everyone. I'll hold on so we can talk. Tom places the call on hold and tells her to block all calls before entering his office and locking up. Tom picks up the receiver while sitting down to listen. Ok, Jack, I am here. Jack explains his worries and the steps already taken to protect everyone. He tells Tom about Reggie's involvement in Aurroyo's schemes and the murders and corruption that have spread. I don't trust many people, just those who are acting on my behalf today.

He tells of Taylor's part and Renton.

The issue is protecting you, says Jack. Get home now. Jack phones Tay to let him know the congressional representative is heading home and to keep everyone out until I arrive and display the BAR's OPEN sign. Jack speeds to Tom's house, hoping to arrive before him, but upon turning into the drive, he spots both Tom's and Reggie's cars. He positions his car diagonally to block any potential escape by car. Jack exits the passenger door, leaving it open, then sneaks through the partially open breezeway door while crouching low. Tom is heard speaking and inquiring about Reggie's reason for being here. Reggie states that there is much to talk about. The complications arising from the death of the bishop are significant. He gives numerous specifics and Tom responds, but it does not make sense. Have you consumed any drugs? No, says Reggie, I have just ended our relationship. Tom yells, is this what Aurroyos has told you to do? It dumbfounded Reggie to learn Tom knows, and says fuck no, I don't need them anymore. That goddamn boss has ordered a hit on me. But I am ahead of them. Tom breaks in to ask; Reggie pulls his gun and fires three times over Tom's head; shut up, you fool! I was doing all my shit directly under your stupid trusting nose, yours, and that bishop. But now, I will show everyone how devious I am. That hired killer called me just to meet and talk, but his talk ended in death, so I arranged a meeting here with the successful congressional representative. I will kill you and your family and then him when he shows up. I'll say how I heard the shots and ran in to find him over your body, and I killed him. I'll be a hero and get appointed to finish your term. This is all I'll need to start my political career.

Just then, Sarah burst in, soaking wet and out of breath, to see Reggie pointing his gun at Tom. Tom, what is going on? Reggie yells, shut up, and where is that brat? At that, Jack steps through the French doors and directly between Sarah and Reggie. Great, are there any more out there? Yes, Jack replies; Reggie says fuck you and lifts his gun as if to fire. Tom moves toward his top desk drawer. Reggie turns halfway to shoot Tom when he realizes his error. Quickly shooting at Tom and spinning at Jack, when he felt the first strike, he heard a shot and felt a second as his eyes glazed over and hit the floor. Sarah screamed and ran to Tom, slumped over his desk. It was only my arm came Tom's voice. Renton burst in, and Jack saw Rachel in Taylor's arms outside the French doors, hugging and soothing her, saying that everybody was alright. The madhouse erupted with Sarah grabbing bandages from a cabinet and mothering Tom, as Renton covered Reggie's body from the little one's eyes. He says, double shot, center mass, respectable job, Jack. Jack tells John about the hitman coming and to set up a perimeter as soon as more men come. Then, start a search pattern for suspects. Jack goes over to sit by Sarah as she continues to bandage Tom's arm. Jack says, keep at that, and you'll cut off the circulation in that arm or run out of the bandage. Sarah struggles to laugh and cry simultaneously. Tom looks at her and asks if she went swimming before coming in to save us. Jack stands up and slowly backs away as Sarah gets ready to unload.

Hours later, after everyone had arrived, including the Navy, Tom is a reservist officer. The FBI and Capitol Police were doubling down. Jack hugged Rachel one last time as she said thank you for saving my mother and father. Both Tom and Sarah pay tribute to Jack's instincts and abilities and offer to call Sam. Jack said I am going right over to see her now. He was exhausted from not sleeping last night and wanted to get to Sam. Jack pulled into the parking lot just in time to see the catering truck getting ready to close for the night. Sam came running out to give him a giant hug and cried; I was so worried when I heard dispatch disclosing gunfire at Tom's house. Why did not you tell me that was where those other two characters were? I scolded them all day in my thoughts for not being around to help you. I could kill you myself. Jack laughed at the way every woman works. She had some food from the truck saved for him, and they all sat to eat and thank God for the day's end.

That night, Sam showed her appreciation for his survival and brilliance in planning. Afterward, they slept in a blissful sleep. Jack awakes in the predawn hours to some nagging thoughts. Why would the bishop climb up all those old stairs of the bell tower? What was he after? Did he believe that was the best place to confess to God himself? No! What might be hidden up there? His mind drifted over each question over and over. Of course, the bishop had once been an early postulate there; he had placed something. Evidence? Documents? A diary?

They got dressed, just an average couple preparing for a normal day of work leading up to a normal night together. Jack drove Sam to the lab for a morning ritual with Tubby, and he would return around 1 pm to take her to lunch. Jack was still bothered by what it might hide at that bell tower. Jack decided that the only way to find out was to look for himself. Jack parked at the front of the church and, on getting out, looked up and up and higher still. Hell, that was a long way to the top. Well, the sooner it started, the sooner it was done. He entered the dark corridor leading to the staircase. He walked up to a separate circular area with stone walls and a wooden staircase of over one hundred years old, buttressed several times to add strength but still shaky. Jack held on with two hands as he climbed up each step, farther apart than the current code allows. They were difficult and gave more pause to Jack's thoughts of a bishop's suicide. After the third landing, Jack stopped to look down and catch his breath. He then noticed the chalk marks where the bishop's body had landed in a spread eagle fashion as if an angel had crashed. Jack thought that is a hell of a way to describe it. He went back to climbing, step by step, ever upward, to heaven or hell. Sweat was pouring down his face as he got to a final landing. Jack looked around and said Christ, it is darker than hell up here. Then he noticed a candle and some wooden matches by an opening to what?

Jack struck a match and lit the candle. A ladder was directly in front of him, and turning around, he noticed the broken section of railing, where Bishop Frys had crashed through and fallen or pushed to his death. Jack picked up the candle and grasped one side of the ladder to begin another climb. He was glad to be inside, so he could not see the distance to the ground far below. Jack slowly and gingerly reached out for each rung until there were no more. Looking around this storage pile in a small attic was difficult and required his hand to do most of the search, hoping they did not encounter movement. Suddenly, the left hand touched a book. It felt like a leather-bound missal used by priests. Jack grasped it and stepped down a rung. A familiar voice completely startled Jack, transporting him back to that frosty night with snow softly falling, Jess slipping from his arms to the icy ground. The voice said, Hello, Jack. Jack's hand slipped a rung, and he held on to the book as if it were life itself. It was the old man with a cane in a raincoat. The voice continued, hand it over to Jack. Why you'll just kill me anyway, Jack said. Yeah, just like the bishop. Jack speaks to stall. Are you the boss of Aurroyo?

If I were, would I be stuck up in this chimney, cleaning up everyone else messes? No, I am just a Janitor.

Jack leaned back, and the Janitor cautioned, Don't, Jack, or you'll never know if I will kill Rachel or Jessica.

Yeah, we thought the big idiot had killed Rachel. Imagine my surprise when I saw her at that congressional representative's place. We were told she had died, but we were told you were dead, too. I was shocked to see the two of you together the other day. If the boss finds out, I shall swallow lots of water. We took Jessica to him in place of Rachel. A kid is a kid. He loves her with you dead; I may not have to kill Rachel. Besides, I owe you; killing that stupid punk for me was perfect. Thanks.

Drop the book, or I'll take it afterward. Jack was helplessly exposed on the ladder, so he tossed it on the floor below halfway to the Janitor. Jack tensed as the man stooped to pick up the book. Jack was prepared to jump and take both to death below. The Janitor held his gun and placed his cane on his knees, keeping his eyes on Jack and feeling with his other hand. Suddenly, a loud voice reverberated off the stone walls and the landing, as did Luc's voice. The old man dropped the cane and reached for the rail, missing it and tripping on the cane. Falling like a snow angel screaming as he passed each landing, which was drowned out by Lucifer's voice saying and echoing," Punishment, can be a bitch! Over and over, that voice's reverberations shock the whole cathedral as if by a giant hand. Jack struggled to retain his grip on the ladder, and just as suddenly, all was silent, as silent as the dead below. Jack slowly climbed down to the landing and gingerly picked up the book with both hands. He walked to the missing rail to look down at the crumbled, broken body spread eagled in the exact place as the chalk marks and stains of the bishop's blood. The expanding pool of blood mingling with Bishop Fry's bloodstains gave an appearance of wine escaping from a broken vessel. Jack, shaken and wobbly, continued climbing down. A few landings down, he stopped to breathe and, holding out the book, looking heavenward, said, thank you, Thank you all! As Jack approached the ground, he came to an abrupt halt and, in a loud voice, asked, Was this God's answer?

Jack looked around into the band of bright white before piercing a dim haze with his blurry eyes, filled with tears, at a spectrum of hate, sorrow, and pain. The sorrow came from the loss of his family, the hate for their murderers, the pain came from gripping the old wooden stair rail so intensely as to crumble in his fist. The stair rail gave way, and Jack stumbled across the cobblestone floor, fell upon the carved religious bench, and leaned against the cold stones of the tower wall. He slid down with legs spreadeagled toward the body that lay before him, the blood of the killer still spilled across the outline of the bishop's body and mused at the sight before him for a hidden message. Can the evil of a devil overcome the posture of angelic good? Jack's head rested on the rock pillows behind him as the mind merged a vision of an evil body overlaid upon a spiritual body to signify a montage of Good versus Evil's justice.

An hour later, a deacon found both still figures. He, at first, thought all were dead until he felt Jack's pulse and called for help. The police were called, and fifteen minutes later, Supervisor Kirby arrived on the scene to take charge. He immediately recognized Jack's symptoms and planned to have Jack taken back to his hospital for protection. He then pried a leather-bound book from Jack's hands and locked it safely away. Then he made calls to his wife to get her over to Sam's, explaining the situation, getting her to the hospital, and notifying the boys about events.

Awakened by the beauty of the multi-colored universe and the hardness of the marble slab, Jack experiences the serenity of Samadhi, which is reserved for those reaching the eighth level of Classical YOGA, Advanta Vedanta, or Buddhism's Noble Eightfold Path.

Jack felt, rather than heard, God's ethereal convenience as to cosmic interactions with humanoid microcosms via a chanting overlay of increasing tempo. Jack's sensibilities were overcome by the sense of a separate individual soul being replaced with a sense of oneness and connection to God, source, and cosmic consciousness.

Jack seemed to float in an aura of multicolored heavens, advancing to the familiar firepit. Jack felt God's presence but could not see him. So, he sat suspended in midair while he in communion with God allowing a transference of Transformational Leadership to increase and balance previous impartations. A familiar voice infiltrated the aura to intrude on Jack's solace.

"Hello Jack, are you well?" After peering around, Jack replies, "Yes, where are you?" "This is my busy Aeon, and my schedule is full. I have provided two surrogate confidantes acquainted with your peculiar scenario; please respect my judgment and collaborate with both of them as they guide you on your personal quest and my mission to cleanse."

Jack slips back into a pragmatic phenomenon, musing on the identity of this new entity, which is aware of the problems. His eyes closed, as did his mind to the ceruleans of this moment in time, and he entered an altered consciousness known as Divine Conscious. This is the Eighth and first level of Fusion, which is the attainment of a symbiotic connection to all creatures. This level allows an awareness of the vibrational frequencies of energy and an ability to channel that over all other creatures.

Jack's embryonic state has transcended the internal state of being and attained entrance into a combined internal/external realm of existence.

This book was written to foster imagination and be educated in a non-academic setting. It was researched thoroughly to allow verification of science and spirituality in a commonsense approach to positive interaction with institutions of all types. Those seeking answers about God's quest for Jack and Tubby, as well as updates on science and space, can expect the release of Book Two Release in mid-2025.

www.ingramcontent.com/pod-product-compliance
Lightning Source LLC
Chambersburg PA
CBHW060629310726
48982CB00003B/719

* 9 7 9 8 9 9 0 6 3 1 1 1 3 *